PENGUIN

Not Quite a

Not Quite a Fairytale is Cee Liddy's third novel – but the first to be published. Cee lives in Clare in a busy household with five children, so how the novel got written at all is a bit of a mystery. When not writing, Cee is a part-time pharmacist and musician.

Not Quite a Fairytale

In which boy meets girl in a car with three wheels but instead of kissing they talk about frogs . . .

CEE LIDDY

PENGUIN BOOKS

PENGUIN BOOKS

Published by the Penguin Group
Penguin Books Ltd, 80 Strand, London WC2R 0RL, England
Penguin Group (USA) Inc., 375 Hudson Street, New York, New York 10014, USA
Penguin Group (Canada), 90 Eglinton Avenue East, Suite 700, Toronto, Ontario, Canada M4P 2Y3
(a division of Pearson Penguin Canada Inc.)
Penguin Ireland, 25 St Stephen's Green, Dublin 2, Ireland (a division of Penguin Books Ltd)
Penguin Group (Australia), 250 Camberwell Road, Camberwell, Victoria 3124, Australia
(a division of Pearson Australia Group Pty Ltd)
Penguin Books India Pvt Ltd, 11 Community Centre, Panchsheel Park, New Delhi – 110 017, India
Penguin Group (NZ), 67 Apollo Drive, Rosedale, Auckland 0632, New Zealand
(a division of Pearson New Zealand Ltd)
Penguin Books (South Africa) (Pty) Ltd, 24 Sturdee Avenue, Rosebank, Johannesburg 2196, South Africa

Penguin Books Ltd, Registered Offices: 80 Strand, London WC2R 0RL, England

www.penguin.com

First published 2012
1

Set in 12.5/14.75 Garamond MT Std
Typeset by Jouve (UK), Milton Keynes
Printed in Great Britain by Clays Ltd, St Ives plc

A CIP catalogue record for this book is available from the British Library

ISBN: 978–1–844–88193–2

www.greenpenguin.co.uk

For each and every one of my frogs,
Wherever you may be . . .

Once Upon a Time

Once upon a time there was a young woman who opened her boyfriend's sock drawer . . .

. . . and what did I find? About twenty or thirty pairs of socks, obviously! What was strange, however, was the way they were arranged. Not in a jumble, but in orderly little rows according to colour. Black ones were grouped together, as were navy, stripes and diamonds. It was, to be honest, a bit weird, but not all that surprising, given the way he likes to have everything just perfect.

I shut the drawer quickly and quietly in case he came out from the en-suite bathroom and caught me snooping. Just then, however, I heard the electric shower being switched on. It meant I had another few minutes so I opened the next drawer down.

This one was full of underwear and, again, it was very carefully organized. By colour, then into briefs or boxers. There was a pair covered with love hearts, which I had never seen and took to be a gift from some former girlfriend. Two swimming togs were tucked in at the back.

Next I opened his wardrobe and found more. His shirts were hung according to a system, as were his trousers and even his T-shirts. At the bottom were ten pairs of footwear. Shoe, runner, boot and slipper, each sat beside its matcher in a line that might have been drawn with a ruler. (Much like my own shoes, I don't think! There always seems to be one under the bed and another in the laundry basket.)

Anyway, I had more or less finished being nosy when the shower was switched off. That meant he would be out in just another minute after drying with a towel. Something was bugging me, though, about the sock drawer. Something small that I now realized was out of place. In a room where nothing was out of place.

I went back over and opened the drawer once more. Hah! As I thought! One pair of socks in the corner was not quite as it should be. I picked them up. Underneath there was a small red box. I reached in and opened it. Inside there was a ring. A big, shiny, sparkly diamond engagement ring.

I took it out and stared at it with my mouth open. Oh, sweet Jesus! For the best part of a minute I simply stopped breathing. As I realized what it meant the key turned in the door of the en-suite bathroom. Feck! I slapped the drawer closed just as he emerged. Thankfully I had my back turned so he hadn't seen what I'd been up to. Or that I was holding the ring.

'It's nothing,' I said, and wriggled past his outstretched arms. 'I just need to . . .' I made straight for the bathroom he'd vacated.

'You just need to what?' he called after me.

I didn't answer. What I needed, however, was quite clear to me. I needed to get inside the en suite and lock the door. I needed to catch my breath. Also, I needed to think about this ring. And the proposal that must surely be imminent.

Once upon the exact same time, on the other side of the world, there was a young man who stood in line to buy a bus ticket . . .

. . . It was one of those automated machines. They have them all over Australia. There was no big queue, just one guy in front of me, so even though the shuttle bus was getting ready to depart I was sure I'd make it. Unfortunately this one guy turned out to be an awful ditherer. For a whole minute he didn't touch the screen but stared at it like 'twas written in hieroglyphics. Which it wasn't. All it asked (in English, not Egyptian) was 'Where do you want to go?' and 'How many of you are there?' Straightforward enough? Not for this guy anyway, because it took him ages to complete his transaction. At which point I leapt into action and typed in my request, chop chop. As my ticket began to print, the guy who'd delayed me stepped on to the bus. By the time the ticket fell into my hot little hand, the door had closed and the bus was pulling out of the station.

For feck sake! A glance at the timetable confirmed that the next shuttle out to the airport would be in an hour. I didn't have an hour. Not if I wanted to be on time to meet the love of my life and hand her the bouquet of roses I was carrying. I wasn't unduly put out, though. All it meant was that I'd have to take a taxi. I walked to the rank and hailed one with a big fat smile on my face. Nothing was going to dampen my joyful mood. Not when I was on my way to see her again, be with her again, at last.

*

. . . Well, my breathing returned to something like normal but otherwise I was in turmoil. About my little discovery in the sock drawer. A marriage proposal was not something I'd been expecting so soon in this relationship and I wasn't sure what my answer should be. He was a pretty decent guy, clever and ambitious, strong, tall and athletic. The kind most women would consider 'a catch'. Yes, he ticked an awful lot of boxes. And yet . . . and yet . . .

There was no need to decide right away. He hadn't offered me the ring and the actual proposal might be weeks off. At least now I was forewarned. It wasn't going to be sprung on me. Over the next few hours and days, I could ponder the matter carefully and have my mind made up by the time he got down on bended knee.

Finished in the en suite, I decided to go back out into the bedroom where I would take the earliest opportunity, while his back was turned, to put the ring back in its box. What I had not counted on was that the door would refuse to open. I turned the key but to no avail. Clockwise, anti-clockwise, jiggling it a bit in and a bit out, it just wasn't catching. Oh, sweet Jesus! Of all the days it could happen. I was locked in.

. . . the taxi had brought me within sight of the airport, which was just a few miles north of Cairns itself. Twilight was beginning to descend, so I could see the bright lights from aeroplanes and runways getting closer. And closer still. Until, all of a sudden, my taxi pulled over to the side of the road. I looked behind to *see a police car with its lights ablaze. It drove up just behind us and two female cops stepped out.*

'This is just silly, mate,' I said to the taxi-driver, shaking my head. 'Haven't those sheilas got any hoons they could be out catching?'

He didn't reply, and in the rear-view mirror I could see on his forehead a single bead of sweat.

One of the cops knocked on the window. She took the taxi-driver's licence and scrutinized it carefully. She said nothing but something seemed to displease her. She demanded his car keys, then went back to the cop car.

For feck sake! I thought once more. This was far from just a routine licence check. This driver of mine must be a criminal. Or an unfortunate illegal immigrant. Whatever he was, it seemed unlikely that he was going to get me to the airport on time. My rendezvous with the most beautiful woman in the world might not happen in the way I'd been picturing it for several months.

I picked up my bouquet of red roses and opened the car door. The taxi-driver made no attempt to dissuade me. Neither did the second cop, who was lying on the tarmac with her head stuck underneath the vehicle. I stepped out on to the Captain Cook Highway. Then I put out my thumb and began walking quickly in the direction of the brightest lights.

. . . How do I manage to get myself into these situations? It took quite a bit of calling and knocking before I got my boyfriend's attention and explained my plight. Not the most patient of guys,

he spent only a few seconds wrenching at the door handle before – bang *– without warning, the door shuddered. He had attempted to barge it down with his shoulder. I stepped back. BANG! He tried again with even greater force. This, however, was a door made by a pretty decent carpenter. BANG! Arrrrrgha! He tried one last time but succeeded only in hurting his shoulder.*

'I think, darling,' he moaned, 'that I'll have to try a different approach. Hang on while I get some tools.'

I heard him stomp away out of the bedroom and within a minute he stomped right back, this time accompanied by another set of footsteps. Altogether lighter and more refined. It could only be his mother.

'Evelyn,' she shouted, as she tried the door handle. 'Evelyn, are you all right?'

'I'm fine,' I replied, wondering why he'd had to go and get her involved.

Then he told me to take out the key and he tried the spare one. No good. Next he attacked the lock with a screwdriver but that didn't work either. Apparently it was the tool's fault for being the wrong shape . . . Eventually he admitted defeat and got his mother to ring a locksmith. She worked through a list in the phonebook but, it being a Sunday, there was only one in the whole of Dublin who was answering his phone. He said he could be over in an hour. Give or take. At which point my boyfriend grabbed the receiver and began to shout blue murder at the guy, saying it was a major emergency and he'd better come over immediately. Or be reported to the police. And so on.

Naturally the locksmith just hung up. And thereafter his number was constantly engaged. There was nothing for it but to try a few locksmiths out in Wicklow, Meath and Kildare. The one who agreed to drive into the city said he might take as much as three hours. Give or take. Four max.

. . . There was very little traffic on the road and the few cars that passed refused to give me a lift. Nevertheless I was still in a positive frame of mind. I could see my goal before me, nestled between mountains, mangroves and the Coral Sea. Step by step, I was getting there. Yes, sir! And whistling all the way.

There was one thing that became increasingly clear about the road I was on, however. Namely, that it wound its way to the airport via a large semicircle. Also apparent from studying my watch was the fact that I was going to be tight for time.

Then I came across a shortcut. It was a red dirt-track, but as far as I could tell, in the last few minutes of daylight, it cut straight through the mangrove scrubland on my right, in a direct line to the airport.

I decided to take it and was soon well pleased with my decision as I made quicker progress towards the bright lights. I was even more delighted when I came across an abandoned bicycle. An old rental model emblazoned with the Bushwacker Bikes logo, it seemed to be in perfect nick. The only problem was my attire. Dressed to impress, I was wearing a cream suit and pinstripe tie. Not ideal cycling gear. Even so, there was no time to waste so I gathered my trouser legs and put them down inside my socks. Then I balanced my bunch of roses on the handlebars. As I put leather shoe to pedal, there was a huge roar overhead and an aeroplane flew past, descending towards a runway. I laughed out loud and pushed that pedal as hard as I could.

. . . An hour is a long time when you spend it trapped in a bathroom. Three and a half hours, the length of time I wound up waiting for that bloody locksmith, is something like eternity. I suppose the only consolation is that I had full toilet facilities, water if I was thirsty and a dilemma to keep me from getting too bored.

'Right!' *I kept telling myself. 'Very soon you'll have to say yes or no to him, so while you have nothing better to do why not decide? Before that door is opened you* must *make up your mind.'*

So I pondered and paced around the bathroom in small circles. Shower, toilet, sink, bath. Shower, toilet, sink, weighing scales!

Aha . . . a welcome diversion! Anything rather than face the situation at hand! I stepped on board and waited for the display to settle. Hmm, apparently I was XX kg. Was that good or bad? *I couldn't remember. Looking down, though, I was forced to admit that my belly was protruding slightly. More than it used to.* Goddamn, *I thought,* if you don't get gym membership soon (and actually go, not just set up the direct debit) you'll be in no position to be so picky about proposals! *On the upside, I could still definitely see my toes.*

And my goose pimples! Truly this was a bad time to be wearing nothing but my underwear (a black bra and completely unmatching stripy pink knickers, if you must know!). All the towels were gone as well, so there was no possibility of fashioning a sarong to cover up.

But most of all, I spent much of those three and a half hours looking at the ring: a gold band with three large diamonds set in a row that sparkled brightly. It fitted me perfectly. Nice. In fact, it was bloody amazing. Just the one I would have picked. Truly he had a lot of excellent qualities as a boyfriend, among them his penchant for perfectly chosen gifts. This was just the latest example of his excellent taste. (Or maybe, just maybe . . . his mother's . . .)

At last, the slow crawl of time did indeed come to an end and a van pulled up outside.

'He's here,' shouted my boyfriend, triumphantly. 'We'll have that door open in a tick.'

Oh . . . and the decision that I'd promised I'd make was still not made. There was positively no more time to put it off.

. . . But the reason why the bicycle had been abandoned soon became apparent. I had only gone fifty yards when the chain fell off. I rolled up the sleeves of my suit and shirt and managed to get it back on. Unfortunately it fell off a second time, just a minute later. This time the repair was more difficult because the chain was greasy and had become jammed between the cog and the frame. In yanking it loose,

I got a black smudge on my nice shirt. And off I set once more . . .

The fourth time it detached, I threw it into the mangrove bushes and looked at my watch. There was no way I was going to walk to the airport in time. I clutched my roses tightly to my chest, put my head down and broke into a mad gallop.

'Run!' I shouted at myself. 'C'mon, John, you can do it!'

Lo and behold, I did indeed make it on time. In fact, I was jubilant to find myself a few minutes early. Which was just as well. I was no longer looking as dapper as when I'd set out and badly needed a trip to the Gents to clean myself up. Remove what I could of sweat and black bicycle grease. Prepare myself properly for the reunion with my wonderful woman.

That was the plan anyway. No sooner had I walked into the airport, however, than I saw her in the distance. Good God, but she was stunningly beautiful! To hell with the plan. I flicked my hair into place, held up my bouquet and made a beeline for her.

. . . I needed a sign.

Yes or no.

From up above.

If only I'd had a coin I would have flipped it.

If only I'd had dice I would have rolled them.

If only I'd had a Ouija board or a tarot deck or a crystal ball, I'd have given any of them a go.

But no. I had none. I knelt down and squinted through the keyhole. My boyfriend and his mother were sitting on the end of the bed. They were talking quietly, which suggested that I wasn't supposed to hear. I cupped my ear to the hole and realized that he was apologizing to her for all the inconvenience. On this the very morning of her birthday.

At which point I had an idea. Without further ado, I stood up and walked over to the toilet. I dropped the ring into it.

'Okay,' I whispered, and put my hand on the flushing lever. 'If this flush carries the ring away, that will be a sign!'

I pulled.

When the cascading waterfalls had run dry and the swirling eddies receded, the ring was . . . still there. Faithful and true, it just awaited my rescuing hand. All I had to do was reach in and . . .

I went back to the keyhole and heard the muffled sound of the locksmith stomping up the stairs. Then I heard my boyfriend greet him and explain the situation. 'It really is urgent,' he said. 'My mother's birthday dinner is in just a few hours.'

Unconsciously, my hand reached again for the toilet lever and I flushed, thinking, Okay, best of three!

The ring finally disappeared, carrying a month of my boyfriend's salary into the city's sewer. He was a pretty decent guy, I reflected, but not *my Prince Charming.*

Outside I could hear the locksmith jangling a set of skeleton keys. I knew I had only seconds before he found the correct one and put it in the lock.

I wondered if there was any point in attempting to hide behind the door.

Or in the shower.

Or . . .

Or under the bathmat?

Or . . .

And then it hit me. In a blinding flash, I knew exactly what I must do.

Frog 1

I

Perhaps flushing a toilet to decide whether to say 'Yes' or 'No' to a marriage proposal seems ridiculous. Evelyn, though, always had great difficulty whenever she faced a big decision in her love-life: paralysis by over-analysis.

Perhaps, too, that man dashing headlong towards an airport rendezvous seems a bit reckless and accident prone. John, however, knew no other way than to charge into romance with the clumsy enthusiasm of a young puppy.

In fact, the behaviour of both parties was consistent with how they'd always acted. And thought. Since many boyfriends and girlfriends ago. Stretching back, into the mists of time, all the way to January 1989 when they'd first met one another and were inches, rather than a whole world, apart . . .

'Yes, I do. He's just gone to get me a drink.'

'And you get on well together?'

'We do, yeah.'

'And how long are ye going out?'

'Three months,' said Evelyn, 'and your point is?'

'Well, what about him?' asked John. 'Maybe this Gary fella is your Prince Charming. Maybe the two of you might just go the distance.'

'Yeah . . .'

'Yeah?'

'Yeah . . . But . . . Look, let me put it to you this way . . . It was so much easier for the princess in the fairytale.'

'How so?'

'Well, lots of reasons. All she had to do was kiss a frog. Then – abracadabra!'

'Her prince appeared.'

'Exactly. But this frog's transformation into a gorgeous hunk of manhood wasn't the best of it. Even better was the fact that there was just one frog. The princess didn't have to pick randomly from, say, ten frogs. She didn't have to kiss one of those slimy creatures knowing nine out of the ten were just regular frogs. That no amount of kissing was going to transform them into princes. That in most cases she'd get nothing for her trouble but the icky taste of frog on her lips.'

'Yes, but what does this have to do with . . . ?'

'My life? Only everything! The princess equals me or any girl. The frogs equal most of the men we go out with. The taste of frog on our lips is the aftermath, when we split up, of disappointment, heartbreak and very likely a nasty cold sore.'

They were sitting facing one another in the back seat of a Ford Cortina. The car was situated in the garden of a student house on Pearse Street and was not going anywhere. There was no driver, it wasn't switched on and, in any case, it had only three wheels. The fourth corner of the car was held up by a concrete block.

They were at a house party that had been gate-crashed and then gate-crashed some more until every room was thronged with revellers, and the garden too. This rusty old banger was parked down by the tool shed. Tired of standing, Evelyn had found a door unlocked and sat in for a rest. Inside she had found this guy she didn't know, half asleep, sitting and sipping from his beer can quietly. They compared notes on who had invited them to the party. That led to a discussion of the on-again, off-again relationship of a certain couple they both knew. Which in turn was the launch pad for Evelyn to begin explaining her many theories on love and romance.

'So let me get this straight,' said John, smiling broadly and getting increasingly animated. 'All men are frogs?'

'Yes.'

'Myself included?'

'Yes, you especially.'

'But then why –'

'Why do we bother kissing you?' Evelyn shook her head. 'That is a bloody good question.'

'Maybe it's because, in fact, things are not as bleak as you make out.' John laughed, then had a swig from his can. 'Maybe because one in ten is not such bad odds. All you have to do is kiss ten frogs and you'll be more or less guaranteed that one will turn into Prince Charming.'

'Aha!' said Evelyn. 'But that is where you're wrong. Because there is another way in which reality fails to live up to the fairytale.'

'Which is?'

'The fact that, in real life, none of the frogs turns into Prince Charming.'

'What?' exclaimed John, his eyes wide in mock horror.

'Harsh but true, sir, harsh but true.'

'You're really sure?'

'Certain. I saw it on TV. A Channel 4 documentary.

Teams of female researchers have recently conducted tests at a variety of wells, lakes and ponds.'

'Really?'

'Oh, sure. And not a single frog was transformed by being kissed. Not even into a regular guy, let alone a prince.'

'Feck! Next you'll be telling me that the Three Little Pigs –'

'– were eaten by the wolf.'

'And the Three Bears?'

'Had Goldilocks for breakfast. Deal with it!'

'Oh, no!'

'Oh, yes.'

'Oh, no.'

'Oh, yes,' said Evelyn, as she reached out to poke his beer can. 'Yes, yes, yes, yes!'

At which point the pair of them burst out laughing and had to suspend the conversation until they caught their breath.

'Come on, seriously! You can't just rubbish all men, say that we're all slimy amphibians. Just because none of us lives up to the fairytale. We're not complete brutes, surely?' John demanded.

'Admittedly,' said Evelyn, 'not complete brutes. Some of ye are actually pretty sensitive. Like my boyfriend Gary, for instance. I've already said that there's no prince, no one hundred per cent perfect man, but he comes pretty close. Maybe . . . I dunno . . . eighty . . . ninety per cent.'

'Sounds good.'

'He is good. But it only raises another problem the princess never had to deal with.'

'Go on.'

'When the princess kissed her frog, the transformation into a prince was immediate. Right there and then she knew she had struck gold. The fact that he was wearing a little crown on his head was a dead giveaway. In real life, though, there is no blinding flash to confirm that you've made the right choice.'

'I see.'

'But do you see,' said Evelyn, 'what it means?'

'Not exactly.'

'If, like me, you eventually want to settle down and get married. There is no perfect man out there, but all the same I'd like to think I'll marry the best one available.'

'Fair enough.'

'But in the immortal words of that great philosopher Ms W. Houston . . .'

'What? Whitney?'

'Yes.'

'She who once sang "How Will I Know?"' he crooned into his beer can.

'The same. How will any of us ever truly know? If, for example, Whitney or, indeed, any girl has a boyfriend and he's pretty decent, with just a very few flaws – say she and he are about ninety per cent compatible – how will she know if he's the best she'll ever meet or whether she should hold out for a better one coming down the line?'

'Hmm!'

'If she settles down with the ninety per cent guy then maybe she's going to miss out on the ninety-nine per cent guy she was destined to meet two years later. On the other hand, if she breaks up with Mr Ninety-per-cent then maybe she'll wind up regretting it, for the rest of her life. A life spent meeting guys who only score seventy or eighty.'

John nodded.

'Because you can't go back. In this girl's life, each boyfriend or potential boyfriend mostly comes one at a time. It would be so much easier if you could gather the whole lot of them into one room on one day and pick the best.'

'That would be so cool.'

'Yes. Instead, though –'

'How would you pick the best?' John interrupted. 'Perhaps a wrestling contest? Let them fight it out until only the strongest boyfriend remained? Or no. Better still. Hand them all a Rubik's Cube and see which lad could get, say, three sides completed first?'

'Instead, though,' persisted Evelyn, 'as each frog comes along you have to make a big decision, stick or twist. If you twist, that frog jumps back in the pond – in all probability never to be seen again.'

They were interrupted by someone opening the driver's door of the car. It was John's friend Brian. He stubbed out his Marlboro Light on the ground and sat into the driver's seat. Then he put on his seatbelt, took a big swig of beer and placed his can carefully on the passenger seat.

'Right then,' he said, turning around to Evelyn and John. 'Where would ye like me to take ye?'

It was apparent from his slurred speech that Brian was not on his first can. Or indeed his second or third. Approximately his seventh, perhaps.

'Brian?' said John.

'I thought I told you earlier, bro – tonight you've got to call me Mr Mojo Risin', okay?' said Brian.

'O-okay . . . Mr Mojo Risin' . . . Surely you realize that this car doesn't actually . . .'

But Mr Mojo wasn't listening. He had turned back to face the steering wheel and begun to make some mechanical sounds. 'Vrooom,' said Mr Mojo. 'Vroom, vrooom, vroooooooooooom, skreeeeeeeeeeek!' he continued, and so set off on an imaginary journey, twisting the wheel this way and that through the mean streets of Dublin, pausing occasionally for another swig of beer.

It became apparent to those in the back seat that they could ignore his presence.

'I don't know,' said John, laughing. 'Your theories are convincing but you're over-complicating matters. Surely whether couples stay together or not all boils down to two simple words, which you haven't mentioned even once – true love.'

'True ick!' said Evelyn, smiling despite herself.

'Oh, ick yourself! It's very straightforward, really. Boy meets girl and, very quickly, in a matter of weeks, days or perhaps even minutes, they fall in love. Or they don't. If they don't, there's no story. Move on to the next candidate. If they do then . . . well, then . . .'

'They what?'

'Well, this is going to sound old-fashioned, I know . . . but I think they get married.'

'And live in a cottage by the sea, perhaps?' said Evelyn, with a smirk.

'Sure.'

'And have babies?'

'Why not?'

'Then grow old together? Die on the very same day? And are remembered fondly by their thirty-six grandchildren?'

'Yes, yes, and yes indeed.'

'Jesus, mister! What's your name again? I take my hat off to you! You truly are a hopeless romantic.'

'Vroom, vrooom, vroooooooooooom, skreeeeeeeeeeek,' said Brian, more quietly than before.

'Enough of these theories,' said John. 'Back to the practical. Howsabout you and this fella – Gary, isn't it? He sounds like a really cool guy.'

'He is. A wonderful and sensitive guy, in fact.'

'So why not him? Maybe he's the one you're meant to be with for ever.'

'Yeah.'

'Yeah?'

'Yeah . . . but I just have this nagging, totally irrational feeling that . . .'

As her voice trailed off, Evelyn's eyes fixed on John's and there was a moment when they both stopped talking. The only sound was from Brian, who was no longer playing at car driver. He was snoring.

What Evelyn wanted to say, but what she couldn't say, was that, although he was wonderful and amazing, she still couldn't quite decide about Gary. She couldn't admit that, despite all her logical arguments, her cynical doubts, she, too, held hopes not so different from John's romantic ideals. For a miracle between her and Gary. A magical moment of transformation when they would share a kiss that lit up the planet like a firework and after which she would see the prince inside the man. And know with total certainty that THIS was THE ONE. So far, that had not happened.

'This nagging feeling that what?' asked John, but the question froze in mid-air. At that very moment, someone outside opened the car door at Evelyn's side. You could only see the bottom half of whoever it was – a guy wearing stone-washed jeans. On closer scrutiny, he was wearing black Doc boots that went halfway up his shins and had fluorescent yellow laces. It had to be Gary.

'Here you go, babes,' he said, and his hand reached in towards Evelyn with a plastic cup of red wine.

And then the door on John's side opened too. Unfortunately he happened to be leaning against it so he fell out of the car, head first onto tarmac. His trailing feet were left sticking up in the air beside Evelyn. Which she would have found hilariously funny, except that there was a quite audible thud.

'Ouch!'

For a moment he lay still, half in, half out of the car, and looked up in a daze. The girl who had opened the door was leaning in over him asking if he was all right. She was very beautiful. Even upside down.

'I'm grand – I'm grand,' he assured her, and began to pull himself together.

'You nearly killed him, Michelle,' said Evelyn, who had got out at her side and come round to survey the damage. 'We should get him to A and E.'

John managed to stand up and began to recognize that it was not his head that had taken the worst of it. There was a very sharp pain emanating from his right arm between the elbow and wrist. 'No, honestly, I'm grand,' he said nevertheless. He reached for his beer can and picked it up with his good hand before realizing that its contents were now soaking through his jumper.

'Is that blood, man?' asked Gary, pointing at a dark stain forming on his right arm.

It was.

'God, no.'

'I think it is, actually,' said Michelle.

Oh, feck, thought John. In considerable pain. Bleeding. Drenched in beer. Most likely looking ridiculous. Being stared at by three people I don't even know, one of whom is the most fascinating woman I've ever met, another of whom is the most beautiful, and all this on the very night I forgot to apply my acne gel. Ouch! 'No, honestly, I'm grand,' he said, wincing slightly. Then he turned abruptly and walked away from them, disappearing into the party throng within seconds.

'Who the hell was that, Evelyn?' asked Michelle.

'Just some random guy,' she answered.

'And what were ye talking about?' asked Gary.

'Oh, y'know . . . the usual trivial things.'

2

That party might have been the beginning and end of it, had they not had another chance meeting just two days later. On the morning in question, John was looking for somewhere quiet to work on his stats project but couldn't use the library as he'd forgotten his student card. Wandering through the arts block, down past the lecture theatres, he found one of the big brown square box things (not quite a chair or a desk) that littered the building.

He sat down and took the maths workbook from his satchel, then a pencil and ruler. Unknown to him, two girls were watching from a distance. They saw a tall, scrawny lad of eighteen with acne and a terrible side-parted farmer-boy haircut. Not for the pleasure of basking in his attractiveness were they staring, but because he looked familiar. When John set to work on drawing his first graph, however, they knew for sure it was him. Because he was attempting to do it with one hand. He leaned in ridiculously close to hold the ruler steady with his chin. The other arm had been bandaged in an extremely amateurish fashion and was hanging by his side.

The girls walked up behind him.

'Well, well, well! If it isn't the unknown stuntman!' said Evelyn, from over his shoulder.

Startled, John turned to face her, feeling like a rabbit caught in headlamps. It was a girl with hair dyed jet black, wearing black Docs, thick black tights and a short lacy black dress. Also black mascara and eyeliner. Her lips were bright red. In other words, a Goth. In other words, though the lighting was very different, the girl he'd met in the car at the party.

'That X-axis doesn't look very straight,' she said, and moved around to face him. 'I don't think we were properly introduced,' she continued. 'I'm Evelyn Creed. First-year engineering.'

'John Fallon. First-year pharmacy.'

'Hmmm. Interesting,' she said. 'So what are your lectures about, John? Do they teach you how to count tablets?'

'No, actually.'

'It must be very complicated. Learning to be a person who counts tablets.'

'That's not . . .' John sighed. Very few people seemed to realize just how much the job of pharmacist actually entailed.

'Pink tablets, blue tablets, red tablets.'

'There's a bit more to it than –'

'Green capsules, white pills, orange, purple and yellow . . .'

John gave up trying to explain. As Evelyn continued to list every colour she could think of, he simply folded his arms and smiled patiently up into her face.

'. . . beige, maroon, gold. So, anyway, what's with the maths book?'

'Because I've been assigned a stats project and I'm no good at it.'

'Aw, shucks.'

'Evelyn, stop teasing him,' said Michelle.

'Oh, all right,' said Evelyn. She stared at John and was lost in thought for a moment. 'Tell me, John,' she continued, 'would you like a little crash course in statistics? Maybe even a little help drawing your graph?'

'Yeah. Sure.'

'The thing is that my friend Michelle here has an A in honours maths. And seeing how she's so sorry for busting your arm, she would be only too happy to give you a quick tutorial.'

'I would?' said Michelle, her left eyebrow raised.

'Yes,' said Evelyn. 'You would!'

'But –'

'Now, John,' Evelyn continued, 'could you come over to our flat this evening?'

Could he?

Of course he bloody could. Although outwardly he did his best to play it cool, John was thrilled at this turn of events. Evelyn and Michelle seemed far more sophisticated than the girls in his own class, who (except for Aoife Hennessy) all wore baggy jumpers and plain blue jeans.

As Evelyn drew out a rough map of their address, John stole a glance at Michelle. She didn't have half as much to say for herself but, my God, she was gorgeous. Really stunning, movie-star gorgeous: tall with brown curly hair, a pretty face and a perfect hour-glass figure. She, too, had a distinctive style. On top she wore a blouse of crushed purple velvet and her long paisley skirt almost touched the floor.

As Evelyn finished her instructions he looked back at her. She was pretty too, but in a more quirky way.

'We'll see you at eight,' she said, 'but now we have to head off to our next lecture.'

'Oh, yeah. Me too.'

'Is it all about how to count tablets?' asked Evelyn.

In fact it was organic chemistry. 'Oh, all right, then! I admit it.' John smiled. 'But it's how to count tablets at an advanced level.'

John's gangly scrawniness was the result of a late growth spurt. In due time, it was inevitable he'd fill out. Likewise his acne was destined to last only a few years and in any case it wasn't the really brutal sort of acne – it was usually limited to about six spots that migrated around his face. Whenever one healed, another sprang up elsewhere to take its place. It was annoying but manageable.

Nevertheless, his acne and his undernourished physique were much on John's mind that evening in his bedsit, as he prepared to visit Evelyn and Michelle. Certainly he gathered together an A4 pad and his maths textbook. Most likely he showered and shaved. More importantly, he went out and purchased a new tube of acne gel. The best one was very expensive, so he could only afford the second best. He put a good big dollop on each of his six spots. Then he made himself a little drink in a mug, comprising a raw egg, which he gulped down in one swallow. This was something he'd seen done by a boxer who was training for his big fight in the film *Rocky*. It felt both highly nutritious and quite manly. Ready for anything, John put on his windcheater and headed for Ranelagh.

Their address was 64 Marlborough Road – flat nine, to be precise. Evelyn had forewarned John that it would be impossible to ring their doorbell when he arrived. The buttons only went from one to eight because theirs was a flat that was not quite like the others. It wasn't in the main house; rather, it consisted of a little prefab out in the back garden. Luckily there was a gravel laneway by the side of the garden, leading to the mews. John's instructions were to walk down alongside the prefab, pick up a handful of pebbles from the lane and throw them onto the flat felt roof.

'Remind me again, Evelyn, why you invited this fine specimen of manhood,' said Michelle, when she heard the stones falling overhead . . .

'Now, now, Michelle. Less of the bitchiness. It's just for one hour. To help the poor guy out. Be nice.' Evelyn stepped out, jangling keys, and made her way across the lawn, through the house and all the way up to the front door to let him in.

John couldn't understand it.

'Are you familiar,' said Michelle, as she scribbled some symbols on an A4 pad, 'with this one for standard deviation?'

$$\sigma = \sqrt{} [\Sigma (X_i - \mu)^2 / N]$$

'God, no,' he replied. 'That's why I'm here.'

'Fair enough,' said Michelle. 'Let's take it back to basics, then. The mean of any sample, which is to say the average, is usually expressed as . . .'

$$M = \Sigma x / n$$

'What's that E stand for?' he asked.

'Silly! That's not an E.' Evelyn leaned in and corrected him. 'It's a symbol that means the sum of a set of numbers.'

'Oh, feck,' said John, already feeling very stupid.

Mercifully Michelle decided to leave the formulae and talk in very general terms about the science of statistics. That went a little better. They were making definite progress until she mentioned the importance of sample size.

'The importance of size?' said Evelyn, with the beginning of a smile.

'Yes,' said John, happy to be on a topic that he even partly understood. 'I read about that in the maths book. Obviously bigger is better.'

'Mmm. So I hear.' She started laughing and gave Michelle an elbow in the ribs. '*Much better!* Michelle is the girl who'll tell you that . . .'

John didn't really understand but found himself blushing anyway. 'It has a big impact,' he said, 'on something called the confidence interval.'

'A *very* big impact!' echoed Michelle, who also seemed suddenly to find this area of statistics funny.

'And does your fella always give you a . . . confidence interval?' laughed Evelyn.

'He certainly does,' giggled Michelle. 'Often several of them!'

What? Who? What were they on about? Being a bit innocent, it took John several seconds to grasp that there must be sexual overtones. None of the girls in first-year pharmacy ever talked like this. For that matter, none of them, in so far as he could tell, had ever had sex. (For that matter, neither, of course, had John.)

Meanwhile his two tutors fell around the room and nearly choked themselves laughing. Their innuendo was funny enough, but what capped it off was the perplexed expression on John's face.

'Right,' said Evelyn, when she finally managed to catch her breath. 'I think it's time for tea and HobNobs.'

So that was the end of the lesson. But somehow John did not go home. Rather (as the two-bar heater was plugged in), he stayed on to listen to Evelyn explaining why the Smiths were the best rock band in the history of the world, for ever and ever, amen. Utterly dismissing his favourite band (Queen), she went on to hold forth on a dozen different topics ranging from the trivial to the deeply existential. Like . . . the wedding of Scott and Charlene . . . the God-shaped hole in her life . . . the hideous perm her mother had forced her to get when she was fourteen, all photographic evidence of which she had since systematically destroyed . . . whether it was possible to be simultaneously pro-choice and anti-abortion . . . the fact that she was born in New York when her parents used to work there . . . a dream she'd once had that could only be explained by Jung's theory of the collective unconscious . . . and how much she hated U2.

It was nearly one a.m. before John took his leave, having learned very little about statistics – but they had all had a good laugh and it was Michelle who made him promise to come again for a further tutorial later that week.

Which he did. In fact, John became a regular caller to the prefab at 64 Marlborough Road. The stated aim of his visits was to work on his stats project, but that always ran aground and they wound up chit-chatting instead. Which he loved. This, after all, was what he had dreamed college would be all about. Hanging around with gorgeous and clever young women, not attending boring lectures on pharmaceutics.

What the girls saw in John was not so clear. Perhaps the fact that he was funny, sometimes on purpose, most often in ways he didn't intend. Naïve and unfailingly enthusiastic about everything, except stats, perhaps he was kind of like their pet. Or a male doll they could play with. Shortly after their first meeting, they took him shopping to try to make him dress a bit cooler. All he bought was a long grey army coat, second hand, in Eager Beaver – it looked sort of Russian. The girls decided it required a name and christened it 'Sven'. On another night they mentioned to John that he badly needed a haircut and volunteered themselves for the task. With a pair of scissors apiece, Evelyn and Michelle each took one side of his head and began to chop. The results were not too bad.

But none too symmetrical either.

3

Nor was John the only regular visitor to the prefab at 64. On most evenings, it was a hive of activity as friends like Joan, Cliona and Niamh dropped in to discuss lectures, eat chocolate HobNobs and figure out where to go on Thursday night. The most regular visitor of all, however, was a lad from second-year economics. A lad who was certainly not 100 per cent perfect but by Evelyn's estimate probably scored at least 90. Her boyfriend Gary.

Although brown-haired and only reasonably handsome, he was (not unlike Evelyn herself) a guy who stood out from the crowd in many ways, most obviously on account of his extremely trendy attire. He never went outside the door without his pair of tall black Doc boots with fluorescent yellow laces. In addition he wore his hair in a quiff and generally sported a red polka-dot shirt with stone-washed jeans. The jeans (of which there were only ever two pairs, one in the laundry and one on his legs) invariably had the bottoms rolled up and slogans written on them in black marker – 'Love', 'Death', 'Anarchy' and other super-cool words. Most distinctive of all was his habit of wearing (not in college obviously, just in the kitchenette of his own flat) an apron.

'Oh, my Lord,' Evelyn had said, on the first occasion that he cooked for her. 'This pork casserole is delicious.'

'It's not just any old casserole, babes. It's Somerset,' he had corrected her, but there was even better to come when he served up a homemade pavlova. It, too, was absolutely scrumptious. Gary, it emerged, was one of a very rare breed: male students who can not only cook but actually enjoy the task. Over the course of the next few months, he treated Evelyn to a variety of other meals, including roasts, salads and, his signature dish, beef Stroganoff. Most of the other guys Evelyn knew subsisted on things like packet soup, crispy pancakes (which were nothing like actual pancakes, just some mince of dog-food quality wrapped in orange breadcrumbs) and meatballs (canned mince of dog-food quality fashioned into spheres).

There were other ways in which Gary was different from the average Joe. From the very first morning when she had met him in the buttery, Gary had impressed her as someone who knew both how to talk and how to listen. A rare combination. As their conversation went deeper over a slice of biscuit cake, she experienced for the first time the intoxicating thrill of revealing her innermost feelings to another human being. When she told him things, stuff about her childhood and her difficult relationship with her mother, her opinions on the latest referendum, his focus was total. She realized that nobody before had ever made her feel so strongly that what she was saying mattered. When he spoke, his comments were fresh with insight and understanding.

Finally there was one other thing about Gary. If asked to describe him in just one word, Evelyn always chose 'sensitive'. This description was really a code. What it meant was that, as well as being able to discuss emotions, he liked to hug. And to cuddle. It also meant that when their clothes were removed and they went to bed together, Gary was a lad who knew there was such a thing as an erogenous zone. And in addition, even with the lights switched off, he had a fair idea of where to find one.

Gary was Evelyn's first proper boyfriend, but their relationship was far from the first time she'd become entangled with a member of the opposite sex. She had already known a dozen loves and crushes of varying intensity. As early as the age of eight she had had a strong attachment to a boy with a nice smile at the newsagent's. When he abruptly stopped working there, she was distraught. His replacement was old and ugly, and when he smiled, Evelyn could see flashes of metal.

It was a few years later that she noticed another nice boy – at Mass with his parents, four rows back in the left aisle. From then on, Sunday became her day to look forward to. Her one guaranteed day when she might watch this boy for the best part of an hour. In due course, she was no longer satisfied to look and wanted to get closer. There was, however, no question of moving over to a pew in the left aisle. Her family never sat on that side. It would be unthinkable. Instead, the obvious time to get near was during the free-for-all of Communion. As the congregation left their pews and headed towards the altar, Evelyn tried to time her approach so as to intersect with the boy's. Some weeks she managed to get a spot in the queue right on the boy's shoulder. Other times she made it so that she was going up just as he was going down. There was almost a collision as she looked into his face and stepped sideways to prevent him going around.

And then one cursed week, just like the boy at the newsagent's, Evelyn's boy at Mass was gone. Presumably his family had moved away. Or maybe they had all been run over by a bus. Not particularly likely was Evelyn's favourite theory that they had switched religion. Possibly emigrated to the USA and become Amish. Evelyn had done a project in school on the Amish people and liked the idea of her boy wearing a broad-brimmed hat and riding around on a horse and wagon.

The teenage years began and Evelyn had several other obsessions, mostly with older boys, once with a girl in sixth year. All of these 'relationships' were unrequited but, on the other hand, she was also kissed by two or three guys. It always happened at the annual discos in the community hall during the summer festival week. They were not guys she really liked, just ones who asked her to dance and were bold enough to grab the moment. The kiss, indeed the entire relationship, generally lasted for the duration of a slow set. 'The Power Of Love' (Jennifer Rush version), 'Wonderful Tonight', 'Two Out Of Three Ain't Bad'. One year a boy grabbed at her breasts and she slapped him in the face. Relationship over. He laughed it off and spent the rest of the week telling everyone that she was frigid. And a lesbian. And a crap kisser. Next year when the festival disco came around, Evelyn decided to give it a miss.

Fifteen, sixteen and seventeen were the years when Evelyn began to dress all in black and listen to music by the Cure, Joy Division and most especially the Smiths.

'There are so many colours in the rainbow,' said her mother.

'I wear black on the outside,' Evelyn replied, 'because black is how I feel on the inside.'

Which annoyed her mother no end. As did the state of Evelyn's bedroom, the walls covered with posters of sad young men who had unusual haircuts. As did the sound of funeral dirges leaking downstairs through the floorboards.

'You'll burst your eardrums and not be able to hear a thing!' she said, after plugging out the cassette player for the nth time.

'Possibly,' said Evelyn, coolly, 'that wouldn't be all bad . . .'

Evelyn wasn't suicidally depressed or anything. Just a bit mixed up, a bit apprehensive of adulthood, just a bit determined to stand out from the crowd. That mass of other girls who wore pastel. And got their hair permed. And wore little gold chains around their necks with their names on. And listened to Madonna on their Walkmans. And went to see U2 in Croke Park with their parka-clad older brothers. And whispered, 'Evelyn Creed is such a weirdo.'

During her Leaving Cert year, Evelyn had a few near misses that owed a lot to the type of boy she usually attracted. Fellow Goths. Shy boys. In other words, guys who gazed at her longingly across the crowded floor of the local disco but never had the gumption to walk right up and take her hand.

At last came the longed-for escape from her small town in Longford to the new gold dream of college in the big city. In the very first week she met Gary. The minor marvel that was Gary. They hooked up after a long day spent walking and talking that culminated in a kiss. For the first time in Evelyn's life the guy she had a crush on and the guy she was kissing were one and the same.

Gary generally slept over in 64 every second night. Michelle, too, had a boyfriend but by contrast he never slept over and indeed never came around. In fact, his identity was a closely guarded secret. Cliona, Niamh and Joan were not told. John hadn't a clue. The only person Michelle confided in was Evelyn and she was sworn to silence.

One night towards the end of January, Evelyn and Gary were lying side by side in bed in a state of post-coital bliss. They were both reading books – Gary a feminist text called *The Female Eunuch*, and Evelyn a novel called *The Bonfire of the Vanities*.

'She seems to think every man is, by definition, an oppressor of women,' said Gary, indignantly. 'She's very unfair.'

'Who?' said Evelyn. 'Michelle?'

'No!' said Gary, pointing at his book. 'This author. Germaine Greer.'

'Oh . . . yes,' said Evelyn, who was in the middle of a very interesting paragraph.

'I don't oppress women, do I, Evelyn?'

'No, of course not, Gary,' said Evelyn, still not looking up as she reached the crucial line where the Mercedes hits the skinny boy.

'I don't, as this Ms Greer claims, take away your joy, do I?'

'What Gary? Ahmm . . . no.'

'I didn't think so,' said Gary, triumphantly, and closed his book. 'Speaking of Michelle, where is she tonight?'

'Gone out with her boyfriend.'

'Oh, c'mon! You can tell me his first name, surely,' said Gary, as he wrapped his arms around Evelyn and began to give her a cuddle.

'No,' said Evelyn, marking her page and turning to face him once more.

'But why not?'

'If I told you why not, then you'd know the thing you're not supposed to know.'

'Huh?'

'Look,' said Evelyn, 'I'll tell you this much. I don't like him. Though extremely good-looking and intelligent, he's not a nice guy. Not like you. I can only see the relationship ending badly.'

'But why doesn't he ever visit her here?'

'Because,' said Evelyn, wistfully, trying to decide how to put it, 'because . . . because he prefers to take her to more exotic locations . . .'

Even as Evelyn spoke, Michelle was in an exotic location. It was a locked classroom on the third floor of the Trinity College arts block. The lights had been switched off and she was lying on her back on the carpet-tiled floor.

Her knickers and tights had been discarded.

Making love to her was the good-looking, intelligent boyfriend. A man who was also a professor in the college. And husband to a wife.

'You should never kiss another girl's frog,' Evelyn had protested, when she first found out. 'That is totally ick.'

'But he doesn't have any children,' Michelle had explained, 'so it's not that bad.'

'It is that bad,' insisted Evelyn. 'He's married. The fact he doesn't have tadpoles is no bloody excuse.'

But Michelle wouldn't listen. Her mysterious boyfriend was a very skilled lover, no matter how unpromising the location. Pretty much simultaneously, they both began to cry out.

4

A week later, Michelle was crying again. This time, however, there were tears too, because her mystery man had dumped her. She was lying in her bed, with Evelyn sitting on the edge trying to console her, when they heard a knock on the door.

John's visits to 64 had become so frequent that he sometimes didn't bother throwing pebbles on their roof. Instead he would clamber over the high wall and straight into the back garden.

'Not good timing,' said Evelyn, as she let him in, 'but maybe you can make yourself useful.' She returned to Michelle's side. 'You have to eat, Michelle. Come on, you haven't had a pick since breakfast yesterday! I'll stay with you, and John can fix you up something.'

So John went to the kitchen and looked around for inspiration. Unfortunately his ability to prepare food was nowhere near that of Gary. Although the fridge was full and the press contained rice and pasta, he decided that the answer was toast. Or, better still, beans on toast.

The girls did not possess a toaster so he decided to use the grill. It failed to come on, though, when he twisted the dial. He went back into the bedroom where the girls were whispering. Evelyn looked up. 'Yes, Einstein, it's broken,' she said testily. 'The landlord has promised to fix it tomorrow. We need that food right now, though. Can you do it or not?'

Bloody hell! thought John. He went back to the kitchen, opened a cupboard and could see no packet soup or even a packet of HobNobs. One thing was for certain: he wasn't going to be welcome in the bedroom without food. His eyes alighted on their two-bar heater and he remembered a trick he'd seen his mate Brian do once. He simply propped the heater up at an angle with some books, plugged it in and placed two slices of bread on the curved metal guard. They were nicely browned by the time he had the tea ready. The only flaw was that they had moulded to the shape of the heater and were a little bit curvy. Which made it hard to get the beans on board. Nevertheless, John persevered and, in due course, offered Michelle two slices of beans on toast.

'Thank you,' she croaked, as she sat up in the bed. 'That looks . . . ahmm . . . nice.'

'I keep telling her,' said Evelyn, 'that he was a total jerk and she's better off without him. I tell her she keeps falling for bad boys who seem wonderful but then break her heart. Next time around she needs to find a nice guy.'

John nodded furiously at this sound advice.

'Someone more like Gary,' continued Evelyn. 'Do you know anyone suitable, John?'

John shrugged. Michelle took a bite of her roundy toast.

The plan for that evening was to meet Gary and various other people down in the Horseshow House bar. Michelle was in no mood to go but Evelyn persuaded her. Later they moved on to the disco at Lansdowne. It was packed and there was a brilliant atmosphere. Brilliant, at least, until Michelle suddenly dropped her glass of Ritz and fled to the ladies' toilets. Evelyn gave chase.

After Michelle had stopped crying, she had to touch up her makeup in the mirror. She wore a grim expression as they came back out and an even grimmer one when Gary asked Evelyn on to the floor for a slow set. Michelle edged over beside John, who had met up with his friend Brian. They were holding up the back wall, refusing to dance until a song came on that they deemed to be cool.

'Buy me another Ritz, will you, John?' Michelle asked. 'No, in fact, please make it two.'

When he returned from the bar, she gulped both glasses back in a minute and then asked did he want to dance. Brian drifted away in the general direction of the Gents.

Me? thought John, as he followed Michelle to the middle of the dance floor. The song playing was not remotely cool, but he decided to make an exception. He began to bend his knees and wave his arms.

Back at 64, quite a few people packed into the tiny kitchen. Besides the two tenants, there were Gary, Niamh, Siobhan, Cliona, Cliona's boyfriend and John. There weren't enough seats or enough cups so they took it in turns to have tea and HobNobs.

Gary sat in a corner with Evelyn on his lap and broached the subject of where everyone intended to go for the summer. New York? Boston? London? Or where? None of the others had given the matter much thought. Gary, however, had a proposal that he wanted to promote: Germany. Specifically a village called Odenwald, about fifty miles south of Frankfurt. According to his cousin, it had a cherry-processing factory where they could all get work easily. Well paid, with food and accommodation supplied, they'd be guaranteed to come home with the best part of two thousand pounds.

'But you don't speak German,' said Evelyn.

'I know,' he said, with a grin. 'That's why you're coming.'

'I am? This is the first I've heard of it.'

'But you did honours German for the Leaving, babes.'

'True but –'

'And, anyway, we wouldn't want to spend a whole summer apart,' he said, 'would we?'

'No, definitely not,' said Evelyn, her voice sounding less than definite. 'We wouldn't.'

'It's pushing three a.m.,' Michelle said. 'Time for bed?'

Everyone agreed, and Niamh and Siobhan departed immediately because they lived just around the corner on Morehampton Road. John was about to do the same when it began to rain heavily. The prospect of walking all the way home to Rathmines, in such conditions, was a daunting one.

'I won't hear of it,' said Evelyn. 'You can crash here.'

Which was grand but where was he to stay when the prefab was so full? The answer was unexpected. Without batting an eyelid, Michelle spoke up and made the sleeping arrangements: 'Cliona, you and your man can have the couch in the front room. Gary will sleep with Evelyn, and John can crash in my room.'

John looked a little bit stunned. Evelyn may, or may not, have flinched slightly. No one made any objection, though. Everyone shuffled towards their place of rest.

All John took off were his boots and socks. And his long grey army coat, the one called Sven. While Michelle was in the bathroom brushing her teeth, he lay down on the floor alongside her bed. Initially he rolled up Sven to use as a pillow but found himself getting very cold. He decided the boots could be his pillow and pulled Sven over himself as a blanket instead.

'What the feck are you doing down there?' asked Michelle, when she came in. She closed the door firmly. She was now wearing just a T-shirt with a print of two kittens on it. A long T-shirt, admittedly, but a lot of leg was visible.

'Ahmm . . . I thought . . .'

'It's freezing,' she said. 'Just get in the bed.'

Michelle switched out the light and John did as he was told. But still tried to position himself so as not to cross the line. A difficult task in a skinny single bed. For a moment they both lay on their backs but there just wasn't room. John tried turning on his side facing outwards while Michelle did the same. He scrunched his eyes closed but couldn't get comfortable. He switched to his other shoulder but it was still no good. He opened his eyes and there was Michelle.

Just inches away and facing him.

Eyes open and a smile visible in the moonlight.

'So, anyway,' John said, 'what was your favourite song at the disco tonight? I was a bit disappointed they didn't play "Radio Gaga".'

Michelle didn't answer. She lunged forward and shut him up with a kiss. A wet, sweet kiss that tasted strongly of Ritz.

There was kissing going on in two other rooms of the prefab at the same time. Cliona and her boyfriend were side by side on the couch in the front room. Both pairs of eyes were closed, however, and they were drifting off to sleep. Evelyn and Gary, meanwhile, shared a perfunctory peck before quickly proceeding to take off each other's clothes and wrapping tightly together.

*

John's experience of kissing, as of many other things, was not extensive. There had been a very quick peck with Elaine O'Mahony in the Gaeltacht and another with Roisin at the retreat house in Spanish Point. In fact, the only one that had involved tongues was with Fiona Carmody on the night after the Leaving results. Even that had lasted no more than a minute before she stumbled away to get sick. This kiss with Michelle was of a totally different order. For one thing, once joined, their mouths did not part for ten minutes. Also, the motions of Michelle's tongue, in and out, round and round, left him in no doubt that he was in the arms of a woman with experience.

Nor were their mouths the only point of contact. Squashed tightly on the single bed, John had little choice but to rest his hand on Michelle's hip. Once it was established there, though, his instinct was to manoeuvre towards an even greater prize. Her breasts. He did it by degrees, slowly migrating his hand up along her T-shirt, millimetre by millimetre. So it might just seem (he hoped) to Michelle that it wasn't moving at all. Until finally he made it to the mountain. His hand was on Michelle Neylon's right breast.

Oh, hallelujah, he thought. Look at me! With one of the best-looking girls in college. *Me?* Ha-ha!'

And then things got better. Michelle pulled open a few buttons on his shirt and put her hand inside on his chest. John felt that therefore he was duly authorized to go under her T-shirt and put his hand directly on her breast. And yes! He was right! He cupped it, caressed it and felt the absolute miracle of it, skin on skin. The softness of it. The considerable weight of it. And the nipple.

In the case of Fiona Carmody, John had only got to do this for about five seconds (uncomfortably reaching up beneath a tight blouse) before she departed abruptly. This time he stayed stroking that breast for what seemed a blissful eternity.

'Sit up a minute,' gasped Michelle, breaking off their kiss momentarily. He did as she said, and had the shirt pulled from his back. Michelle followed up by removing her own T-shirt and her breasts swung free.

Oh, good God! John thought. If the world should end right now, then I really wouldn't mind. At least I can now say that for one night I lived. Truly, truly lived.

At which point Michelle picked up his hand and placed it on her knickers.

Evelyn was naked and lying in bed with the quilt pulled up as far as her chin. Gary was not alongside her. Rather, he was under the quilt, halfway down along the bed, and tracing tiny circles with his tongue. Half a centimetre from exactly the right spot. He paused for a moment. 'Here?' he asked.

'Just a bit lower,' Evelyn gasped.

Which he duly did and then there was no more talking.

Michelle pulled out the drawer of her bedside locker and rummaged inside.

'Here,' she whispered, and handed John a condom. She even sat up and put it on for him before lying back down.

Oh, good God! John thought. Good God!

For John and for Evelyn, events came to a similar conclusion. Gasps for breath and a collapse into bliss.

5

I love her, thought John. I absolutely love her.

It was the morning after the night before and he was walking through Donnybrook on his way to a lecture in the School of Pharmacy at Shrewsbury Road. But he wasn't simply walking. He was strutting to a mental soundtrack of 'Stayin' Alive' by the Bee Gees. He felt even taller than his actual six feet. Seven feet, perhaps, eight or nine. He was bouncing on the soles of his shoes.

I love her. I love her. I love her, he thought. I love her. I love her. I love her. I love her.

He loved Michelle and was overwhelmed with the realization of how wonderful life could be and how simple it was to find happiness.

I have located Heaven, he thought, and it is neither in the clouds nor at the bottom of the sea. It's here. It's in a prefab on Marlborough Road, Dublin, Ireland. In a freezing cold bedroom. On a bed. And last night it was contained within my arms.

After they had made love, John had spent an hour stroking Michelle's hair, long brown wavy tresses that fell past her shoulders. He traced his thumb along the curve of her figure and then back up to her face. He circled her eyes and he loved her. He circled down to her chin and he loved her. He kissed her gently on the lips and he loved her.

It was only then he had noticed she was snoring lightly. He loved her. Also he became aware that she was lying on his right arm. It was stuck in under her neck and getting quite numb. He couldn't really feel it properly. But he loved her. The obvious thing to do was pull it out and yet he couldn't. That would have seemed unromantic. Instead he kept on kissing her face and touching lightly the curve of her breasts until sleep finally overpowered his discomfort near daybreak.

He loved her so very, very much.

Skreeeeeeeeeeeeeeeek.

'Sorry, sir.'

'Will you look where you're going, you big eejit?'

Crossing the junction at the Stillorgan dual-carriageway, he had failed to look left or right and stepped out in front of a truck. The driver hit the brakes in time and there was no damage done. John jogged across to the safety of the footpath and continued to float along to his ten o'clock lecture, basking in the afterglow of a night spent with a goddess.

The goddess in question was also out walking, on her way into Trinity for a fluid-mechanics practical accompanied by Evelyn.

'To be honest, I wasn't looking past last night,' said Michelle, rubbing the tiredness from her eyes.

'No way,' said Evelyn, who was a lot more awake. 'But he's just what you need right now. You should go out with him. He's a great guy.'

'Na-ah.'

'He is too!'

'Fine, Evelyn. If you say so. He's great. But it doesn't matter. Last night was just last night. A ration of passion.

All I wanted was to put my ex further behind me and now I have. Anyway, did you bring the lecture notes? I need a glance at them or I won't have a clue.'

'I did,' said Evelyn, and produced a handful of A4 sheets from her bag. She held them towards Michelle, then pulled them out of reach again. 'But you're not getting them until you at least consider some of John's good points.'

Michelle sighed. 'Go on.'

'Okay. Now I know this probably sounds a bit educational,' said Evelyn, smirking and adopting the accent of their old school principal back home in Ballymahon, 'but I've this list in my mind of qualities I think are essential in a man. They might be even more important for you to learn than anything you'll get from a college lecture.'

'Here we go again. Lucky me! Advice from my very own relationship counsellor.'

'No, listen, I wouldn't even charge you money for this session, Michelle. The way I remember them all is with a mnemonic I made up last summer. It's GITH-TH-SSS.'

'Wow, Evelyn, it really trips off the tongue.'

'Want to guess what each letter stands for? GITH-TH-SSS?'

'No, I don't! Just tell me.'

'Okay. Now listen close. He must be . . . a good person.'

'Hmm. Possibly . . .'

'Intelligent, trustworthy, and have a sense of humour.'

'Just how many items are on this list?'

'Must be taller than you, handsome, slightly scruffy, unafraid of spiders and have a nice smile.'

'Yeah, okay,' said Michelle, 'that probably covers everything. Can I have those notes now?'

'Not until you admit that John ticks most of those boxes. Except maybe the bit about spiders – we haven't seen him deal with one yet.'

'Sure, Evelyn.'

'So there's no reason you shouldn't go out with him.'

'There is. You know and I know that he's just not my type.'

'But he should be your type,' implored Evelyn.

'Well, he isn't!' said Michelle. 'You're the confused romantic who still half believes in fairytales. I, on the other hand, am very much not.'

But then she softened her line slightly. Because she wanted the lecture notes. 'Oh, what the hell? I suppose it can't do any harm. Okay. If it makes you happy I'll go out with him for a week or two. Just for a bit of fun.'

'For a bit of fun? You're so –'

'Yes, I'm unromantic. We've already established that. Can I have the notes now?'

'But why?'

'Because I want to read them.'

'No. I mean why are you so unromantic?'

'Blame it on my father, Evelyn. Or my mother. Or both. Their marriage. Whatever. I'm not looking for Prince Charming. I just don't believe in that frog crap you go on with. I just believe in men and women. Sometimes having sex. When the mood takes them. And, thanks to the invention of contraception, with no further consequence.'

Evelyn shook her head and sighed deeply.

'And what about you, Ms Relationship Counsellor?' said Michelle. 'Let's turn the spotlight on you for a change. Did I imagine it, or were you a bit thrown last night when Gary told you where you are spending this summer?'

'. . . No.'

'Yes, you were,' laughed Michelle. 'Don't try to deny it.'

'Was not!'

'And as for this checklist of yours, how many of those vital qualities does Gary have?'

'Oh,' said Evelyn, 'all of them, obviously.'

'All of them?'

'Yes. He does absolutely.'

'Absolutely?' Michelle raised her eyebrows a fraction. 'Well, Evelyn,' she continued, 'if Gary really does tick every single one of your boxes, I can only conclude that you've got a box missing.'

'Why you absolute bi–' said Evelyn, laughing at her cheek.

They were walking through the Nassau Street entrance to college and were greeted by Cliona and Joan so there was no time for Evelyn to construct more of a reply.

Gary, meanwhile, was back in his own flat. He was sitting at his table, with a biro in his hand, and before him were two sheets of paper. One was blank and on the other there were four questions about microeconomics. He had decided to skip three lectures in order to write up this assignment, which had to be in by two o'clock. He had already failed to hand up the last two such projects, each worth 10 per cent of the year's overall result, so he could ill afford to drop more marks.

As the seconds and minutes drifted by he sat motionless at the table and put not so much as a dot of ink on the blank page. He stared out of the window at the drainpipe as a crow landed on it. He watched it preen itself with its beak before flying away again.

1) Define the Price Elasticity of Demand.

I wonder, thought Gary, how much it would cost to buy a Vespa.

His flat was all the way out in Rathgar, which made for a long walk home from college or else the hassle of dealing with buses. Standing waiting for a 15A or B. Which often turned out to be full and drove past without stopping. Or if it did stop, it did so several yards past the bus stop, causing the queue to dissolve into chaos. Those people near the back would be delighted, pressing forward towards the door, instead of waiting for those at the front who were entitled to be first. It wasn't pretty.

Then there's the price of petrol. And insurance.

1) Define the Price Elasticity of Demand.

The tennis court in college, Gary pondered. I wonder how you go about booking a game. Maybe there's some club you have to sign up for. I doubt that you can just turn up with your racquet anyway. There's bound to be some sort of timesheet where you get marked down for a slot. I must check it out tomorrow. I have the racquet. I have a few balls. I –

1) Define the Price Elasticity of Demand.

If the truth be known, Gary had not much interest in economics. He was doing the course to placate his parents. Fortunately the first year had been a bit of a doddle. Most of the material was just common sense and he had managed a 2:2 without much effort. The second year was proving a bit harder. One actually needed to consult the textbooks and attend the odd lecture. And, upon attending, actually listen to what the lecturer was saying.

1) Define the Price Elasticity of Demand.

Eventually accepting that the deadline was not going

to be made, Gary took off his Doc boots with the yellow laces and put on his slippers instead. Then he reached for his apron and moved over to the kitchenette to cook something nice. He looked in the tiny fridge. Egg, cheese, bacon, mushroom. Yes, an omelette would be just the job.

6

So, John and Michelle became boyfriend and girlfriend. In fact, they were together for seventy-three days, much longer than Michelle had planned if perhaps shorter than John had hoped. His daydreams (of marriage and a cottage by the sea) had never been a realistic possibility, though. Their future was never going to involve him standing at the altar as Michelle's father led her down the aisle. (Unless, just maybe, he had decided to become a priest.) Nevertheless their first thirty days, in particular, were happy ones for John as he wandered around in a state of permanent elation. Michelle and he met up almost every day, in college, in the prefab at 64 Marlborough Road or occasionally at his flat, and did a huge amount of kissing, snogging and cuddling.

Some other highlights included: their first proper date, *Young Guns* starring Emilio Estevez, Kiefer Sutherland and Charlie Sheen at eight forty-five p.m. in the Carlton – it was watchable but by no means a classic, which was probably for the best as they spent most of the second half with their tongues in each other's mouth; the disco at McGonagles where John noticed for the first time Michelle's adorable style of dancing, which was all in her shoulders with very little movement below the waist (Brian said it looked a bit weird but Brian was an idiot: it was, John declared, the loveliest thing).

When John went to look for Michelle in the Lecky Library she was away from her desk. He recognized her bag and the lecture notes scattered all around. Something caught his eye in the margin of one. He leaned in closer to look. It was a doodle of a heart with an arrow through it. Inside were the names 'Michelle Neylon' and 'John Fallon'.

Valentine's Day. John wasn't sure what to write on his card. Obviously 'I love you' would feature somewhere, but what else? Just how far should he go in expressing that his feelings would last until the end of time? John sensed that might seem too much, too soon. He stuck with a simple 'I love you' and three Xs. And a bunch of flowers. And a brilliant mix tape of Queen and Billy Joel songs he'd made especially for her.

He went to 64 to bring Michelle to dinner at Banjo's diner and presented her with the gifts. 'Oh, feckity feck,' she said. 'I'd almost forgotten. Hang on while I get yours.'

She went into the bedroom and returned holding a green box. 'I don't understand,' she said. 'I had a card for you as well but it's not where I left it.'

Evelyn breezed into the kitchen as he opened the box to reveal a pair of braces. They were orange, with a blue paisley pattern. 'Hey there,' she said.

'You wouldn't happen to know where the card's gone, would you?' asked Michelle, eyeing her suspiciously as John picked up the braces and put them on straight away.

'Who – me?' said Evelyn, with a big smile, and swiftly changed the topic. 'Those are some cool braces, John.'

'Thanks. You look . . . pretty good yourself.'

In fact, she was not dressed up at all. She was in her most worn-out clothes and an apron. Gary's apron.

'So you're sure, Evelyn,' said Michelle, 'that you don't know where the card is?'

'I think,' said Evelyn, 'ye'd better hurry. A classy diner like Banjo's won't hold that table for two for ever, y'know!'

Also highly significant for John, though not directly involving Michelle, was the Wednesday morning when he went to play five-a-side indoor soccer in the sports hall.

'I heard from Brian that you're shifting Julia Roberts,' said one of the lads in the dressing room.

'Huh?' said John.

'Michelle Neylon, first-year engineering,' explained another. 'That's what we all call her.'

'Oh,' said John. 'Michelle. Yes, I suppose I am.'

'You fucking jammy bastard, you.'

There were nods all round. And when the game started all the lads tackled John much harder than was really necessary, whether the ball was in his vicinity or not.

That same period was also an eventful one in the liaison between Evelyn and Gary. To begin with, the relationship had gone swimmingly but then one or two little things happened, which Evelyn found slightly annoying.

The reason Evelyn didn't get dolled up on Valentine's Day, the reason she wore an apron, was because she had decided to cook a meal for Gary. He had done it for her on numerous occasions and she wanted to return the favour. Also, she wanted to prove that she was actually capable of making something more complicated than spaghetti Bolognese. To that end she made extensive preparations, hauling several bags of raw materials from the supermarket in Ranelagh and even going so far as to ring her mother and ask her to confirm the exact ingredients for apple crumble.

Unfortunately, things did not go exactly to plan. The problem was nothing to do with Evelyn's cooking abilities and everything to do with the limitations of the prefab where she lived. In order to cook the meal, she needed to use the oven, the grill and all four rings simultaneously. Therefore she needed quite a bit of electricity. In a regular home that wouldn't have presented a difficulty but in the prefab the electricity was metered and had to be paid for by feeding in 50p pieces. Normally this was fine when all that was switched on were a few light bulbs and perhaps the two-bar heater. In this case, however, the demand was much greater and the money was eaten up a lot faster. By the time Gary arrived, Evelyn was stressed. There was the effort of trying to co-ordinate so many ingredients as well as the fact she was on her last coin and most of the food was still not cooked. Gary had come without any change so the electricity abruptly cut out. They stood in the darkness for a moment while Evelyn made a decision.

Whether to laugh or cry.

'It's no big deal, babes. I can go back out to Ranelagh,' said Gary. 'There's bound to be somewhere I can get change.'

Evelyn decided to laugh. She threw her arms around him and searched for his mouth with her lips. A few minutes of cuddling later, Gary lifted her onto the table. She unbuckled his belt and they proceeded to heat up even as the half-cooked food went cold.

Not so wonderful, however, was a night two weeks later when Evelyn was lying in bed with the quilt pulled up as far as her chin. Gary was in the bed too but not alongside her.

'Oh, well,' Evelyn murmured, glancing over at the radio

alarm clock, 'though it's not for the want of him trying, it's just not happening tonight.'

'Sorry, babes, what did you say? Are you cool?' said Gary, his voice muffled through the 13.5 tog quilt.

'Very cool,' Evelyn replied. 'Perfectly cool, in fact . . .'

'What exactly do you mean by that?' said Gary, his voice much clearer as he poked his head out from under the quilt. She couldn't see his expression in the dark but he sounded aggrieved.

'I just think,' said Evelyn, awkwardly, 'maybe it's not going to happen. Why don't we leave it for tonight? You can just . . . y'know . . . do your bit.'

'Are you trying to imply I don't turn you on any more?'

'No. No.'

'Or that I haven't a clue what I'm doing?'

'Of course not.'

'Well, then, what?'

He sounded very hurt. With a touch of sulky. Evelyn started to regret opening her mouth. 'Nothing, Gary. I'm not trying to imply anything. Why don't you just go back to what you were doing? Give it five more minutes.'

So Gary did. Evelyn meanwhile closed her eyes.

And then there was another night in bed when their love-making had been more satisfying. Very satisfying indeed. They lay naked with bodies entangled in the warm after-glow.

'Ooooh,' said Evelyn. 'I can still feel tingles.'

Gary dragged over his jeans and produced from his pocket two little blobs of blue wax.

'What the hell are those?' she asked, even as he began to stuff one into each ear.

'They're to block out the sound of traffic,' he said, a bit too loudly. 'I'm finding it wakes me in the night.'

'Oh,' she said. 'I didn't realize.'

But Gary couldn't hear and didn't reply. He turned over on his shoulder and was very quickly asleep.

7

And then, one day in the middle of March, questions were asked that put the exact state of each relationship into the spotlight.

'So I went into the Aer Lingus office on Dawson Street and checked,' said Gary, as he lay on the couch, having been stricken with a headache, in the front room at 64. 'They have direct flights to Frankfurt with Aer Lingus for two hundred and seven pounds. After that it's just a short bus-ride to Odenwald. So, what do you think, babes? Will I book them tomorrow?'

'I think . . .' said Evelyn, who was perched on the floor beside him, holding a damp cloth to his forehead. 'What about accommodation?'

'I already told you! They have two hostels right at the Konserven. One for men, one for women. Theoretically, anyway. I gather from my cousin that there's no problem with a bit of . . . ahmm . . . nocturnal visitation as long as we're discreet.'

'Hmm. And what's the story with food?'

'All paid for. Although it helps if you're not too picky. Apparently, there's this thing called schnitzel. It comes in a foil-wrapped box. If you're still hungry, there's a shop in the village.'

'Okay . . .'

'Okay? C'mon, babes, you're making this migraine

worse with your total lack of enthusiasm. I'm relying on you to teach me the basics of German.'

'Ahmm . . . yeah. And what does the actual factory work involve again?'

'Cherries. It's a processing plant. They take in the cherries, remove the stems and the pips, wash 'em, dry 'em and fill them into jars. We'll each get a place somewhere along the production line. Don't worry – by all accounts, it's a doddle.'

'Okay . . .'

'We even get provided with our own apron. C'mon, Evelyn, don't you see this is going to be a big adventure?'

'I –'

'Owww,' Gary interrupted.

'What happened?'

'It's nothing, babes. Just try to keep the cloth in place, if it's not too much trouble.'

'Sorry.'

'I don't understand it, babes – you're normally so up for trying something a bit out of the ordinary. It's like there's something bothering you about the whole trip that you're not telling me.'

'No . . .' said Evelyn. 'Not really . . .'

But there was something. Something like this . . .

The approach of summer was a bittersweet promise for any student. On the one hand there was an end of listening to lecturers and the opportunity for a working holiday (an adventure!) abroad. On the other hand – exams. Similarly the prospect was mixed for students in a college relationship. It begged the question, and sharpened it, of whether to stay together. Yes or no? If the answer was yes, should the couple travel together? Perhaps even live together? Far away from mammies and daddies. Yes or no? The alternative was to do their own thing, trust that the relationship could survive the distance and live on letters until October came around once more.

Those were the choices facing Evelyn and Gary. Or, specifically, Evelyn. Gary didn't even know it was an issue but Evelyn could think of nothing else. She hated making any big decision with regard to her love-life. It tended to bring out the huge conflict in her logical yet romantic nature. Yes, Gary was a wonderful guy and she did (whisper it) really, really like him. A lot. Maybe even . . . But was he The One?

Evelyn reached over to Gary. She closed her eyes and, with her left hand, she pulled his face closer and their lips met for a kiss. Meanwhile her right hand was tucked behind her back and two fingers were crossed.

The kiss was long and lingering, as passionate as any they'd ever shared. When it was finally over, Evelyn opened her eyes, looked at Gary and saw . . . Gary.

'So, what is it, then?' he asked.

'I'll tell you what it is,' said Evelyn.

But then . . . she somehow lost her nerve. 'Odenwald sounds great,' she said. 'Why don't we go and book the tickets this afternoon?'

The same day, Michelle and John were snogging in the quiet seclusion of the alley behind the microelectronics building. Everything was going well until John took his tongue out of Michelle's mouth. 'I love you, Michelle,' he said.

'Me too,' she replied.

Me too? It had been her standard reply for as long as they'd been together and John still didn't know how to take it. Did it mean she loved him back? Or did it mean Michelle also loved Michelle? Surely not.

John waded in further. 'We're a month into this relationship,' he said, 'so what do you think about . . . ?'

'About what?'

John tried to explain. 'About . . . What I meant was . . . I dunno . . . I've told you a fair few times how I feel about you . . . that I . . . love you, like . . . so I'm just wondering how you feel about . . .'

God, it was embarrassing to have to say the word out loud.

And yet John went ahead and said the word out loud.

'Me.'

'You?'

'Yes. Me.'

'Okay,' said Michelle, with a sigh, peeved that John couldn't just be satisfied with snogging. 'I do like you and I think it's great. For now. But I almost definitely don't want anything serious. Or long term . . .'

'Oh,' said John.

'Does that answer your question? Happy now?'

'Yes,' said John, while thinking, No, no, no, no, *no*!

'Fine,' she said, reaching back to unclasp her bra.

These breasts, thought John, reaching up under Michelle's blouse, never disappoint. If only I could have a relationship . . . just with them.

'Goddamn it,' said Evelyn. 'I've just put a fifty-pound deposit on an airline ticket to a place I'm not sure I want to go.'

She was alone in her bedroom, talking to no one except, perhaps, the ceiling.

'Gary is a wonderful guy and he ticks all the boxes but there's something missing. I just don't know what it is.'

Certainly there was no question of her confiding such doubts to Michelle, whose sole response would undoubtedly be 'Told you so!'

'And now I'm committed to spending the summer with him in some godforsaken boondock called Odenwald.'

She sat up in her bed and grabbed her deposit receipt from the locker. Dublin–Frankfurt, Frankfurt–Dublin. There was info on the departure times, the arrivals, the baggage restrictions, procedures to be adhered to when bringing your pet, and down near the bottom some tiny script about the cancellation policy. The policy was for the airline to keep all of your deposit.

This is a good thing, thought Evelyn. I was being silly again. Gary is a wonderful guy and us going to Odenwald together will probably turn out to be brilliant. I've just got to cop on, stop daydreaming about the fairytale romance and embrace reality. In fact, I'll go and visit that wonderful boyfriend of mine right now.

'For feck sake!'

John, too, was lying on his bed. Thinking. Several thoughts per second.

My girlfriend has stated explicitly that she doesn't love me and we have almost definitely no future together.

This should not be happening!

I've met the wonderful girl. Check.

Managed to hook up with her. Check.

Fallen in love. Check.

But has she fallen in love with me? No.

And there will be no more checks.

So where did I go wrong? My relationship is almost definitely doomed.

Doomed!

DOOMED!

He took a break from thinking and went to look in the mirror. He stared at his acne. Might the spots be the reason? Or could it be his teeth? His armpits? He sniffed at one and it was not entirely pleasant. He had an inkling, however, that it was something else.

Not something I am but something I'm doing.

Something I'm doing wrong.

Or something I'm failing to do right.

But what?

He gritted his teeth and growled at the mirror in an effort to psych himself up. There was still hope. What of all the hours he and Michelle spent kissing and cuddling? What of the lovely braces she'd bought him for Valentine's and the magical little doodle he'd seen on the margin of her lecture notes?

And she said she 'liked' me.

Also with regard to us having a future, she said *almost* definitely no.

So there is hope.

But now is a time for action.

Plainly I have been sailing along on the warm breeze of her loveliness and not done a tap to encourage similar emotions within her. I thought it was enough to just turn up and go with the flow. I thought it would come easily. That her love would just fall from the sky. I haven't made enough of an effort to woo her. I haven't yet earned her love.

I haven't.

Yet.

But I will.

Just before it closed, John revisited the shop where he'd previously bought the second most expensive acne gel. This time he bought the very best.

8

So Evelyn threw herself into her relationship with renewed vigour.

'Please close the curtains!' moaned Gary, late one evening. 'Please, babes, if it's not too much trouble?'

'Of course,' said Evelyn, and she moved quickly to do as he asked. She had already got him a glass of water and two paracetamol but his headache was getting worse.

'It's the light,' whispered Gary, who was in his bed. 'I can't stand it.'

They were in Gary's flat in Rathgar. Evelyn had been there all afternoon and had been about to leave when the migraine struck. It was particularly bad timing because at that stage of the evening the No. 18 bus only ran at hourly intervals. Nevertheless Evelyn was happy to stay on and nurse her boyfriend when he was in such distress.

'There's still some light leaking through, babes,' Gary said. 'Could you put up a few towels as well?'

Again Evelyn did as she was told while Gary scrunched his eyes closed. He then popped in his earplugs and pulled the quilt over his head. Evelyn sat down at the table.

'They're definitely increasing in severity and frequency,' Evelyn said aloud, before realizing that she was talking to herself. 'What could be causing them?' she wondered.

On the table in front of her was a sheet of paper with a series of questions about Social Studies. There were spaces on the page in which you were supposed to write each answer. Spaces that were still spaces.

During the subsequent Easter break, Evelyn demonstrated the extent of her devotion. Because she and Gary were apart for all of two weeks she wrote him a letter that ran to seven pages and went through several drafts before she deemed it good enough. It was all about their time together and she poured on to the page all her hopes and fears for the future. In fact, the letter turned out so well that she thought it might just move their relationship on to a whole new level. She awaited Gary's response. When he rang her on Easter Sunday, however, he never mentioned it. She subsequently confirmed that he had never received it. It had, presumably, been lost in the post. Was probably lying somewhere in a mailroom down behind the filing cabinet. Or perhaps delivered into the wrong letterbox, opened by the wrong hands and read by the wrong eyes. This piece of paper on which she'd written her deepest, most intimate thoughts.

'Oh, sweet Jesus,' she fumed. It just wasn't in her to attempt to write it all out again.

Eventually, in April, Gary's avoidance of his college lectures and assignments reached a critical point. A morning finally came when he decided to get notes from all the lectures he had skipped. One of the class swots obliged and Gary made photocopies down in the basement of a bookshop on Nassau Street. Then he settled into the library for a few hours to get a sense of what he had missed. The answer was . . . a massive amount. An unbelievably massive amount. A stunned expression appeared on Gary's face and refused to leave as the realization sank in of just how much material there was. Now, for the first time in a long time, he knew how little he knew.

'Damn, damn, damn,' he said, when he met Evelyn and Michelle for lunch in the dining hall. 'There's just no way that I'm going to get it all covered. I'm going to fail. Definitely!'

'I'm sure it's not that bad, Gary,' said Evelyn, as she put a consoling arm around his shoulders. 'You're an intelligent guy.'

But Gary didn't want to be consoled, preferring to rant about all he needed to learn. And, to top everything, he still hadn't written up assignment five.

Evelyn unloaded her lunch from the tray and then tried to hold his hand. He pulled away. Then she had another idea. 'Why don't I do the assignment for you?'

'But how?'

'Well, not necessarily to a very high standard, Gary. But just give me your textbook and I bet I'll be able to bash out something that'll get you a pass.'

'Oh, would you, please?' said Gary, and his face lit up at last. He reached out and hugged her. 'Oh, Evelyn,' he whispered. 'You're the best.'

'Yes, Evelyn,' said Michelle, pausing to examine a piece of boiled celery on the end of her fork, 'and also you're a very big eejit.'

John, too, poured lots of energy into his relationship, trying harder than ever to make Michelle see it as more than just a temporary fling.

One morning, instead of going to his pharmacognosy lecture, he went into the Thomas Davis theatre and found

Michelle and Evelyn. They greeted him warmly but were a bit surprised when he sat down and didn't leave as their lecturer took the podium.

'You do realize,' whispered Evelyn, with a worried frown, 'that this lecture is just for first-year engineering?'

Of course he did, but there were two hundred seats in the theatre and little chance of the lecturer noticing his intrusion. The lecture was about hydrostatics.

'That was fascinating,' John said at the end. 'Where's our ten o'clock?'

Michelle, however, didn't seem as pleased as he'd hoped.

'Our?' she said, with a puzzled expression. '*Our?*'

A week later John announced that he'd applied for two tickets to the Trinity Ball.

'That's nice,' said Michelle, but she didn't seem as excited as he'd hoped. Instead she went on to drop the news she had decided to go to New York for the summer. John was stunned. And heartbroken. There was no way that he could possibly follow suit as his father had already lined up a load of work for him. Then Michelle went on to talk about the requirements for a J1 visa. She would need a letter from her aunt in Long Island, the return flight ticket and a bank statement showing £500 in her account. This last was going to cause a problem. Michelle had just done the calculations and discovered she'd be a hundred short. Her daddy was going to have to be rung a.s.a.p.

'Oh, no,' John insisted. 'I've plenty to spare. Let me loan it to you.' That was stupid. He didn't have plenty to spare. He was going to be left with very little to live on.

Then the Easter break arrived when all the students

went home to their parents' houses for the fortnight. In John's case this entailed lugging home two large black bin bags in addition to his backpack. They were full of laundry for his mother to deal with. Nevertheless he found room for a huge chocolate egg and delivered it to Michelle on his way to the bus station.

'That's nice!' she said, but she didn't return the favour.

Luckily for John, it turned out that his mother had bought him one.

9

Because it was nearly exam time, Michelle and John decided to see a bit less of each other. Well, in truth, she decided and he went along with it.

'The important thing is quality of time together,' he said, putting a positive spin on the arrangement. 'Not quantity.'

One Friday he was supposed to hook up with her by the front gate of college at quarter to twelve. They were then going to meet Evelyn, Gary and Brian to play pool in the JCR. Michelle didn't show, and after twenty minutes there was still no sign. Then John remembered it was the day she was collecting her J1 visa. He took a stroll towards the USIT office.

Well before he reached it, he came across the queue. It started all the way out on Dame Street and snaked down the length of Anglesea Street. Nor was it a queue of the fast-moving variety: there were many students sitting down on the pavement, some looking bored, others half asleep. John looked along carefully but there was no sign of Michelle until he came to the USIT office itself. Through the window, he could see that it was jammed inside. Nevertheless he spotted his girl just a few yards from the counter. She was talking with great animation and enthusiasm to three guys. Presumably they were comparing notes about where they were going in the US, with whom they'd stay, jobs they'd lined up, etc. As John watched her trace an imaginary map with her index finger, he was struck by how very beautiful she was.

Two security guards were manning the door so there was no question of him popping in to say hello, but he wanted Michelle to know he'd figured out why she was late for their rendezvous. He knocked on the window pane. For a split second Michelle looked over and John was sure she saw him. Just as quickly, however, she switched her focus back to one of the guys she was with.

John knocked on the window again. No response. He called out, 'Michelle.' He shouted it and thumped the window at the same time. Almost everyone else in the USIT office turned to look at him. One of the security guards glanced over and scowled darkly. But Michelle never moved a neck muscle. In fact, she didn't flinch. That guy she was staring at, whatever he was saying must've been the most fascinating thing she'd ever heard: not for a second did her eyes leave his lips.

'Hey, you,' growled the security guard, as he approached and put a fist on John's shoulder. 'Feck off to the back of the queue.'

'Top pocket on the left.'

Push, click, roll, plop. Evelyn potted the black just as she'd called and Brian was left with his seven stripes still sitting on the pool table.

Evelyn laughed. She was in a great mood and certainly on form, having already beaten Gary. While Brian shoved another 50p piece into the slot, Gary came back from the jukebox to tell her something.

'*Dankeschön* again,' he said. '*Mein* beautiful *Fräulein*.'

In his hands were assignments six and seven, which

Evelyn had just finished writing up for him. 'Sorry about lumbering you with these,' he continued. 'I've just been feeling so overwhelmed by it all.' He reached out to Evelyn and hugged her.

'*Ich bin* . . . really *dankbar* for the typing and *es tut mir leid das* I was such a drag. So, babes, do you forgive me?'

'Of course I do.' Evelyn smiled.

'Anyway,' he continued, 'I take it that you remember today's the big day?'

'Huh?'

'Y'know – the day we have to pay the balance on our tickets to Germany.'

'Oh,' said Evelyn, who had forgotten, who had in fact been trying not to think too much about this day of reckoning. 'Yes, of course. Odenwald! Brilliant! Can't wait!'

'*Guden Fräulein!*' said Gary, and gave her another squeeze. 'The thing is, babes, that I've lectures all afternoon, which I actually propose to attend! So I have to go up there right now. Want to come?'

'No way,' said Evelyn, no longer smiling.

'No way?' he said. 'What do you mean?'

'Sorry.' She recovered. 'What I mean is that . . . um . . . my afternoon lectures have been cancelled so there's no rush on me, and my ATM card isn't working so I'll have to go into the bank first and go through all that withdrawal-slip crap and ahmm . . .'

Both of these excuses were lies.

'Fine, fine,' said Gary. 'Just as long as you do it at some stage today. The deadline is half four. Any later, you'll lose your ticket and deposit and all.'

'Hey, sis, do you want to break this time?' interrupted

Brian. He had taken up the triangle and was poised to begin the next game.

'No, go ahead,' said Evelyn, absently. Gary, meanwhile, went over in the direction of the Gents. Evelyn watched him go. She looked at him, really looked at him, from head to toe. All the way from his quiffed hair, right down to his fluorescent yellow bootlaces, he was exactly the kind of guy she'd always thought she wanted. So why wasn't she stone mad about him? Why did she feel such uncertainty? Why had her recent attempts at really pouring herself into the relationship made not a jot of difference? It just didn't add up.

Gary reached the door of the Gents. At that moment he did something – it was a small gesture, which maybe he did or didn't do regularly but which Evelyn, in any case, noticed for the first time. He reached for the handle of the door and, rather than touch it directly, pulled his sleeve over his hand.

What was that? Evelyn thought. The Gents is very icky, no doubt . . . Thus the handle of the door to the Gents may be icky too . . . But no . . . No!

Gary's refusal to touch a door handle with his bare hands made her feel uneasy about him in a way she couldn't quite understand.

'Remember as well,' said Gary, when he came back out (while giving her a goodbye peck on the cheek), 'that tonight I'm taking you out to dinner at Fat Freddie's – okay, babes?'

'Okay,' said Evelyn, and turned to watch him go. She was no longer in a great mood. Her eyes couldn't focus properly and she found herself staring into space.

'This can't go on,' she said softly.

'You're right, sis,' said Brian. 'I'm on stripes this time and got one down while you were smooching with Mr What's-his-face.'

The game that followed was a complete reversal of their previous frame with Brian tearing into a commanding lead. This wasn't due to any great improvement in his form: Evelyn's game had collapsed. Suddenly she could hardly hit a ball, let alone cut an angle. Miss followed miss and the only ball she potted was the white on several occasions. Thoroughly annoyed with her form, Evelyn took a break and went over to choose a tune on the jukebox. She threw in 20p and turned away as the song began, military drum rolls and obscure lyrics about birds, snakes and earthquakes.

Right, then, she thought. Enough is enough. My mind is addled trying to decide whether or not to go to Odenwald with Gary. I am going to let this pool cue decide. If my next ball is a miss, I'm going. If I pot it, I'm not.

So Evelyn strode back to the pool table with a purposeful look on her face and sized up the situation. Her only available shot was an extremely tough one, the full length of the table with a 45-degree angle and the white ball uncomfortably close to the cushion.

It looks, Evelyn, she thought, like you're going to Odenwald.

Nevertheless she hunkered down to the shot.

'Have you any idea why John didn't show up?' asked Brian, just making conversation.

'No,' said Evelyn, firmly, and closed her left eye to take aim.

'It's not like him,' said Brian, 'and Michelle as well.'

'Shut up!' said Evelyn, a little rudely. Brian could have

no idea that the fate of her summer, possibly even her entire future life, was hanging on the outcome of this shot. He stopped talking nevertheless.

Push, click, roll, plop. With a brilliant shot, Evelyn potted it, let out a long sigh of relief and her face collapsed onto the cushion. At last the decision was made. There would be no walking up Dawson Street to pay for the rest of the ticket. No going to Odenwald. No summer spent with Gary, ultimately no more relationship. He was a wonderful guy but something just wasn't right and at last she had fully admitted the obvious consequence of that. Now all she had to do was tell Gary. The obvious time was at Fat Freddie's that very night. But she felt overwhelmingly tired and wanted to go home for a nap.

'That's just one ball, sis,' said Brian. 'You've a few more to go to catch me.'

Evelyn was about to reply when John walked through the door, looking less than happy with the world. 'The very man,' she said, and handed him the pool cue. 'John, I need to go home. Take over this game from me, please.'

'So tell me, bro,' Brian said, as soon as Evelyn was gone, 'how're things with Julia Roberts?'

'Who – Michelle?' said John, taking a deep breath. 'Absolutely excellent.'

Over the next few balls, he did, however, give Brian an edited account of events at the USIT office (not mentioning the embarrassing fact that Michelle had blanked him, just the bit about being jealous of her talking to other guys).

'Well, bro,' said Brian, and stroked his stubbly chin thoughtfully, 'when you're with a fine-looking woman like that, it's what they call an occupational hazard.'

'It is.'

'Every man who sees her is gagging to be shagging.'

'They are,' John admitted, swallowing hard at the prospect.

'Except me, bro, obviously. I want to assure you of that. I'm still holding out for Aoife Hennessy.'

'Good to know.'

Brian took some more time to stroke his chin. He was trying to look thoughtful. There was also the fact that part of his face had become itchy since he'd stopped shaving. It had been several weeks yet the beard was still very much in the developmental phase, consisting of just a few scattered sprigs. Many men would have admitted defeat, but not Brian. He'd already devoted eighteen months to growing his hair to his shoulders, and a beard was next on the list. The aim was to look like Jim Morrison *circa* the *L.A. Woman* album. And nobody was going to stop him. Nobody! He didn't give a feck what his parents or the lecturers might say.

'Well,' he said, 'I think that . . . when all is said and done, you're just a guy going out with a girl. Don't take it so seriously and simply enjoy the ride for as long as it lasts.'

'Hmm . . .' said John. This was not exactly what he wanted to hear.

'If you love someone, bro, then you must set them free.'

Definitely not what John wanted to hear.

'It's not as if,' Brian added, with a chuckle, 'you can actually stake your claim on her, is it?' John shook his head, as Brian went on, 'Not like the olden days when you woulda been able to brand your woman with a hot iron, huh, bro? Let all them other feckers in the USIT office know who she belongs to.'

Brian thought the idea very funny. He leaned back down to the table and hit a ball. Nothing went in. 'Must get a packet of fags,' he said. 'Mind you don't pull a fast one while I'm gone.'

Far from cheating, John didn't even take his shot. He was too busy thinking about what Brian had said. Simply 'enjoying the ride' and 'not taking it so seriously' seemed sensible but John turned the words over in his mind and three things became very clear.

Brian hasn't a clue what it's like to be really in love.

He can't know the depth of my feeling for Michelle.

His advice might be useful for other people . . . but doesn't apply to me.

Then John's thoughts turned to Brian's other (intended to be sarcastic) remarks. Of claims and how they might be staked. John thought of how an explorer claims the mountaintop by planting a flag. Of how a tourist marks his poolside recliner by leaving a towel. And a dog uses piddle. And the mother of a schoolchild sews a name-tag on to the little cardigan . . .

But how does one nail down a girlfriend? he wondered.

The obvious answer struck him as Brian returned and lit his cigarette. 'You got nothing down?'

John nodded distractedly. The idea of asking Michelle to marry him was crazy. And yet why was it so crazy? He loved her, didn't he? And by common consensus she was the best-looking girl on the campus. He wasn't going to find a prettier one.

So why not? The worst that could happen was she would say no.

No . . .

That didn't bear thinking about.

If she said yes . . . well, John's anxieties would melt away and the world return to the wonderful state he had enjoyed in the first few weeks of their relationship.

'Come on to feck, bro. It's your shot again,' said Brian, impatiently.

'Bloody hell!'

He'd had no idea that engagement rings were so expensive. After finishing the game with Brian, John's first stop was Weirs Jewellers on Grafton Street. H. Samuel on Henry Street was his last. In between he saw a lot of diamonds and every carat of gold. Not one came remotely within his tiny budget. He needed to do something he didn't want to do. He found a phone box.

'Hi, Dad, can I speak to Mum?'

'No. You can't.'

'Why not?'

'Because she's gone into the village.'

Damn.

'Dad,' John said, and took a deep breath, 'is there any chance you could put money in my account? There's three textbooks I simply have to buy.'

'Have to buy?'

'Yeah. Or I'll fail the year.'

'We wouldn't want that.'

'So can you?'

'Can I what?'

'Can you give me some money?'

Silence on the line while John fidgeted and wondered how long before his mother would be back.

'I'm kind of in the middle of a big job,' said his father,

eventually, 'but I think your mother put in a hundred only yesterday. Have you checked your account recently?'

John hadn't! 'That's brilliant, Dad,' he shouted, so excited he said the wrong thing: 'That means I can withdraw the money and buy one of the cheaper rings right now.'

'The cheaper what?'

'The books, Dad,' he corrected himself. 'The books I need to pass my exams.'

10

When planning to break up with a boyfriend, especially one who has done you no wrong, a girl must dress carefully. Which is to say carelessly. The last thing you want is to be looking your absolute sexiest. That would be just too cruel. Hence the full hour Evelyn spent that evening rummaging in her wardrobe before going out to meet Gary at Fat Freddie's. Hence the decision she finally arrived at to wear her most hideous ensemble: brown corduroy dungarees and check shirt. Her mother had insisted she bring them to Dublin. Evelyn's older sister in America had sent them under the delusion they were some kind of fashion.

By contrast, when planning to propose marriage, it makes sense to aim for the optimum conditions. John knew that Evelyn was due to go out to dinner with Gary so if he called over to the prefab around nine p.m. Michelle would most likely be alone. After buying the ring he spent the late afternoon in careful preparation, even ironing a proper shirt for the occasion. Then, at eight thirty, after guzzling a mug of two raw eggs, he set off.

The garlic bread was fabulous at Fat Freddie's, as were any of the pizzas, although the house speciality was calzone. Seated at the last available table for two, down in the basement, Evelyn and Gary enjoyed their main courses and agreed to share a giant portion of Death by Chocolate.

Once the waitress had gone, Evelyn felt the moment of truth had arrived.

'I've got something I need to say,' she told Gary.

'I want to say something, babes,' said Gary, at the exact same moment.

'Oh,' said Evelyn, startled at this interruption. 'You first, then.'

'No,' said Gary. 'You first.'

'Well,' said Evelyn, trying to be as gentle as possible, 'the first thing is that I really do think you're a great guy, Gary.'

He nodded.

'And also . . . throughout this relationship you've never been anything other than a model boyfriend.'

He smiled.

'You have loads of qualities I really admire but –'

'Stop, babes,' said Gary, with a big grin, 'before you make my head explode. You don't know how delighted I am to hear that's how you feel. Recently I was starting to worry and to wonder.'

Michelle was not expecting John so the usual procedure when he got to 64 would've been to throw pebbles on the prefab roof. That, however, would have spoiled the surprise. From his jacket pocket, he took out the little red furry box containing the engagement ring. He opened it and there, shining back at him, was a nine-carat gold ring, mounted with the smallest of diamonds. Not too impressive, yet it was sparkling and new. He hoped Michelle would like it and would understand it was the best he could do for now. He would promise her better, more expensive rings as soon as he left college and got a job.

He climbed over the wall and jumped into the back garden. The light was on in the kitchen but otherwise there was no sign or sound of life. Probably because Michelle was studying hard, he guessed. Playing 'Eine Kleine Nachtmusik' on her Walkman or whatever. Stealthily, he tiptoed as far as the prefab door and went down on bended knee on the welcome mat. Then he knocked.

There was no reply. No sound of keys jangling on the other side of the door. As he waited on bended knee, he could feel a vague tremor. The prefab was vibrating slightly. John put his hand to the wall and could feel it. He knock-knock-knocked again.

No reply.

The vibrations were getting stronger. Someone or something was most definitely at home. As John knocked for the third time he heard what must have been Michelle. She was making a noise . . . and through the door it was muffled and indistinct but . . . There was no other word for it: it sounded like . . . yelping. As he listened in frozen horror, the yelps became louder and more frequent. Then suddenly . . . silence.

He knocked one last time and Michelle opened the door.

'Did you know it's our six-month anniversary tonight?' said Gary.

'Of course,' said Evelyn, alarmed that she'd lost control of what was meant to be a break-up. She had to bring it back on track. 'But listen, Gary, I haven't really got to my point, which is –'

'Now I know how you feel,' he interrupted, 'I'm looking forward more than ever to our summer together in Odenwald.'

'– which is that I don't think we should continue –'

'*What?*'

'– to see each other –'

'*What?*'

'– or be together.'

'*What?*'

'I mean I want us to break up, Gary. Split up. No longer be boyfriend and girlfriend.'

'What, babes?' said Gary.

Michelle was dressed in nothing but a long T-shirt and didn't look especially pleased to see John, but he was already down on one knee so he decided to go ahead with the plan.

'Michelle,' he said, 'will you do me the honour of marrying me?'

He closed his eyes for fear she would say no.

'No,' she said, and as John opened his eyes she closed the door.

Oh, feck, thought John. I've scared her off. Jumped the gun. Of course she wasn't ready yet to contemplate marriage. I should have left it a few more weeks. Stupid. Stupid. Stupid.

He stood up, put the ring back in his shirt pocket and resolved to recover the situation. He knocked again and, after a minute, Michelle opened the door again. For the first time he registered that the T-shirt she was wearing was not one he was familiar with. 'Never mind what I said earlier, Michelle. How about I just come in for a bit?'

'No,' she said, and slammed the door.

*

'It's just there's something missing, Gary. I dunno . . . some kind of chemistry. Spark. Flame. Some kind of . . . magic.'

Gary was not buying Evelyn's line about him being so wonderful and there being absolutely nothing wrong bar the absence of 'magic'. As he pushed her to explain further Evelyn had to resort to talking about frogs. Prince Charming. Her utterly irrational desire to be given a sign of perfect romance.

'*But why?*' said Gary.

'It's not you,' said Evelyn, 'it's me.' (And also, she thought, the fact that I potted a ball at the pool game earlier today.)

John gave it one more go. Knock-knock. When Michelle came out for the third time he simply asked if they could still see each other on Sunday night as planned.

'No, John,' she said. 'You and me . . . it's over.'

'*But why?*' said John.

'If you must know, it's because . . .' and Michelle leaned down to whisper the answer in his ear.

His cheeks reddened.

'Death by Chocolate,' said the waitress, and placed a large dessert bowl between Evelyn and Gary: chocolate sponge, topped with butter chocolate truffle, flooded with rich chocolate mousse and sprinkled with chocolate curls.

'I don't really feel like it,' said Gary, reaching for his jacket on the back of his chair.

'Oh,' said Evelyn, 'but . . .'

'But what . . . babes?' he said, looking her straight in the eye, with just a hint of bitterness.

Evelyn realized that it was 'but nothing'. Given what she had just done to him, his wanting to leave was perfectly reasonable. Before she could object, he had thrown a twenty-pound note on to the table and was making for the stairs up to the ground floor. Turning in her chair, Evelyn watched him go. He did not look back. He started up the steps and the very last she saw of him was the heels of his high Doc boots. Complete with flashes of the fluorescent yellow laces.

'What have I done?' she asked herself. 'A perfectly good boyfriend! WHAT HAVE I DONE?'

She pulled the dessert bowl closer and picked up a spoon.

John had to get away. No longer bothering to tiptoe, he ran around the side of the prefab. The window of Michelle's room was now open and he could see smoke curling out. As time slowed to a crawl, he saw a hand emerge to tip cigarette ash. A hairy hand. A male hand.

John vaulted on to the wall. He wanted to be somewhere else, anywhere but on Marlborough Road – to be in Ballsbridge or Ringsend or Rathmines or Harold's Cross. He wanted to put distance between himself and the scene of his wretched humiliation. But as he landed on the other side his foot came down awkwardly and he went over on his ankle. 'Aaargh!'

His desperation to get away made him drag himself upright immediately but the pain was excruciating. Limping very slowly, he made his way to Marlborough Road and began a long and miserable journey home.

On one leg.

Then it started to drizzle.

Soon it was raining torrentially.

When he got back to his flat he flopped down on the bed and discovered that the engagement ring was no longer in his pocket. It must have dropped out somewhere along his route. There was no way he was getting up to go back to look for it. In fact, he thought, holding his throbbing ankle, which had swollen to the size of a tennis ball, there's no way I'm ever getting off this bed again for any reason.

Whatsoever!

Ever again!

NEVER! NEVER! NEVER!

Amen.

11

The inside of Evelyn Creed's skull was not a nice place to be over the following three weeks. With exams looming, she was always either studying or feeling guilty about not studying. On top of that she had a blazing row with Michelle (about her tryst with the guy from the USIT queue, about the way she'd treated John, about every little petty annoyance that had built up over a year of living together in a small wooden box). Harsh words had been thrown on both sides and they were (at least temporarily) not on speaking terms.

The worst of all the things making her unhappy, though, was the break-up with Gary. It was a complicated kind of misery. A mixture of extreme sadness and stinging remorse. She missed him desperately, even though she had pulled the trigger. So she couldn't expect much sympathy. Joan, Cliona, all of her friends assumed that since it had been her decision she must be fine. But she was not fine. She was wondering had she just made the biggest mistake of her life. Now that Gary was out of her life (and the threat of Odenwald lifted), he seemed more perfect than ever and her desire for something more utterly ridiculous. She daydreamed of evenings when he had cooked her beef Stroganoff wearing nothing but his apron. She daydreamed of him warm in the bed beside her, wearing nothing at all. She pined for how he used to listen each evening to the details of her day.

Beset by all these troubles, therefore, Evelyn spent her days looking forward to night when, at last, she could sleep, when, at last, she could relax into the comfortable bliss of unconsciousness.

John's misery was not so complicated. It wasn't so much that he wanted to kill himself. It was just that he wanted to be dead. He gave only a little thought to what method he might employ to make it happen. (Any such method could not involve leaving his room, after all.) Whether he might . . . slit his wrists with the potato peeler, hang from the belt of his dressing-gown, stick a fork in the electric socket, take all hundred capsules of the vitamin tonic his mother had bought him (but he'd never opened), or simply stop eating until July.

Mostly John preferred to concentrate on the aftermath. The hours and days after his death. When his body would be discovered and the news got out. That John Fallon was dead.

Yes! That John Fallon!

John: son, friend, classmate and valued acquaintance.

John: the guy who until very recently had been Michelle Neylon's boyfriend. Damn near her fiancé. And if only things had been different, potentially, eventually, her life-long lover and husband.

Many people commit suicide in order to escape pain. John's (imagined) suicide would have been quite differently motivated. Yes, his being dumped by Michelle and his discovery of her infidelity had been excruciating. Yes, they had prompted him to go to bed and stay there for nearly three weeks. But the attraction of being dead was not primarily about stopping the feelings of rejection, humiliation and despair. It was not about the effect of his death on himself: it was about its effect on others.

Well, one other, really. Michelle. She'd be sorry, wouldn't she? She would finally be forced to wake up to what a nice guy John was and what a fool she'd been to throw their relationship away, like a used tube of acne gel. His death would stand as a beacon to the intensity of the love he'd felt for her – a love that comes along only once in a lifetime if you're lucky but that she'd taken for granted. And now it was gone. Gone, soon to be buried six feet under the clay with perhaps just the faintest hint of the spirit of it floating on the summer breeze and the laze of a bumble bee under the fluffy white clouds of a Ranelagh morning.

Gone.

Oh, good God, how wretched Michelle was going to feel when the enormity of the calamity finally hit her. It almost made John feel sorry for her. He still loved her after all. He would never want to hurt her. It was such a shame that her actions were going to have such dire consequences for them both.

Nor was it enough that John's death showed Michelle the error of her ways. It was important that he be there to witness her reaction. Crucially, he was relying on having a death in which his spirit would float up and away from the corpse and be free to move around. He would glide invisibly to many places and witness the reactions of people when they heard about his death. The thought of his mother's face lined with tears was not something he liked to contemplate. On the other hand, he looked forward to hearing other people paying him lots of nice compliments. Finally saying all the flattering things for which they'd assumed there'd be another time. Surprising him (John's spirit) with just how much he meant to them.

'He really was such a great guy. I didn't just want to be *like* him, I wanted to *be* him!'

Then John would glide to 64 and hover invisibly when the word came through to Michelle about his death. He would witness her looking stunned. He would hover closer and watch while the true height and depth of it percolated down into her consciousness.

And then the tears.

Too late.

Her whispering, 'I loved him.'

Too late.

The realization that she'd been embraced by the Ultimate Love and failed to recognize it. That if only there was something she could do to turn back time – anything! Anything at all! – she would do it in a heartbeat. Too late.

And John's spirit would stay with Michelle throughout the next three days and nights. Always on her shoulder during daylight, sleeping in her bedroom during darkness, making spoons, trying to comfort her while she wailed and gnashed her teeth.

As she dressed to go to the funeral, John would be captivated even in death by her beauty. As she shook hands with his grieving parents, wanting to explain and apologize.

As she followed the hearse to the graveyard.

Watched his coffin descend.

As the congregation walked away and the men arrived with shovels.

As she heard the muffled sound of the hole being filled in.

And clamped her hands to her ears.

And unleashed a cry of utterly abandoned desolation.

So John stayed in bed for three full weeks, thinking about death. But not literally for every single second. There were breaks to go to the toilet. And to make occasional meals of cheese on toast.

John's confinement coincided with the time of year when many people holed up for some serious exam study. In so far as anyone in college noticed his absence, they put it down to that and didn't worry. One person who was concerned, however, was Evelyn. She knew the gory details of how his relationship with Michelle had ended. She had since made several attempts to visit him, but when she rang the doorbell he shouted, 'Go away.' At least she knew he was still alive.

Eventually an early May morning came when Evelyn rang John's doorbell and he got up and answered it. He was dressed in just his underpants and the grey coat called Sven. He found she was holding a razor blade.

'Hey, lanky boy, I thought you might need this.'

The blade glinted in the early-summer sunlight. It looked new. And very sharp.

'Hey . . . What?' John mumbled, his mind confused and his tongue grown rusty from lack of use.

'Let's just get straight on with it, shall we?'

'What?'

'I'm going to help you do it. God knows, it's obvious you need assistance.'

'But –'

'No buts. Just show me to your sink. I'll try to keep the mess to a minimum.'

Bewildered at this sudden acceleration of events, John led Evelyn to the sink. She put the blade down on the rim and turned on the hot tap. 'Don't worry. It'll only take about three minutes,' she said.

Three minutes . . . thought John. THREE MINUTES!

After all his contemplation of death, he was now only 180 seconds away from departure. 'I . . . Evelyn . . . I'm not sure,' he whispered.

'Don't be silly,' she said. 'You know it has to be done. And with a sharp new blade the pain will be minimal.'

'I . . . Evelyn . . . No . . . No, please no. I've decided definitely I don't want to.'

'Of course you have,' she said. 'Typical you to bottle out just when the water's warm enough. That's why I'm here. To make sure it gets done.'

John tried to move away from the sink but Evelyn caught him by the elbow. She had a surprisingly firm grip.

Damn! John thought. She's absolutely right. It's time to take action.

With her other hand Evelyn reached into the pocket of her jacket and John closed his eyes as she fished around for something. 'Don't worry,' she said. 'I'm just doing the preparations. Obviously I'll let you wield the blade yourself.

'Lean in over the sink,' she continued, and he did as he was told. He pulled up the sleeves of his coat and placed his hands in the hot water, wrists facing upwards. His eyes were still closed so he was taken by surprise when Evelyn began to dab at his face with a facecloth, then to cover it with some sort of cream. He opened his eyes, looked in the mirror and thought, Aha . . .

The lower half of his face was plastered with shaving foam.

'Heavy stubble really doesn't suit you,' said Evelyn. 'You look like crap.'

She handed John the shiny new blade. It had been slotted into a shaving razor.

'But . . . how did you . . . ?'

'Know you'd let yourself go?' She laughed. 'It wasn't too hard to figure. Being the foolish romantic eejit that you are. And being averse to soap and water at the best of times.'

John put the razor blade to the top of his cheek. 'And how is . . .' he ventured.

'Michelle? I wouldn't know, John. She and I are not such good pals at the moment and she's moved out from 64. She's kipping with Joan for the last few weeks of term.'

John scraped the blade downwards to the bottom of his jaw.

'I've tried to visit you before,' said Evelyn. 'Have you spent all that time in bed?'

'Pretty much, yes.'

'And done no study, I'll bet.'

'Pretty much, no.'

Evelyn laughed and shook her head. 'You must be well rested so your little holiday is over. When you're finished shaving, I've got a busy day planned for you.'

'You have? Like what?'

'Well, first I want you to take a trip into D'Olier Street and get yourself measured for a tuxedo. Hopefully they still have a few left for hire.'

'Huh?'

'The Trinity Ball. It's tonight, remember? You still have that double ticket, don't you?'

John nodded.

'Great. So you're taking me.'

Okaaaay . . .

'Just as friends, obviously. Collect me at 64 this evening at eight.'

Again he nodded dumbly. It sounded fair enough. He didn't have any better ideas.

'Once you've got your suit, I think you should scoot into the library and do a bit of study. Perhaps you've forgotten that your summer exams start next Wednesday. I know your mother would hate to see you flunk the year.'

She was right. John had frittered away weeks of study time and needed to cram like crazy.

As he got on with the shaving, Evelyn gave him a little pat on the shoulder and let herself out.

12

Somehow John found a tux and somehow he even studied some microbiology before collecting Evelyn that night. She was dressed in a black cocktail dress, her hair up, and her lips were especially red. She looked stunning. They met up with Cliona, Siobhan and their boyfriends in O'Neill's and hit Trinity at half past ten.

Wow!

The first thing to strike them when they entered was the purple light that bathed the whole front square, making the familiar seem very strange indeed. The second thing John noticed was Michelle. He hadn't seen her in three weeks and was startled by how wonderful she looked . . . She was standing outside the exam hall snogging the face off some guy. He took his right hand from his pocket and raised it to cup her breast.

Oh, for feck sake, John thought. I really should have stayed in bed.

'Come with us,' said Evelyn, giving him a dig in the ribs. 'The Golden Horde are starting on the main stage.'

Freddie White, Toasted Heretic, Something Happens and the intriguingly named Hank Halfhead and the Rambling Turkeys. The ceili tent, the country-and-western marquee and a videowall disco in the dining hall. All of these and more provided them with an excellent night's entertainment as they traipsed around the cobbled grounds of the college from venue to venue. By three a.m., though, several of the gang were starting to flag. Cliona's borrowed high heels were cutting into her ankles and (despite the desperately slow service at the various bars) Siobhan's boyfriend had become obnoxiously drunk. Both couples made their apologies and headed away for taxis, which left Evelyn and John. They got themselves baked potatoes and plastic forks. There being nowhere else to sit and eat, they perched side by side on a chain near the Campanile.

'I still don't understand why,' said John.

'Why what?' said Evelyn.

'Why you . . . did what you did.'

'Why I did what?'

'Why you dumped Gary and ripped his heart into shreds.'

'Yeah.' Evelyn smiled to hear him put it so bluntly. 'The truth is, John, that I can hardly explain it to myself. I was waiting for something but it never came. Like the number thirteen B bus. Why don't we talk about you and Michelle instead?'

'Well,' said John, 'I've spent three weeks in bed thinking about it, but there's quite a few things that still don't add up.'

'Like what?'

'Like . . .' John searched for a good example. 'Okay, here's one. I once saw a doodle that she'd made on the margin of her lecture notes. It was like a heart and had our names, Michelle Neylon and John Fallon, inside all joined up together.'

Evelyn shook her head. 'I'm afraid that was me, John,' she said. 'I drew that doodle one day to tease her.'

'Oh . . . Well, then, what about those braces she got me

for Valentine's Day? They were really nice. That showed genuine thoughtfulness.'

'You're welcome,' said Evelyn. 'It was me who bought them. Michelle hadn't bothered to get you anything and I didn't want your feelings to be hurt. At that stage I was still holding out hope that a proper relationship might develop between two of my favourite people. Not to be, though, not to be . . .'

'You bought them?' John was incredulous.

'Yes. And I also swiped the Valentine's card she was going to give you – because the message wasn't up to much. I knew it might cause a split right then and there.'

'What did the card say?' he whispered.

'"To John. Have a good one! Michelle."'

John swallowed hard, embarrassed to think of his own card with its stupid declarations of love. He got up off the chain and threw the remains of his potato into a nearby bin. Then he turned to Evelyn. He started to laugh. 'Well, feck me,' he said. 'I didn't think it was possible to feel more ridiculous. Not after what Michelle told me about my failings as a boyfriend the night we broke up.'

'Go on,' said Evelyn. 'Tell me. That girl is always very good at justifying the unjustifiable. Tell me why she did what she did.'

'Hmm,' said John, 'I'm not sure I want to.'

'Was it your acne?'

'No.' John smiled. 'Thank God.'

'Your not-always-as-freshly-showered-as-they-should-be armpits?'

'No, no, no.' He laughed.

'Well, what, then?'

'I could tell you but . . .'

'But what?'

'I can hear the blues a-calling me.'

From the arts block came the sound of a woman singing. Apparently she had woken up that morning. Subsequently it emerged that her baby was gone.

Mary Stokes was a great singer but John spent most of her set staring into the distance. He was thinking about the engagement ring he'd bought for Michelle. He was wondering if someone had found it or whether it was still on a street or pavement between Ranelagh and Rathmines. He was thinking, too, of his relationship with Michelle and how it had never really been right. How something had always been missing, a special connection. And he was struck, too, by something else, which it seemed he'd always known but persuaded himself to forget. The fact that there was another girl with whom he did have that connection. A girl who might not have the classic looks of a movie star but was nevertheless sexy as hell – and was standing right beside him. A girl who was Evelyn.

'Exit stage left,' she shouted in his ear, and tugged at his sleeve. John followed her and she led him away through the crowd. Down along past the Walton and Swift lecture theatres she walked. Eventually she parked herself on one of the big brown square box things. He sat beside her.

'It was Gary,' she said. 'I just saw him to the right of the stage and wasn't in the mood for an encounter.'

They were away from the crowd.

This is it, John thought. This is my moment. I must strike while the iron's hot.

'Evelyn,' he said, and she turned to him.

'John.'

'Evelyn, I wonder if, maybe, that is, if you don't mind, I could possibly be so bold as to . . .' He gave up on finishing the sentence and simply made a lunge to kiss her cherry red lips.

Evelyn dodged him, leaning back just in time. 'Whoa! What was that about?'

'I just thought maybe . . . y'know?'

'No, John. I don't think it would be a good idea.'

'But we get on so well together.'

'Yeah, sure we do. But the timing is all wrong. Now that I'm not going to Odenwald for the summer I've decided to go to London instead. I'll be getting a place with Cliona. Also, we've both got our exams starting next week. This isn't the time for us to be getting together.'

'But I thought we had . . .'

Evelyn smiled and reached out to take his hand. 'John,' she said. 'We do. That's all the more reason why I don't want to spoil it. You're a really nice lad but I'm still in turmoil after splitting with Gary. My emotions need a break. So do yours after Michelle.'

John looked into her face and pondered. 'So maybe we could get together in October when we come back after the summer?'

Evelyn smiled. 'Yeah. Let's do that.'

Then she leaned forward and gave him a hug. They held their embrace for at least a minute.

'I think,' she said finally, 'that we'll give the Disco at Dawn a miss. Let's go and get breakfast in Bewley's.'

'You never answered my question,' said Evelyn, as they tucked into two full Irish. 'Remember? About why Michelle did what she did?'

'Yeah,' said John. 'I've been trying to figure out how to phrase it politely and I can't. She dumped me because . . . I was a crap lover. Inadequate between the sheets, if you will.'

'Oh,' said Evelyn, not knowing where to look.

John started to butter his toast. They did not make eye contact for a minute as she tried to think of something positive to say. Eventually she put a consoling hand on his shoulder and said, 'I suppose that before you go home you'll walk me back to 64?'

'I will.'

'Well, I think it's best if you come into the prefab for a minute. I've got something I want to give you.'

Cosmopolitan, a.k.a. *Cosmo*. It was a magazine with articles about fashion, beauty products and celebrity gossip. A women's magazine. Nevertheless, at Evelyn's insistence, John walked away from 64 with six issues under his arm, dated November 1988 through to April 1989.

When he got home his plan, because he'd been up all night, was to crash out and sleep. He brought the mags to bed with him, however, and just by looking at the covers he soon grasped the reason for Evelyn's unexpected gift. One other topic formed the bulk of the subject matter, one other topic that was covered from every angle, whether it be regarding positions, techniques or the exact location of certain significant zones.

Suddenly not feeling so sleepy, John got up and fixed himself a mug of raw egg. Then he dived between the covers and learned lots of useful information in a short space of time. There was a lot more to sex than John had been led to believe by the lads in his secondary school. He even did a few of the little quizzes and was not surprised to find he scored poorly. He could see quite clearly why Michelle had left him. But he was learning. When finally he drifted off to sleep, it was with visions of tongues in circular motion dancing in his head.

Evelyn lay awake, trying to study a lecture on fluid mechanics. Her eyes kept glazing over and all she could think of was John. And how he had tried to kiss her. And how it had come as such a surprise.

But on reflection it didn't seem all that surprising. More to the point, it didn't seem like such a bad idea. In fact, it seemed like something she should have allowed to happen, then see where it might lead, instead of being so damned sensible. Making excuses about bad timing and emotional turmoil and blah-blah-blah when actually John and she – together – might just be a good match.

As she threw down the lecture notes, Evelyn remembered John's suggestion that maybe they could get together in October after the summer holidays. She had agreed just to humour him.

But now . . .

Now she fell asleep and imagined a scene where the leaves were falling.

Frogs 2, 3, 4, 5, 6, 7 and 8

13

'Snow White!' said Evelyn. 'Also Cinderella, Sleeping Beauty and Rapunzel. Just like the frog princess, each of these fabled heroines ended up in the arms of dashing Prince Charming. What has never been properly established, though, is whether the prince was the same man in each case.'

'What?'

'Well, hopefully not. The stories all end reassuringly with a promise of happily ever after, not with a divorce, or fights over the custody of children and who gets which castle after the split. It would certainly be hard to feel enthused about Snow White's marriage if the prince had two ex-wives – Cindy and Rapunzel – who were sending snotty letters demanding more maintenance money.'

John laughed. 'Ssh now, Ev,' he said. 'Your complicated theories will only disturb our woolly friends.' He opened the gate and together they walked into a small field enclosed by tall stone walls. It was night but there was a full moon and light enough to see quite clearly without a torch. Everywhere they looked there were sheep – 219, to be precise – comprising a mixture of ewes, hoggets and rams. Some were standing at round-feeders, munching hay, and there were a few at the water trough. Most of them were lying down, asleep.

With John leading the way, he and Evelyn quietly threaded a path through the animals towards the centre of the field. Some of the sheep that were awake ambled away from them. Others stood their ground and stared. John proceeded all the way to the big sycamore tree. Once there, Evelyn paused to take in the scene, the shades of grey all around her. She could hear the sheep so clearly. From all sides came the sound of their breathing, interrupted by snores, and further away the scraping of two that must be butting and fighting. 'There's so many of them,' she whispered, 'for a field so tiny.'

'It's only temporary,' replied John. 'My father and I herded them in here earlier so they'd be handy when the vet comes tomorrow morning. After that they'll be released back on to the Kyle.'

'The Kyle?'

'That hilly field just above the avenue. All the fields have a name, you see. Like, for example, the Fort, the Riasc, the Sluggguradh. How else would we tell them apart?'

'I suppose,' said Evelyn. 'It just seems a bit weird giving names to rectangles of grass. Weird and surprisingly sentimental.'

'Believe me,' said John, 'I'm not one bit sentimental about the place or the woolly creatures. Just bloody glad to have escaped! I only come home for a weekend once a month out of a sense of duty. As regards helping my father, I feel it's the least I can do.'

But it was Sunday night now and time to return to Dublin for work next morning. Normally John would have taken the bus but on this occasion Evelyn had come in her car to give him a lift. 'I'll be at home, too, that weekend, Johnny, and it's on my way back to Dublin,' she had said. 'It's no bother to pick you up.'

But that was patently untrue. Cappataggle was not on

the route from Evelyn's home in Ballymahon to Dublin. The real reason had more to do with what Evelyn had been doing while at home: attending the massive car showroom in Moate, with her father brought along for advice, and buying herself her very first car, a sparkling, metallic blue Opel Corsa. In the event she had not arrived until it was dark, when it was hard to appreciate just what a wonderful shiny machine it was. Then John's mother had insisted that Evelyn stay for a meal. Something small. Not so small, however, that it didn't involve putting a pot of potatoes to boil. While they waited, John had given Evelyn a pair of wellies and taken her outside for this little walking tour of the farmyard and livestock.

'And another thing worth pondering,' whispered Evelyn, as John rummaged in his pocket for something, 'is the manner in which the heroines managed to snag their prince. It breaks down like this: Rapunzel, by being an enchanting singer and having lovely long hair; Snow White, by having perfect skin and being the fairest of them all; Sleeping Beauty, by being beautiful and simply waiting on her bed for as long as it took; Cinderella, by wearing fancy clothes and being a lively dancer.'

'Okaaay . . .' said John, as he found what he was looking for – a penknife.

'Do you see the pattern emerging?'

'I guess I don't, Ev.' John turned towards the wide sycamore and cut into the bark.

'These girls were all so beautiful they simply had to sit and wait for the prince. Completely passive. Sleeping Beauty, for instance, was asleep during her courtship. Rapunzel never left her bedroom, and as for Snow White, when she first met her prince, she was actually clinically dead!'

The first letter John cut was E.

'Cinderella, though, Johnny, was the odd one out. A hard worker and not afraid to damage her nails, she was the only one who showed a bit of initiative. When she wanted her prince she bloody well had to make an effort to get dolled up and go out dancing. My conclusion? Cinderella is the most fitting role model for the modern girl. For that is what we do, those of us who seek the man of our dreams – just like Cinderella, week in, week out, we get dolled up and go to discos and clubs.'

Then the letters V-E-L-Y-N-C-R-E-E-D.

'Howl at the Moon, Leggs of Leeson Street, Peg Woffington's – God knows how many Saturday nights I've spent with Cliona and Michelle trawling through those hell-holes in search of romance.'

Followed beneath by the letters P-R-I-N . . .

'What's that going to spell?'

'Princess, of course.' John laughed. 'And now let me just add the date.'

S-E-P-T '94.

Evelyn came alongside him to trace the letters with her finger. The white bit inside felt gooey to the touch. 'That's really nice, Johnny,' she said. 'But why do I get the feeling you're not fully listening to me? In case you haven't grasped, it's my life I'm talking about. Only trouble is that I haven't met with Cinderella's level of success. Six? Seven? How many boyfriends have I had over the last few years without one turning into a prince? I don't know what I'm doing wrong. Maybe I need to invest in some glass slippers.'

'C'mon,' said John, tapping her on the shoulder and turning to go. 'I reckon your dinner will be on the table by now.'

'Or I could start arriving to the nightclub in a carriage,' she called after him. 'I could trade in the Corsa.'

He turned and smiled at her. 'C'mon, will you?'

She followed him and they meandered back through the labyrinth of sleeping animals in the direction of the gate. A wisp of cloud crossed the moon, dimming the light. John could still see enough, though, to detect something standing in their path. Two small orange eyes stared at them defiantly. He made to go around a different way but the animal shifted its position and blocked that path as well. Evelyn could hear its breathing very clearly as the moon shone out brightly once more. It was one of the bigger ones, a ram.

John stepped towards it.

'Couldn't he just make a wild lunge with his head,' said Evelyn, trying to whisper but in a voice quite shrill, 'and knock you down?'

'Theoretically, yeah,' said John, 'but not really. It's like my father once said. I'm a descendant of my great-great-grandfather, Peter Fallon, who started farming here in 1875. Similarly, that sheep is a descendant of whatever sheep were here at that time.'

'Okay. So how does that help?'

'It means, Ev, that all I have to do is maintain eye contact. Remind him who's boss. Who's always been boss.'

And so it proved.

'Get out of my way!' said John, in a commanding tone, advancing on the ram and pushing it sideways with his knee.

Evelyn hurried along to join him again and they went indoors. After slipping off their wellies they found that 'something small' had evolved into a lavish five-course meal.

14

It was now more than five years since Evelyn and John had first met. They were not boyfriend and girlfriend, rather 'just' the best of friends. The promise of them getting together in college had never worked out. Instead their relationship had slipped into a comfortable, companionable groove and they got together on a weekly basis to discuss their lives, loves and half-baked theories. Usually on a Sunday. The day after the night before.

Although they were not going out with one another, neither had been idle in that department. During the intervening years, John had had a few liaisons, which had all ended the same way: with him being dumped. Evelyn had kissed many frogs and deemed them all unsuitable. Sometimes the decision had been difficult, with a guy close to perfect but not quite. Other break-ups were more straightforward: something was plainly not right.

Frog 2
Darren. She'd met him during her summer in London, while sharing a squalid house in Golders Green with ten other Irish students. He seemed very intense and knew an awful lot about English politics. They bonded over an argument about the electability of Neil Kinnock and by the end of the week were sharing the same mattress.

Back home in Dublin that autumn, though, Evelyn began to tire of Darren's fixations on a socialist solution.

When she tried to steer the conversations on to fresh ground he always wound up talking instead about his second great passion: science fiction. Not, Darren would emphasize, the juvenile lizards-and-lasers kind of sci-fi but the more hardcore ideas-based end of the genre. Thus Evelyn learned more than she ever wanted to know about the genius of Philip K. Dick and Isaac Asimov. Darren was even generous enough to loan her *Our Friends from Frolix 8* and all three books of *The Foundation Trilogy*.

One week later he asked Evelyn what she thought of them, and she admitted she hadn't read them yet. That didn't go down well. In fact, Darren got into such a sulk that Evelyn realized, for the sake of the relationship, she was going to have to make an effort and try at least one. That evening she opened *Foundation*, read a few pages and had to put it down. Sweet Jesus, it was awful stuff! Life was too short. She resolved that her relationship with Darren was over.

When he next came to visit her (she was back in the prefab at 64 for second year, sharing it with Cliona as relations with Michelle were still not healed), she told Darren and he was very angry.

'I protest!' he shouted. 'You can't do this. I'm going to come back down here every night until you change your mind.'

And that was what he did. Night after night for three weeks, Darren came to try to get Evelyn to reverse her decision. Around half nine, he would throw some gravel on the roof and she'd go out to him. He would try to persuade her and she'd listen politely before confirming that the answer was still no. And so on. After a week, Evelyn stopped going out to him but he kept throwing gravel on the roof – several fistfuls, night after night. It was a wonder there was a pebble left in the lane by the time he finally gave up.

Frog 3
Tony. A brother of a friend of a friend, Evelyn met him at a birthday party in Mozart's. After a bit of chat he asked her out to dance the slow set. By the time the DJ spun 'Another Day in Paradise' their tongues were in each other's mouth. Though the fast songs started again, they remained in a clinch and kept snogging through to the end of the disco, all the way to the chipper and right back to the friend of a friend's parents' house in Donnybrook. As everyone else settled down for a game of spin the bottle, they found a couch in the sitting room. Though the friend of the friend had ruled the room off limits, Evelyn brazenly locked the door and unbuttoned Tony's shirt.

Tony was very sweet and bursting with enthusiasm for life. Over the next few weeks, they met every second day and Evelyn found herself quite smitten. Sadly there was one problem she could not overlook.

'I wish I didn't have to say this,' said Evelyn, when she phoned him from the coin box in the front hall at 64. 'But we both know that you and me is not sustainable.'

'What?' he said, sounding genuinely surprised.

'C'mon, Tony. Don't be awkward. You know well why.'

'No, I don't. Is it the living on opposite sides of the city?'

'No. Come on, haven't you even noticed that when we walk down the street holding hands, people point at us and turn around to gawk?'

He didn't answer.

'And doesn't your neck feel the strain every time we snog?'

'Yes, but surely *that* isn't enough reason to finish something so good?' he pleaded.

Evelyn didn't answer. For a few moments there was silence on the line and then the beeping started, which warned they had just twenty seconds left of the call. Unless Evelyn put in more coins to prolong it.

'So what are you saying, Evelyn?' Tony whispered.

'That it's over,' she said firmly. 'You're a nice guy but it can never work because . . . you're too tall.'

And with that there was an abrupt click. The call was over, as was Evelyn's relationship with Tony.

'Darn it!' he shouted, and felt like throwing his parents' telephone out through the sliding door. 'And blast! Here we go all over again.'

And who could blame the poor lad for feeling bitter? Yet another girl was laying the entire fault on him, simply because he was six foot nine. Just once in his life, Tony would have liked to hear a girl take some bloody responsibility. Like Evelyn, for instance, for being five foot five.

Frog 4

Alan. He was a really lovable guy in many respects with by far the best sense of humour Evelyn had ever come across. However, though he could make her laugh until her ribs hurt, he took the stereotypical male student's disregard for hygiene to an extreme. He was just too messy, untidy, scruffy, stubbly and unclean. He didn't seem to have grasped the concept of daily showering. Most likely he was more of the old school – a weekly bath. Nor did he brush his teeth overly often.

If ever.

Evelyn eventually discovered that he didn't even own a toothbrush. Saying goodbye to this boy was one of her easier decisions. And he wasn't at all bitter. When she next saw him in town, months later, he smiled at her from across the street – making quite a display of his sparkling teeth.

Frog 5

Gerard. This was quite a long-lasting relationship, stretching as it did to the nine-month mark. He was a natural-sciences student, and Evelyn had noticed him around the physics building when they were both freshers. He was strong with curly brown hair and a nice line in polo-necks. They finally hooked up one night towards the end of fourth year outside the Pav and, wow, he was a most excellent kisser. The omens were good.

Outwardly, the routines of their relationship were in many ways similar to how they had been with Gary, daily meetings in college for tea and a snog session, passionate nights spent on a single bed in a tiny room, this time at Gerard's place in Grove Park.

'Let's give each other,' he used to say suggestively, 'a right good seeing-to!'

And they generally did.

On an emotional level, things were not quite as intense. Gerard was much more of a man's man. He didn't like to talk too much about feelings or, indeed, to listen to Evelyn talking about hers. That might have been okay if it wasn't for Evelyn's problem with Gerard's friends. Or, to be precise, one friend in particular called Sean. The situation was that Gerard was a member of a very close-knit gang of five guys who were classmates and Sean was effectively their leader. Not that he ordered the others around exactly, but he did manage to control their activities. No matter what was happening, be it a trip to the cinema, the pub, a kick-about, or just a night out in the Stag's Head, Sean was always the organizer, always the one setting the time and venue, making the phone calls and bookings. Thus Evelyn soon began to realize that Sean controlled a considerable portion of Gerard's life – which meant that since Evelyn wanted to be with Gerard, Sean controlled a considerable portion of her life too.

She didn't like it and eventually decided to make a stand.

'How about Saturday night?' she asked Gerard. 'I want to try the Palace Bar.'

'Oh, no,' said Gerard. 'Sean said he's getting the gang together at the Lincoln. Why don't we just go there?'

'Sunday, then?' she persevered.

'No. Sean's organized for us all to go to the greyhounds in Ringsend. But why don't you come too?'

'How about Monday?'

'Feck, no, Evelyn. I'll be wrecked at that stage. And broke! Needing a night in, definitely. Come on over and we'll give each other a good seeing-to . . .'

'Do you know what, Gerard?' said Evelyn, through gritted teeth. 'You can shove it! Why don't you get Sean to come over and give him a good seeing-to instead?'

Frog 6

Manus. He was another guy whose failing was easily identified: his American accent. Which was not to say that Evelyn hated American accents *per se*: it was just slightly incongruous in a lad who was from County Offaly. She had found it amusing on their first get-together in Buck Whaley's but after a while it became extremely grating.

'What-*eh*-ver!' he used to say.

'I am *so* not going there!'

'Could you *be* more wrong?'

Nor was this tendency to emphasize the middle syllable a result of Manus having spent a large part of his life Stateside. In fact, the sum total of his time there was a summer spent working on Long Island. Possibly more significant was that he spent much of his spare time watching CNN and ABC on satellite. Whatever the reason, the final straw came when Manus began saying to Evelyn, 'You *go*, girl!'

It was meant to be a positive thing. An all-purpose way of saying that he approved of whatever she had just done or said.

It didn't sound positive to Evelyn's ears. It sounded stupid. And a bit camp.

'You *go*, girl!' he said, once too often.

So she did.

Frog 7

And then there was Fintan. Good-looking, good-humoured, tick-all-the-boxes Fintan. Like an older version of Gary, he really was quite a catch and, what was more, he satisfied Evelyn's desire for magic. Spontaneous romantic gestures were Fintan's style from the very first time they met, on a freezing cold night. He had hailed what appeared to be the last taxi in Dublin when Evelyn appeared on the scene, looking the worse for wear, a refugee from the last late-opening nightclubs, sporting an outfit none too suitable for the Arctic conditions.

'No, go on,' he said gallantly. 'You can have it.'

After she insisted that they share, they both squeezed into the back seat, and by the time they got to Cowper Downs, she was inviting him in for a coffee. An hour later, she leaned over on the couch to kiss him, but instead of one thing leading to another, Fintan said he must be going. He wanted to do things right, he explained. He wanted to take her on a proper date first.

So they went out to dinner the following night . . . and then rushed home to make love.

Many more sweet, romantic gestures followed, such as flowers when it wasn't even Valentine's Day. Also notable was the little 'poem' he wrote on her birthday card. It went something like . . .

> Ramalama ding dong
> My popsalisha wing wong
> With you no thing thong
> Can go wrong
> A Super Mario scenario
> Some day I want to marry you
> And love you for ever
> Till my heart goes bong!

Truly lovely . . .

Fintan's one drawback in Evelyn's eyes manifested itself one morning after they'd been going out for about a month. By then they were sleeping together more or less every night and on this occasion Fintan had stayed over at Evelyn's apartment. (Now a working girl, she was no longer living in a glorified shed, but in one of the really nice apartments in Cowper Downs. Cliona and Michelle, with whom she'd eventually patched things up, were sharing with her.) On the morning in question the phone rang at eight thirty a.m., and what did Fintan do? He answered it! Evelyn watched in mortification as her worst fears were realized and it became apparent that her mother was at the other end of the line. No doubt she would want to know why a man was answering Evelyn's phone at that hour of the morning. No doubt she would go ballistic when confronted with this blatant evidence of shameful pre-marital sex.

But Evelyn's mother did not go ballistic. Rather, Fintan managed to persuade her that he had just arrived in the apartment and the purpose of his visit was to make her daughter breakfast in bed.

'Oh, that's so lovely,' purred Evelyn's mother. 'I can tell you, neither my husband nor any man of his generation would think of doing such a thing.'

The conversation continued, with Fintan being so charming that Evelyn's mother was thoroughly taken with him. When Evelyn was finally put on the line, her mother had forgotten what it was she'd rung about in the first place.

So, Evelyn's mother liked Fintan. And, indeed, vice versa. Some women might have seen this as a positive development, but not Evelyn. Her mother had spent so long criticizing Evelyn's hair, her clothes, her choice of career that for Evelyn to hear such ringing praise from her was a novel experience. A disorienting experience. Perhaps a suspicion began to grow in Evelyn's mind: if she and her mother disagreed about everything else and Fintan was so much her mother's kind of guy, could he really be hers too?

Over the following months, Fintan's relationship with Evelyn developed nicely, but unfortunately he also had a few more friendly phone conversations with her mother.

Matters came to a head when Evelyn's parents decided to have a party for their wedding anniversary and insisted that the young man come along. Evelyn's mother invited him in person over the phone so there was no way Evelyn could 'forget' to ask him. Once again she was presented with one of the big decisions that tangled her thoughts and emotions into a knot.

To bring Fintan home to meet her parents would definitely be to move their relationship to a new level. Evelyn had never got to this stage with any of her previous boyfriends so it would certainly be a signal that Fintan was special. More than just another boyfriend: a – *whisper it* – potential future fiancé and then son-in-law. Which was fair enough, in a way. She did really, really like him, and he was wonderful in so many ways. Also, this trip to the anniversary party was something everyone else seemed to want. Fintan was enthusiastic, as were her parents, so why did Evelyn feel as if she was being shoved over the edge of a cliff?

On the morning of the party, Evelyn was racked with indecision over what to do. She had one of her characteristic breakdowns. Her gut feeling was that it just wasn't right. Bringing Fintan to the party, where her mother would undoubtedly like him even better in person, would tangle things even more tightly. Any future break-up would be further complicated by her mother cheerleading from the sidelines and telling her she was mad for letting him get away. And immature and possibly a bit stupid. (From her father's side, of course.)

But still Evelyn couldn't quite make the decision. She picked up a copy of *Company* magazine and read her horoscope (Taurus).

With Venus in opposition and Mars ascending, you must tread warily on the 14th. Though keen to rush into new things, you must know when to back down. Travel plans do not look good but the 16th is an ideal day to ask your boss for a raise. Beware of leaping out of the frying pan and don't count your chickens just yet.

Which seemed quite conclusive to Evelyn.
And that was the end of that relationship too.

15

Of course, breaking up with a series of boyfriends was not the only thing Evelyn did during those years. By and by she had also managed to wean herself off all-black outfits, which was quite an achievement. Her opaque black cotton tights in particular hadn't seen the light of day in two years and she had even been known to experiment with a sky-blue blouse on the odd occasion. Her hair, though still long, was a few inches shorter, and the lipstick she favoured was no longer cherry red, but Sunset, an altogether subtler shade.

She also made progress at college, just about scraping through each summer exam, and finished with a 2:2 degree. A month before graduating, she did an interview with the Electricity Supply Board and duly got a job. Possibly this was because they looked past her mediocre academic results and saw her potential for greatness. Alternatively, it could've been because Uncle Pat, her mother's brother, was a senior man in the planning division.

John was not quite the same boy he'd been either. His acne was down to just a single spot and his hair had improved since the desperate days when he used to let Evelyn cut it. Now also a member of the working world, he complained about it when they finally got on the road to Dublin in Evelyn's brand new Corsa.

'I have an important announcement to make,' he said,

making a drum-roll gesture. 'After two years working as a pharmacist I'm finally ready to admit that it isn't quite what I'd hoped.'

'No kidding, Sherlock! I did warn you that it was nothing but counting tablets.'

'It is not, Ev! There's a lot more to it. Anyway, the problem is not that it's particularly hard or disagreeable – not by comparison to sheep farming anyway. Like most jobs, I suppose, it's sometimes stressful but mostly just terribly boring. It's quite a shock to the system after the excellence of being in college.'

'True. Totally true.'

'Look at the crappy holiday entitlement, for instance, of just four weeks a year. Worse still, though, is that this job is a real one, not like the pretend jobs we all got each summer. Whereas formerly any employment, no matter how unpleasant, was purely a temporary inconvenience, this job stretches out to infinity, or at least the rest of my life. It's not a pleasing prospect.'

'Yes, it's absolutely ick,' said Evelyn. 'My own job is exactly the same, totally uninspiring. I mean somehow . . . I never really believed it would come to this. Somehow I always hoped that, instead of taking my place among the working masses, I'd branch off sideways into something more exciting.'

'Like being plucked from the crowd at an Ireland match?' asked John.

'Like what?'

'You know, when all three substitutes have been injured in a freak accident and it's the last minute of extra time and the score is one all, but we've won a penalty and the manager wants me to come on and take that penalty, which

I duly do, dispatching it to the top right-hand corner, thereby winning the team qualification for the World Cup and a professional contract for myself in the process.'

'Em . . . Something like that, yeah,' said Evelyn, smiling. 'Let me put it to you another way, Johnny. When you were younger, what job did you imagine you'd wind up doing? I'll bet it wasn't pharmacy.'

'No,' said John, wistfully. 'I wanted to be Tarzan.'

'Okay . . . and when you got over that?'

'The Incredible Hulk.'

'And then?'

'Evel Knievel.'

'Oh, come on, Johnny. Didn't you ever want to be something at least slightly practical?'

'No, Ev. I didn't think like that. As a kid I just assumed that I would take over the farm from my father. I didn't necessarily want to, but it was expected of me and it seemed utterly unavoidable.'

'Really?' said Evelyn, turning to face him with one eyebrow raised.

'Keep your eyes on the road,' said John, 'or you'll miss the turn-off at Athlone.'

'It's just . . . I know you've told me that a hundred times before but, now I've met them, they seem lovely people. Your father is just so . . . I dunno . . . so quiet and big and gentle, your mother so warm and friendly. They don't seem the kind who would have forced you to do anything.'

'Not forced exactly. You don't get it. It was more a matter of duty and guilt. In school, I used to feel jealous of other boys who hadn't a clue what their daddy did for a living. I knew all too well what mine did because I was doing it too. Every evening after school I had a list of chores. In summer, school "holidays" were spent picking up stones and putting them into a bucket behind my father on the tractor and harrow. Which is not to say that I was treated unfairly, not at all. The work expected of me, aged twelve, was probably far less than he had done at a similar age. The problem was that most lads in my class were spending their evenings watching *The Man from Atlantis* and *Gemini Man*. They played Pac-Man while I was out with my father rounding up sheep to check their hoofs for foot-rot. And no matter what work I did, my father was doing more. After completing my chores, I generally skimmed through my homework and then lay on a couch in front of the television. My father, meanwhile, kept on going and going until darkness, through drizzle, rain or even sleet. Again, there was that contrast with other boys my age. Their fathers' work happened far away. My father's was just outside the window. I felt guilty. Though entranced by whatever episode of *The Six Million Dollar Man*, I kept half an eye out so I'd see him coming in from the yard when he was finished. I couldn't let him find me lying on the couch in my socks. I had to look busy. As he came through the porch, I'd lever myself up and dive into the kitchen. I would clear the table, or set it, or pick up a cup and wash it under the tap.'

'Okay, okay,' said Evelyn.

'So that, Ev, was Plan A. To the tiny extent that I could ever imagine escaping it, my Plan B was to jump a motorcycle over eleven cars and five buses. Is that so wrong?'

'Point taken, Johnny. It doesn't detract from the fact that I still found them to be lovely people. Your mother especially. My God, but she's an amazing hostess. She just couldn't do enough for me. Was she always like that?'

'She was,' admitted John. 'Is, was, ever will be, hopefully.'

'She just made me feel so relaxed,' said Evelyn, 'which is quite a contrast to the way I feel about my own dear mother, let me tell you. To be honest, the woman is borderline psychotic. All she ever does is complain about one thing or another. Very often me. No. Sorry. I lie. There is one other thing she's taken to doing in the last few years and that is renovating our house. She started six years ago by adding on a conservatory at the back, and since then she's been working her way through, room by room. Wooden floor here, stone facing there. Refitting the bathrooms and stripping out wallpaper. Whenever I go home she has a project ongoing and there are dust sheets everywhere and the roar of some piece of machinery.'

'Not exactly the perfect recipe for a restful weekend then,' said John, as he reached back into his rucksack and retrieved a can of Coke. He offered Evelyn a sup.

'No, thanks,' she said, as they reached the roundabout at Athlone and pulled into the left lane for Dublin. 'Well, anyway . . . I was hoping when I asked about your childhood ambitions that perhaps, like me, you wanted to do a job that really mattered and benefited less fortunate people. Something that would leave a permanent mark on the world. Something challenging, but fulfilling enough to make you bounce out of bed in the morning, happy to pour all your effort into something worthwhile.'

'Hmm,' said John, taking a long, satisfying slug of his drink. 'All I really wanted was to swing through the jungle on vines wearing nothing but a loincloth, but that sounds good too.'

'Yet it was just a daydream. I didn't actually do anything to make any of it a reality. I drifted along through college, doing barely enough to keep the wheels turning. Getting from first-year engineering to second and so on. In fact, I've now begun to appreciate that my life up to this point has always been like a conveyor-belt. Think about it: starting in junior infants, every September brought me up a grade into seniors, first class and all the way to sixth. Then the cycle was repeated in secondary school and finally in college. Always I have made progress – or at least appeared to – without any particular effort, just by hanging on in there, simply because the conveyor-belt of the education system was moving beneath my feet.'

'Indeed!' said John, almost spilling his Coke.

'Yes,' said Evelyn. 'Why do you think Michelle has gone back to college to do a master's? It's to regain that sense of progress for a little while longer. But all she's doing is putting off the inevitable. Our education is over. We have plopped off the end of the conveyor-belt into the stagnant waters of young adulthood.'

'Yikes.'

'Yikes is right, Johnny! And all we're doing now is just bobbing up and down in those stagnant waters. Going nowhere. Do you know, it's exactly two years yesterday since I started with the ESB? I tore off the date on the calendar and there it was, staring back at me. It made me wonder what's changed in that time. The answer is: almost nothing. I'm still working in the same cubicle at the same desk doing the same pointless –' Before she could finish the sentence, Evelyn's train of thought was interrupted by the sight of a puppy crossing the road in front of her. She had to brake hard. Very hard.

'Arrgha!' yelped John, as a big splash of Coke landed on his jeans.

Meanwhile the puppy took his own sweet time to amble to safety.

'Isn't he cute?' said Evelyn, as she slipped back into gear. 'So, where were we?'

'No, he is not bloody cute,' said John. 'And where I am is looking a lot like a fellow who just wet himself.'

'Not to worry, Johnny,' laughed Evelyn. 'Promise I won't tell anyone.'

'I think,' said John, dabbing at the stain with a tissue, 'that you were giving out about the utter meaninglessness of your existence.'

'Oh, yes, that was it. So, Johnny, what are you going to do with your life?'

'What? Besides drying my jeans? I dunno, but I'd want to be figuring it out soon. I'm not sure if I can take another winter stuck in that dispensary.'

'I can second that. And do you realize that, at our next birthdays, we're both going to be a quarter of a century old?'

'Feck!'

'Feck is right.'

'I just don't know,' said John, looking away out the window as if maybe the answer might be hovering in the hedge somewhere.

'Well, I'll tell you one thing. There will be no more progress for either of us unless we make it happen,' said Evelyn. 'But I don't think we're going to solve it today. Tell you what, how's about we both promise to think about it this week? When we meet again we'll see what we've each managed to come up with.'

16

Monday

Aspirin 75mg daily	1/12
Furosemide 40mg tabs daily	1/12
Co-proxamol 2tds	1/12
Isosorbide Mononitrate bd	1/12
Alendronate 70mg weekly	1/12
Hydrocortisone 1% crm	30G
Lactulose 10ml bd	2 bottles

John typed the customer's name into the computer. She had had all seven items before so there was no need to check for interactions. He simply tagged and repeated from the existing record. The printer generated labels for each as he went.

Next he had to find the actual medicines from the vast array on the shelves of the dispensary. Hundreds of them covered every square inch of the three walls around him, packed in jars, tubes, bottles but mostly small boxes. Many were stored in simple alphabetical order. Exceptions to the rule were the inhalers, which were grouped together, likewise the eye drops, the creams and the contraceptive pills. The children's antibiotics were squashed above the sink so there'd be water to hand when making them up.

The customer, a Mrs Mildred Glynn, returned from the neighbouring Spar with her paper and cigarettes. 'Sonny, are they done yet?' she called, her voice rather louder than it needed to be.

'Almost,' he replied, having just located the first of her seven items.

'Jaysus!' she said, turning to a shop girl who was using a pricing gun to tag products in her section. 'But yer man is very slow entirely.'

Going as quickly as he could, John found the medicines, all seven, counted out the requisite quantities, then stuck the labels on and bagged the lot. He wasn't quite finished, though. The prescription was of the medical-card kind so it needed to be stamped and the five-digit serial number of each drug filled in. He looked up in time to see two more customers approaching the counter. The shop girl collected three prescriptions from the woman with the buggy and one from the elderly gent.

'Here you go,' she said. 'Isn't there always a bit of a rush come Monday morning?'

John went out to Mildred with her finished prescription. 'Sorry for the delay,' he said, making an effort to put a smile on his face. 'Would you like to ask any questions about these medicines?'

'The only question I have, sonny,' hissed Mildred, as she grabbed the bag, 'is why you bloody well took ten minutes when the girl said you'd be five.'

John could say nothing. That was one of the joys of being behind the counter. The customer could be unreasonable and the employee had to stand there and take it. If something similar happened outside the shop, John would have defended himself. But the ordinary rules of courtesy don't apply when speaking to a shop employee. Shrugging it off and sneaking a wry smile at the shop girl, he went back into the dispensary and started on the next prescription.

Tuesday

Evelyn's cubicle, smack bang in the middle of the floor, was not one of the good ones. She accepted that. After all, she was still only a junior engineer in the line-maintenance section. It would be at least two more years before she was considered for one of the window cubicles – and as for the corner offices . . . Only if she made it to senior management would she ever be in a position to look out at both Fitzwilliam and Merrion Squares.

There was something else, another marker of her subordinate status, that Evelyn found harder to accept. Especially on a day when she had been asked to collate all the recent inspection data on the Cavan–Cootehill line. Having gathered the relevant graphs and reports, she was expected to write an abstract of the salient points, then make twelve copies of all items in time for the meeting at three p.m.

No problem. All of that technical stuff she could do. What really annoyed Evelyn was when she came to the last step of the process: putting together the reports. What ground her progress to a halt – and was an infuriating example of her lowly standing – was her stapler. Her stupid, gammy, keeps-getting-clogged-up-just-when-most-needed fecking stapler.

And, no, she couldn't just go up to the supply cupboard and grab a new one. Owing to suspected pilferage of stationery, the storeroom was locked and the keys held by Betty McCormack. If you wanted anything you had to persuade Betty first. Evelyn had already asked Betty for a new stapler and been rebuffed.

'It works fine,' said Betty. 'Some of the time. And we're on a tight budget around here, missy. I can't be doling out new staplers to every junior in the division. There'd be questions asked! Come back to me when it's completely banjaxed.'

So Evelyn had stormed back to her cubicle with the stapler and tried to see if she could break it entirely. Throwing it into the wastepaper basket did not do the trick. When she picked it back out, the stapler was still gammy, but not banjaxed. Next she opened its two arms apart and dropped it on the floor. Still no deterioration in its capability. She did manage, however, to put two neat holes in her thumb.

'Ouch, feck, ouch, feck,' she fumed. Quietly. Lest someone in a neighbouring cubicle be moved to look over the partition and see what she was up to.

The report on Cavan–Cootehill sat on her desk. It still needed to be stapled and the stapler was jamming. No doubt if she gave it a rest and tried again in a few hours' time it would be working perfectly, but by then it would be too late. Evelyn's next best option was simply to borrow a stapler from Killian in the cubicle to her right. She'd had to do that several times before. Yes, that was the simple solution. Evelyn stood up from her desk and walked out into the corridor. On her way around to Killian's, she passed by Mary-Anne's cubicle. It was empty.

Probably out on another sick day, Evelyn thought. She was making a big production of her sniffles yesterday.

Mary-Anne was not there – but her stapler was. It was sitting out on her desk in a position of prominence. Evelyn stopped walking. She realized she still had her own gammy stapler in her hand. She glanced around to see if anyone was looking. She stopped breathing, went into Mary-Anne's cubicle and was back out in two seconds.

Stapling of the Cavan–Cootehill line report was completed a short time later.

Wednesday

Much the same as Monday and Tuesday. The only item of interest occurred at Evelyn's workplace when she noticed Mary-Anne strolling past her cubicle. She was carrying a stapler. Carefully, Evelyn poked her head out into the corridor and watched Mary-Anne walking away. Except she wasn't walking, not exactly. There was something stealthy, sneaky even, in her gait and it was apparent that she was looking into each cubicle she passed. Searching for an unoccupied one, presumably so she could unload the small device she was carrying.

Thursday

Time was when tablets all used to come in big brown jars of 100 or 500 or 1000. That was very much the exception now. They came in their own little boxes wrapped in a patient-information leaflet. They were generally in blister packs to reduce the risk of children taking an overdose. This had led to one area of contention.

The vast majority of tablets had a dose of simply 'one daily' and were typically prescribed by doctors for a month at a time. So how many tablets should the standard box contain? Thirty, said some. Twenty-eight, said others. Nor was this a trivial matter. If the pharmacist gave the customer thirty at a time, there would be twelve dispensings in a year, hence twelve payments. If he/she were to give twenty-eight in each box, there would be thirteen dispensings in a year, hence thirteen payments. In the case of medical-card patients, that was not permitted. The upshot of this was that part of a pharmacist's day was wasted in opening another box, taking out a sheet of tablets and cutting off two to add to a twenty-eight.

Sometimes, when John's shop was quiet, he liked to cut up sheets of tablets into twos and have them ready for when the pressure came on. He was thus employed, when he had the pleasant surprise of a visit from a young man with a beard and long hair. He bore a vague resemblance to Jim Morrison *circa* the *L.A. Woman* album. John called him into the dispensary and Brian explained that he'd just come from the airport. He'd been on a midweek break in Paris.

'You lucky fecker,' said John.

'And I haven't even told you who I was with yet.' Brian smiled enigmatically as he produced his cigarettes and rooted for a lighter.

'Go on.'

'Aoife Hennessy.'

'*The* Aoife Hennessy?'

'Yes,' said Brian, lighting his cigarette and trying to remain looking cool. 'We hooked up a fortnight ago and, well, I dunno, one thing kind of led to another.'

'Such as . . . ?'

'Well, I took her to see Jim's grave. Y'know. It's in Paris. Père Lachaise graveyard.'

'Nice one.'

'Hmm. Yeah. Very nice one. The thing is, John, old pal, as a result I need a bit of a favour.'

'Okaaay . . . What sort of favour?'

'The big kind.'

Friday

By Friday morning Evelyn was starting to sweat, and it got worse as the day progressed.

Since Wednesday she had been observing her old stapler land in one cubicle after another. No sooner had Mary-Anne palmed it off on Seamus, while he was in a meeting, than he too was up and about looking for a swap. Fergal – gone to the toilet – was next and after that the stapler served briefly on the desks of Trish, Jack and Ronan.

Thursday was even worse, with the stapler taking a grand tour of the line-maintenance section. Evelyn watched in growing horror as, one after another, various engineers, both junior and senior, emerged into the corridors with a familiar expression on their faces. It was almost comical but Evelyn wasn't laughing. She knew in her bones that it could only end one way.

At one minute to five she was proven right. Almost ready to go home for the weekend, Evelyn poked her head out into the corridor and saw Betty McCormack approaching. On the warpath.

'How dare you, missy?'

'Sorry?'

'Bloody right you're sorry,' said Betty. 'I'll be letting your boss know about this little stunt.'

In Betty's hand was the stapler. Evelyn's defective old stapler. Betty was holding it between two fingers as you would a soiled nappy. With a heavy sigh, Evelyn realized there was no point in fighting it, no point in explaining that she had only swapped with Mary-Anne, who'd swapped with Seamus, etc., etc., etc. Evelyn picked up the good stapler on her desk and handed it to Betty.

The clock struck five.

Sunday

'So what did he want?'

'To tell you, Ev, would breach all kinds of ethical principles.'

'I repeat, Johnny. What did Brian want?'

'Oh, all right. I can't help it when I've got two pints inside me,' said John, draining the last of his glass. They were in Rody Boland's pub and Man U were playing Everton on the big screen down the end. 'Brian wanted the morning-after pill. Not for himself, obviously. For Aoife.'

'What?'

'You heard me. They had sex. Unprotected sex. Without condom or pill.'

'But –'

'If you need more detail, I can reveal that they did it standing up. Against a dead rock star's gravestone.'

'It's just Aoife –'

'Then Aoife was nervous about going to her family doctor for a prescription in case her mother might find out. So Brian prevailed on me to cut out the red tape and give it her directly.'

'Cut out the red tape? You mean you broke the law?'

'Indeed. Putting my licence on the line, Ev, because, well . . . that's just the kind of crazy guy I am.'

'Or not.'

'I suppose. I will admit to having had very little sex on musicians' graves but I do stand ready and available to provide morning-after pills for those super-cool people who do.'

'It's a thankless job, Johnny,' Evelyn smiled, 'but luckily there's someone like you there to do it.'

'Four years in college, Ev. They didn't go to waste.'

'Yeah, well, anyway,' said Evelyn, as she signalled to the barmaid for two more drinks, 'it certainly sounds like your week at work was more productive than mine. All I have to report is that I did something stupid with a stapler.'

'I did that once too. Damned painful!'

'You have no idea, Johnny. In more ways than one. To be honest, it was a final straw of sorts.'

'Go on.'

'I will,' said Evelyn, 'but only if you stop sneaking little sideways glances at the soccer match.'

'Right,' said John, tearing his eyes off a free kick that was being taken by Giggs. 'You have my full attention.'

'I spent yesterday working on my letter of resignation.'

'You what?'

'And checking the situations vacant. I've decided to make the break and look for a new job. Something meaningful and fulfilling obviously.'

'Nice one,' said John. 'But also a bit spooky. It seems we were on similar wavelengths without knowing it.'

'How do you mean?'

'Well, I too spent yesterday plotting an escape from my job.'

'Sounds intriguing!'

'Well, yes, intriguing but also quite obvious. Brian's visit, fresh from Paris, was just the trigger. I mean, it's bad enough that, unlike me, he made the right choice and went with the industrial-pharmacy option. Now he has something like a proper career going on in Leo Laboratories while I'm a glorified shop-keeper. Anyway, I decided that the time had finally arrived to eat the peach. I went into USIT yesterday and am now the proud holder of a plane ticket.'

'To where?'

'To all around this little world of ours.'

'Excellent!' said Evelyn.

Her attempt at an enthusiastic expression seemed slightly strained.

'Good man,' she continued. 'And your itinerary?'

'First stop on the way out is Egypt, then Singapore, Bangkok, Bali and Darwin. On the way back I'll fly out of Sydney to New Zealand, Hawaii, California and New York.'

'I'm impressed, Johnny,' said Evelyn, biting her lip and turning towards the television rather than look him in the eye. 'Didn't think you had it in you. When are you going? How long will you be gone?'

'The flight's in five weeks,' said John. 'I'll be gone a year.'

Evelyn still didn't turn to face him. She was surprised at herself: she felt far more emotional than made any sense.

'So, Ev,' he said gently, 'will you miss me?'

'Abso-fucking-lutely brilliant!' said Evelyn.

'Sorry?'

'Sorry, John, what did you say? I was distracted. Look at it there on the replay. That goal by Lee Sharpe. What a player he is! And pretty cute as well.'

17

Alice Springs,
18/12/94

Hey, Ev,

So, yes, I have seen King Tut, the River Nile and the pyramids (they're all a bit shorter than they appear on TV). After that came Thailand, where I danced at a Full Moon party on the beach and was in a constant state of anxiety lest I felt attracted to any ladies who turned out to be ladyboys. Then there was Darwin, where I spent the last two weeks in Kakadu Park tiptoeing around koalas and crocodiles. I also came damn close to drowning at one stage rather than admit to the tour guide I'm a crap swimmer. There were these two holes in the sheet rock near Twin Falls, about ten yards apart. The idea was to dive down into one, swim along underwater, under rock, and pop up again in the other hole. So off I went but I had imagined that the underground bit would be a simple tunnel leading from one to the other. IT WASN'T. It was a cavern and I got lost. I couldn't find the second hole and I was too panicked to get back to the first. My lungs started to burst and in the midst of being totally petrified I had two distinct thoughts simultaneously.

One was: For feck sake, I'm going to die.

The other was: How embarrassing. What will my

father say when the foolish circumstances of my demise are explained to him?

So, anyway, here I am in Alice and in philosophical happy-to-be-alive mode. Travelling mostly alone as I have these past two months has given me lots of time to think. About life, the universe, the significance of the number 42, everything! It's also, if I may be so bold as to say it, afforded me a lot of opportunities to look at women. Fine, fine-looking women. I suppose I have to admit that my purpose in coming out here has been twofold:

1) To make a complete break from the rut into which I had fallen, learn about the world and, in the process, learn about myself. Become a new man, one capable of really grabbing life by the lapels.
2) To make sweet, sweet love to some women . . .

Something John hadn't done in quite a while. On the very last night before he left Dublin, somewhat drunk, he had admitted it to Evelyn. 'It's been almost a full year since I unfastened a bra!'

'Ick!' said Evelyn. 'That's poor. Why, I unfastened one myself only last night.'

Not that the years since John had broken up with Michelle had been entirely devoid of sex or romance. In fact, now that his acne had cleared he could almost be considered handsome. He had had a few snogs and at least two proper girlfriends. Both relationships had proven ill-fated. His connection with a classmate, Valerie, for instance, had shown a lot of promise until one drunken night he did a stupid thing.

They were on the third-year pharmacy tour to Brussels and, as the evening was balmy, stayed outside drinking until very late. Someone had a madcap idea. Why didn't they have piggyback races across the patio? They all paired up into teams and naturally John volunteered to carry Valerie. She wasn't too heavy and for a minute he really thought they were going to win the race. But then he stumbled and Valerie fell sideways on to the patio. For a moment there was silence and John thought that everything was going to be okay.

It was not okay. Rather, that quiet was the sound of Valerie taking a deep breath. Once her lungs were full, she unleashed a deafening howl.

'I'm so sorry,' said John. 'Where does it hurt?'

'Every-bloody-where!' she shrieked.

In truth, Valerie had merely sustained a few scratches and one bad bruise. Her tolerance for pain was not very high. Though John tried to nurse and console her, she would have none of it. When he ran off, then returned with two paracetamol and a basin of warm water, she made it clear there was no longer a relationship.

Fate had not been on John's side when he was with Avril either. He went out with her one summer after meeting her at a twenty-first party for one of his co-workers. All was well until the day when she took him by the hand and suggested they compare notes on their previous partners. Her list of ex-boyfriends made John jealous but that was as nothing to the effect on her when he mentioned Michelle.

'What? You mean Michelle Neylon from near Athlone?'

'Yes.'

'Tall girl, slender, quite pretty?'

'Ahmm . . . Yes, I suppose many people would indeed consider her pretty.'

'One brother?'

'Yes . . . that's right.'

'Well, then . . .' Avril trailed off and let go of John's hand. 'That is a pity. A terrible pity.'

It emerged that Avril was a second cousin of Michelle's. They had only ever met face to face on three occasions at big family gatherings but nevertheless Michelle's name was all too familiar to Avril. This was because her mother had been in the habit of 'encouraging' Avril by telling her all about the exploits of second cousin Michelle Neylon. Michelle, who was so studious and did well in the Inter and Leaving Certs. Michelle, who was so graceful and won medals for Irish dancing. Michelle, who was so blah-de-fecking-blah.

'So,' explained Avril, 'there is no bloody way on earth that I'm going to settle for Michelle Neylon's cast-off boyfriend.'

Sometimes, thought John, Ireland can be a very small bloody island.

There was one aspect of these break-ups, however, that provided John with a small measure of consolation: in neither case had there been any suggestion that he was inadequate between the sheets. He thanked *Cosmopolitan* for that.

. . . So far, item (1) is coming along okay but (2) is decidedly not.

Nor is it like I haven't made any attempts. I can't count the number of times I've been in discos or tour groups and tried to make eye contact with a good-looking girl. And on the odd occasion they haven't turned away. There have even been some conversations, really good conversations! But somehow, some way, when it comes to the moment at which I must close the deal, lean in a little closer and form my lips into an O . . . I can't do it. I am gripped by fear and the hope that if I just wait another minute it's going to get easier. But it does not get easier and the moment goes past the point of ripeness. Her friend comes over to say the taxi is here, and before I know it I'm alone. Returning to the backpackers' hostel and a night in the bottom bunk below some snoring surfer from Holland.

Well, no more, Ev! NO FECKIN' MORE! That's the lesson I have taken from the waterhole in Darwin. The thing I have been forgetting is that out here in Oz nobody knows me. So feck it! I'm going to reinvent myself! As . . . I'm not sure what but someone a bit cooler anyway. Starting tomorrow on a tour to Ayers Rock, which I note has been heavily subscribed by a gang of girls with Spanish names. Watch out, señoritas!

Anyway, must go now. The barbecue in the hostel tonight is serving kangaroo burgers and ostrich meat. Then next week I'll be experiencing an even greater weirdness: Christmas in sweltering heat. A tough job, but I suppose half the world has to do it!

Please say hello from me to Michelle and Cliona and do send me a reply to the post office in Sydney. After trawling the Great Ocean Road I should be there in three weeks' time. Meanwhile I hope you are well and wonder what your new job is like. Also, how's the love-life? Any new frogs on the horizon?

Yours upside-downedly,

John

What was her new job like?

Much like my old one, thought Evelyn, as she put John's letter down and typed in the password (4LSHARPE) on her work computer, except a small bit worse.

And how was her love-life?

Non-existent! thought Evelyn, as one of her co-workers ambled past her cubicle. Mid-fifties, with a fine big belly, he was scratching inside his ear with the point of his car key. And not a single frog in view. Certainly not in this office anyway.

Out of the frying pan of the Electricity Supply Board and into the fire. Evelyn's new job at Margaret Leamy Ltd had not turned out quite as she'd hoped. No major challenge, no major fulfilment and no real sense of making progress. The bottom line was, she'd been a junior engineer in the ESB and was a junior at Leamy's.

Along with the absence of any benefits, the new job also had some drawbacks when compared to her old one – the age profile of her co-workers for one. In the ESB there were two dozen juniors in their twenties like herself, but in Leamy's, a much smaller outfit, she was the youngest. There were also very few women. Although the managing director was one, the only other female junior was Helen. Most of the staff were married men between thirty and sixty. Hence her working days were no longer made more bearable by the innuendo and banter of colleagues her own age.

Which was not to say that the rest of the staff ignored her. Far from it. Unfortunately, the attention she received was mostly from a disgusting old lech called Eugene. Always careful to admire her clothes, he liked to be 'helpful' – but for some reason this always seemed to involve placing his buttock on the corner of her desk. Or leaning in over her shoulder, supposedly to see the computer screen but more likely to peer down into her cleavage.

I need a cup of coffee, thought Evelyn, after reading John's letter through once more. The jammy fecker! That is really living!

She walked down the corridor to the little kitchen. As the kettle boiled, Helen came in and brought to her attention an announcement on the company noticeboard.

COMPANY SOCIAL TRIP TO MANCHESTER
See premiership match
Man U vs. Aston Villa
At Old Trafford
On 4th of Feb
Flights, 2 nights accom and match ticket £200
Contact Adrian to book place
Ext. 192

'C'mon, Evelyn,' said Helen. She was petite, blonde and always enthusiastic, whether the subject was peace on earth or the tender for sewerage works in Leitrim. 'It'll be great *craic*! I'm definitely going, and it's not particularly for the match. There's supposed to be fabulous shopping over there and brilliant nightclubs too. Like the Hacienda.'

'No way, Helen!' said Evelyn, and went about the business of making a coffee. By the time she had got back to her desk, however, she was thinking better of it. It would indeed be a chance to check out the nightlife in Manchester. It was bound to be an improvement on the scene in Dublin, with which she was beginning to feel a little exhausted. She'd already searched all the clubs and come up with nothing. Was she condemned to keep circling them until the end of time? And what the hell else was she going to be doing that weekend? Another thing . . . When else would she get an opportunity to see Lee Sharpe in the flesh?

Those legs . . .

In those shorts . . .

Oh, what the feck? She went over to Adrian's desk and put her name on the list.

18

One fat hen.

One fat hen.

One fat hen and a couple of ducks.

One fat hen and a couple of ducks.

One fat hen and a couple of ducks, three brown bears.

One fat hen and a couple of ducks, three brown bears.

One fat hen and a couple of ducks, three brown bears and four running hares.

One fat hen and a couple of ducks, three brown bears and four running hares.

So far, so good. The first four rounds of this drinking game, held in McKenzie's Bar of Sydney, were no bother to John. It was when Jason called out the next line that the trouble began.

First Jason took a sip of his beer.

'One fat hen and a couple of ducks, three brown bears and four running hares, five fat freckled females sitting sipping Scotch.'

The girl to his left followed suit perfectly, sipping her G and T before reciting the line. As did the next girl and then the other guy. It came to John's turn and he screwed up by beginning his recitation without first taking a sip. That incurred a penalty of two fingers, meaning he had to gulp down his beer until he'd lowered the level by two fingers' width down his glass. Then he took one further sip and began to speak.

'One fat hen and a couple of ducks, three brown bears and . . . four . . .'

He was already struggling even before he got to the hard bit, and the other players around him began to laugh.

'Running hares!' he shouted triumphantly. 'And five fat . . . freckled women sitting something something.'

'I'm sorry but no,' said Jason, shaking his head with disappointment, like a teacher with a kid who refuses to do homework. 'That's another two-finger penalty, I'm afraid.'

So John guzzled two more fingers of beer and listened intently as Jason called out the line once more. At the third attempt, he finally nailed it. Jason moved on to line six.

'One fat hen and a couple of ducks, three brown bears and four running hares, five fat freckled females sitting sipping Scotch, six simple Simons sitting on a rock.'

John looked towards the bar and signalled for another beer.

Since Alice Springs, John had spent many nights pretending to be someone who was a lot cooler and had reaped the benefits in terms of romance. One of the pretty Spanish señoritas, for instance, had fallen for his charms on the trip to Ayers Rock. They had made love *al fresco* on the night when the tour group slept outside, under the strange constellations of a southern sky. In the morning she kissed him tenderly but the desert tour was at an end. They were due to get on buses going in opposite directions: he was going south, to Adelaide, and she north, to Darwin, where he had already been.

'*Adiós,*' she whispered in his ear, '*mi príncipe por una noche.*'

A week later, John managed to bed another woman, although this time it was not really to his credit. Neither was their meeting as romantic. Her name was Sharon and she was from Watford. Without wishing to be cruel, it would only be fair to say that she was not beautiful. Which is to say, she was quite plain. Or, to put it absolutely bluntly, her figure was more like a nought than an eight and there was hair between her nose and upper lip that was badly in need of removal. And yet John slept with her for the simple reason that she put herself on a plate. While he played cards with three guys from Sweden, she sat on the bench beside him and laid her hand on his knee. Then his thigh. Then higher still. John had simply not had enough sex in his life to be turning down a pass like this. Finishing his card game prematurely, he turned to Sharon and introduced himself. He didn't have to say much more as she was a very talkative girl. Later she sneaked him into her bedroom in the hostel and they did the deed as quietly as possible. Though perhaps not as quietly as her friend in the lower bunk would have liked: she stormed out of the room in a huff, pulling her sleeping bag behind her. Shortly afterwards, their 'lovemaking' concluded, Sharon lit a cigarette and started to talk.

Much to John's horror, he was overwhelmed by a wave of revulsion. Now that the lust had drained from his body, Sharon was transformed in his eyes from a reasonably desirable woman into nothing more than a blob of flesh. A big blob of talkative flesh.

It felt like sacrilege to be naked with her. Without lust in his veins he didn't even like, let alone love, her.

It felt like a story that he would never be telling Evelyn – or even Brian.

It felt like eternity before exhaustion finally overtook his 'lover' and he could make his escape.

Last and also least was an encounter with an American girl called Cassie in Millicent. Clearly, his last experience hadn't taught John much. Again the venue was a backpacker hostel. The trouble was that both of them were staying in shared rooms with five other occupants. Having sex with that many other people in the room was not a runner.

Hence, having snogged for absolutely ages and feeling the need to progress matters, the pair began to wander around the hostel, searching for some location, any location, where they could have complete privacy for half an hour. Sadly there was no spare room, or even a closet, in which they could find shelter.

They were at the southern tip of the continent so it was quite a chilly evening and there was no question of lying down on the grass. Instead they just stood behind the hedge. Cassie opened his zipper.

Once it was done she said she wanted to get back inside quickly before she caught a cold. It was, thought John regretfully in his bunk bed, a horribly functional ending to their evening together. He wondered if it really counted as sex. Could he, for instance, include it when he'd got home to Ireland and was telling Brian how many women he'd been with? He thought so but wasn't really sure.

In the aftermath, as his bus set off again for Sydney, he felt empty and ashamed. He had sampled casual, meaningless sex and found it less wonderful than he'd expected. Next time around, he would set higher standards. Next time around, it must be with a very special kind of girl.

*

One fat hen
and a couple of ducks,
three brown bears
and four running hares,
five fat freckled females sitting sipping Scotch,
six simple Simons sitting on a rock,
seven Sinbad sailors sailing the seven seas,
eight egotistical egomaniacs echoing egotistical ecstasies,
nine nubile nymphomaniacs nib-nib-nibbling on nudds, nadds and nicotine.

'And that,' said Jason to his fellow players, 'is that. There is no more.'

There didn't need to be. Not for John, at least. He had drunk so many penalties that he was incoherent and unable to take part long before the ninth round. In the latter stages of his involvement there had been an embarrassing situation in which he had run out of beer and also cash. Unable to buy another drink, he had instead gathered up the dregs from a neighbouring table. He had poured them all together, leftover lager, vodka and wine, into one big glass. Then he played the game with this horrible concoction until he was stumbling over 'ecstasies'. After draining it, he slid sideways off his seat and made no attempt to get up.

It was really quite decent of his fellow players. Though they didn't know him from Adam, they carried John back to his hostel and into Reception.

'You okay from here, mate?' someone said.

'Essssss,' he managed to slur.

But John was not okay from there. He got lost on the winding corridors that led down to his room and then he had a sudden urge to look out of the big bay window. He tried to pull back the floor-length curtains but couldn't seem to find the centre and got tangled up. Eventually finding a way through, he pressed his face against the glass and enjoyed the cooling sensation. He slumped to his knees and then down on to the floor. It felt nice to be lying on the carpet. As soft and warm as the most comfortable bed in the world. It was like he had his own tiny little room inside those curtains and it was cosy and lovely and *zzzzzzzzzzz* . . .

At about seven the next morning, John was awoken by sounds from the corridor just outside the curtain. Someone was using the Coke machine on the landing. But it wasn't straightforward. Something was wrong.

John reached for the bottom hem of the curtain, lifted it slightly and peered out. He had to adjust his head a little but he could see quite clearly. It was a girl, a very thirsty girl, and she was putting a coin into the machine. It fell out into the reject slot. Then she put it in again and it was rejected once more. The coin was an Aussie dollar, enough to buy a Coke, but defective in some way. It must have been her only change because she tried it ten times in a row before giving up. Then she sighed and walked away to her bedroom.

John dropped the curtain hem and disappeared once more into his tiny living space. The girl was gone but she had been standing there for long enough. He had noted her blonde hair, a violin-shaped figure and a truly lovely face. He had also had time to reach a definite conclusion, despite exhaustion and an impending hangover. He knew to the very core of his being that she was, without exception, THE MOST BEAUTIFUL GIRL HE'D EVER SEEN IN HIS LIFE.

19

Dublin
8/2/95

Greetings, Johnny,

As I may have mentioned, approximately 1000 times, it's time to branch out and try new things. It was with that in mind that I allowed myself to be convinced by a colleague to go on a naff work weekend away to Manchester. Like a school tour, but with drunken co-workers. Well, anyway, to begin with the trip was just one annoying screw-up after another.

My workmate Helen pulled out at the last minute – after nagging at me to go on the trip in the first place! I was less than impressed when she rang the night before to say that she'd developed a massive cold sore and just couldn't face it. That left me as the only girl on the trip – or so I thought.

I was at the airport before I realized that the company's owner and managing director, Margaret Leamy, was coming along. Her office is on the top floor, so I'd only ever seen her once or twice. Also in attendance was her son, Andy, pretty much the heir apparent, second in command. Being as low as I am in the food chain, I hadn't had many dealings with him either.

As far as I was concerned this was not good. How could I let my hair down when these people were around? It was too late to back out, though, so off we flew!

The next annoyance was when we got to our accommodation in Manchester. The hotel was supposed to have sorted our tickets for the match but for some stupid reason it turned out that they'd left our party two short. Many voices were raised but it was no use. Old Trafford was totally sold out and no force on earth could get us those two extra tickets. A decision had to be made. Two people from our party of fifteen would have to volunteer not to go.

I don't need to tell you that Miss Fool here was one of them. Despite my longings for Lee Sharpe's fine legs I had to admit that there were guys who'd been major Man U fans their whole lives and they deserved a ticket more than me. Surprisingly enough, though, the second person to volunteer was Margaret Leamy . . .

On the morning of the match, the Leamy group had set off for Old Trafford hours before kick-off. They had wanted to soak up the atmosphere, see the statue of Sir Matt, visit the superstore and buy some merchandise. That left Evelyn and Margaret Leamy alone together. The plan was that they would spend the day shopping.

They took a taxi together into the Arndale and Evelyn felt suitably awkward and shy in front of the most senior person in her company. Then they divided up for a while, as the shops they wanted to visit were quite different. Margaret went to John Lewis, Debenhams and Boots while Evelyn took in Next, Topshop and the biggest HMV she'd ever seen. They met for lunch in the centrepiece restaurant at one p.m.

'So what are your plans for the rest of the afternoon?' asked Margaret. 'More shopping, or do you fancy the cinema maybe? I see they're still showing that Anthony Hopkins thing in the Omni.'

'Neither, to be honest,' said Evelyn, acutely aware that this was not the ideal way to reply to one's boss. But what the hell? While shopping she had begun to feel the whole weekend might be a complete waste of her time. Until, browsing in HMV, she'd been struck by an idea. 'There's something else I want to see.'

Evelyn explained about her love of music. All the bands she'd been so passionate about during her teenage years and how so many of them had come from Manchester. New Order, Joy Division, the Buzzcocks – but, most especially, her favourites of all time, the Smiths. Only together for five years, the band had produced six albums but their masterpiece was the fourth, called *The Queen Is Dead.* Inside the gatefold sleeve of that LP, Evelyn explained, was a photo of the band standing outside a grim and grotty community hall in one of the roughest, most derelict parts of Manchester. The sign overhead said 'Salford Lads Club'. Evelyn explained that she had brought her camera. She wanted to find this place and have her photo taken outside.

'What a charming idea,' said Margaret Leamy, much to Evelyn's surprise. 'I've had enough of shopping too. Count me in.'

. . . After a bit of detective work we did eventually find the exact same place looking just like the classic photo!!! While we were there, these tough-looking little skinhead kids, only about ten, ran over and

offered to sell us some power tools that they were carrying in a plastic bag!!! The taxi-man was good enough to take a photo of me and Margaret standing there. And he didn't even steal the camera.

What was really weird, though, was that Margaret Leamy was not one bit fazed. In fact, the whole escapade led to me and her having this amazing conversation that took up the whole rest of the day. I dunno, it just created this bond between us and the whole employer/employee barrier just fell away with all the laughing we did.

By the time we got back to the hotel she was telling me how she must get me more involved in the top projects at work. By the time we had joined up with the soccer gang (one–nil, Cole) and were clubbing late that night (Margaret wore a figure-hugging dress that had quite a few of her male employees staring with their mouths open), she was telling one of the seniors that I reminded her of herself when she was younger, that I was like the daughter she'd never had . . . She'd had quite a few drinks at this stage.

Then, because I hadn't ever really met him properly, she introduced me to her son and second in command, Andy.

Some time after midnight came the first few defections. The more sensible married men made their excuses and headed back to the hotel. Then came those who had been drinking ever since the final whistle and could drink no more. Next to leave were two men from Accounts (in their forties) who had pocketed their wedding rings and spent an hour chatting up two girls (in their twenties) who went to the Ladies and never came back. That left Evelyn, Margaret, Andy and Eugene (the lech). Perhaps Eugene was thinking that his chance had come at last to make a proper pass at Evelyn. After one more drink, though, Margaret suggested he might like to go to bed.

'No, I'm not a bit tired,' he said.

'I think you are, Eugene,' said Margaret, with just a hint of steel in her voice. 'I'm quite certain that you are.'

Eugene looked a bit bewildered, but eventually made his excuses.

And then there were three . . .

. . . Not quite sure what possessed me. It's not that Andy isn't good-looking. He is. Very much so, actually, with blond hair that he wears short and sharp, military style. Also if I go through my mental checklist of qualities I want in a man, he does satisfy quite a few. Very intelligent, extremely ambitious, strong and athletic. On the dance floor, he was able to spin me like a top. On the other hand, he was so cocky. He had that whole South Dublin upper-middle-class thing. The effortless confidence which is only a hair's breadth from arrogance. The certainty that he knows what he wants and wants it now. Nevertheless, the fact is that I got off with him. And it wasn't really because of his good points or despite his bad ones. It was because of – don't laugh! – his mother.

There were just the three of us and we were getting on so well. Then Margaret made her excuses and it was just Andy and me. Somehow I felt it was expected of me. Like it was what Margaret wanted and I didn't want to disappoint her. When he leaned in for a kiss . . .

Anyhow, it turned out he was quite decent in the sack . . . and . . . oh, enough about all that. I don't want to get you overexcited with the gory details, John! I just hope that you are having a wonderful time, you jammy fecker!

Evelyn

PS I was going to enclose a copy of the photo of me and Margaret standing outside Salford Lads Club. When I got back to Dublin, however, the film was finished and I didn't rewind it properly. When I took it out, I exposed all twenty-four to the light, thereby ruining them.

Oh, ick!

The Monday after the Manchester trip, Evelyn received the first confirmation that her newly forged bond with Margaret Leamy was not just a passing whimsy. Eugene dropped by to inform her that she was being promoted to senior engineer. 'And about time too,' he said smoothly, easing his bum on to her desk. 'I've been telling anyone who will listen what a very talented girl you are.'

Evelyn was so delighted that she almost wanted to give this bearer of good news a hug. Almost.

Later that day, she got the second confirmation that things were changing when a bouquet was delivered to her desk. 'Congrats from the top floor!' read the little card. 'Any chance of you meeting me for drinks tonight to celebrate?'

Yes, of course she would. Evelyn picked up her phone to ring upstairs and give her reply.

She dialled 101.

'Oh, feck!' she gasped, and slapped the receiver back on the cradle as quickly as possible. For some reason she had dialled Margaret's extension before the penny dropped that the flowers must be from Andy: 102.

20

John was not a particularly good soccer player. Lacking in skill and composure, his main contribution to the teams he played on was as a tireless runner who kept trying to the very end. Nevertheless, through years of playing, he had noticed how very occasionally he would have a game in which everything he attempted came off. His passes found the man, his dribbling left tacklers flat-footed and his shots at goal burst the net. Pure bliss was it on such an afternoon to be alive. The next week the upsurge in form was gone and he went back to being barely competent.

If it could happen in soccer, perhaps it could happen in other areas of his life.

After his kamikaze *One Fat Hen* session, John was desperately hung-over and stayed in bed for twenty-four hours. When eventually he arose it was only to answer a phone call from a pharmacy called Medicine Supermart. They were impressed by the CV he'd dropped in and wanted to interview him. Considering the state he was in, he was grateful when an appointment was made for the next day. He duly presented himself the following morning and was hired on the spot to start the very next week. Yes, John was an impressive candidate. Also, it helped that New South Wales was suffering from an acute shortage of pharmacists.

So that was the first good thing which happened to John that week. His savings had carried him this far but the time had come to do some work and replenish the bank account. The plan was to stay and work in Sydney for six months and that was now on a firm footing. The second good thing, though, was ultimately of far more consequence. He was strolling back into the hostel (looking better than usual, perhaps, in a short-sleeved shirt and tie) when he came across the girl he'd seen at the Coke machine. This was the girl he had been so certain about: she was THE MOST BEAUTIFUL GIRL HE'D EVER SEEN IN HIS LIFE.

This time John was perfectly sober but his judgement was the same. Her hair was blonde, her face so very pretty and her body curvaceous as hell. Without missing a beat, not giving himself time to be overwhelmed by his unworthiness and shyness, John walked straight up to her and asked if she would please have dinner with him that night.

She put down a book she'd been reading called *Miss Smilla's Feeling for Snow*. She looked him over, up and down. She said yes.

Unlike John's previous Australian encounters, his liaison with Sophie (for that was her name) followed a more old-fashioned trajectory. Instead of proceeding straight to sex within a few hours of meeting, their first night was almost all conversation. He took her to dinner on Darling Harbour, and they sat at a table overlooking the bay. There was an initial period of awkwardness, but Sophie was a fellow backpacker and they were soon comparing notes on what places they'd already been to in Australia, and what they missed about home (she was from Cheshire). Then they swept on to families, schools, favourite books and movies. By the end of the evening they had established quite a rapport, but there was no physical intimacy, except for the last few hundred yards before they reached the hostel when they held hands. Then they went into Reception and let go again.

The next day, Saturday, was their second date and it lasted all day as they went out to the Blue Mountains. Trekking along forest trails and admiring views, they walked side by side throughout. Their conversation dug deeper than it had the previous day, touching now on subjects like love and children and the pursuit of happiness. Even the meaning of life received an airing, though not, perhaps, a solution. On the back seat of the bus going home they finally had their first kiss, which they kept going all the way back to King's Cross. Still, when they got back to the hostel, it was to two separate rooms that they retired in exhaustion.

After they'd had breakfast the next morning, John said he wanted to show Sophie something and they went for a stroll. Down the street he stopped outside the nearby four-star hotel, an extremely classy-looking joint.

'I, uh, hope you don't think . . . that you don't mind, but I . . . I've booked us a room. Would you . . . ?'

'I thought you'd never ask.'

So they checked in and, in their room, took their clothes off so fast the door had hardly shut behind them. They would not put them on again for almost twenty-four hours. Three, four, perhaps five times they made love. In between they lay in one another's arms. And watched television. And shared a bath. And ordered room service – twice.

On Monday morning at seven thirty, it was time to say goodbye. Sophie had arranged to meet friends and was headed north to Coff's Harbour. John, meanwhile, was committed to Medicine Supermart and his first day of work.

After swapping home addresses and phone numbers they promised to keep in touch. He saw her off from the bus stop, then hurried to his new job in the city. Somewhere around Pyrmont, he realized he was crying.

It was a hellish first day at work. He didn't know their computer system and all the drugs had different names from the ones he was used to. On top of that, John's brain was operating on only a fraction of full capacity. He thought constantly of Sophie and of the time they'd spent together over the previous three days. Of the things she had said. Of the way she had looked when she laughed. Of the moment when he had finally unclasped her bra. Of . . . How could he have just let her go? It was a crazy mistake to have made. Sophie was the kind of girl you met once in your life if you were lucky.

But, on the other hand, what of his plan to stay in Sydney and work for six months? John was already slightly overdrawn and badly needed this time to recharge his finances. He spent five days agonizing, but in the end the decision was no decision at all. At the end of the working week he resigned from Medicine Supermart and booked himself on to a bus all the way north to Cairns. First stop: Coff's Harbour.

Sophie had a week's start on him and had most likely moved even further north by now to who knew where? On a continent the size of Australia, it could be a case of searching for a needle in a haystack.

But so be it, thought John. I *am* going to find her.

21

After several years of stagnation, the next few months finally saw major advances in the life and times of Evelyn Creed. She had at long last been promoted to senior engineer and that was just the beginning. Owing to her brilliantly innovative work on the Morgan project that spring, she was rewarded with an upgrade to the status of junior associate. Summer brought fresh challenges and a potential disaster for the company, as the deadline for the Gribbin development loomed large. A multi-million-pound contract hung very much in the balance for a fortnight, but thankfully the necessary audits were completed in time – by a team Evelyn headed. Her achievement was recognized by advancement to the rank of associate (above which there is only one further level: partner).

Despite the pressures at work, things went well for Evelyn with Andy too. He really was, she soon began to appreciate, a pretty decent guy. Like Fintan, he was a master of the spontaneous romantic gesture. On the other hand, on the only occasion that he spoke to Evelyn's mother on the phone, he was polite but showed no sign of forming any special connection with her. (When he handed the phone to Evelyn the conversation was a short one. Her mother wanted to renovate Evelyn's old bedroom and was looking to discuss a new colour scheme. Evelyn wanted it left the way it was. Mostly black.) In another way, Andy bore some resemblance to Gary by being quite a good listener. Utterly unlike Gary, he was well capable of telling her if she was blathering on a bit much. His favourite phrase was 'Cut to the chase!' His second favourite was 'Put it in a nutshell!'

But there was one thing Andy had, which absolutely all of her previous boyfriends had lacked: money.

It was not that Evelyn had become in any way materialistic. Still, though, it was nice to see how the other half lived. To go to posh restaurants like Chapter One and give no thought to the cost. To have a seat reserved in a box at the Gaiety. To be whisked away for a surprise weekend to Edinburgh, London, Paris. And then there were the presents, jewellery and perfumes. Never had Evelyn met a man who produced such perfectly chosen gifts.

There was, however, an aspect of her new life with which Evelyn was not entirely comfortable. The business of sleeping with Andy. Well, not the sleeping bit exactly or, of course, the sex (which was always vigorous, if sometimes a little quick), but rather the staying over at his place. Or, rather, his mum's place. Or, really, her boss's place. Although he often talked about buying an apartment on the quays, Andy still hadn't got around to leaving home.

The upshot was that Evelyn much preferred to have Andy over to her apartment, but inevitably would wind up on occasion staying at his house. The first time it happened, legless drunk after a party nearby, she awoke in the morning conscious that someone was moving around the room. Naturally, she assumed that it was Andy but no . . . He was motionless in the bed beside her. At which point, Evelyn sat bolt upright, convinced that it was burglars or, worse still, Margaret Leamy, come in to see exactly what she was up to with her only son. In fact, it was the family maid, rummaging in the laundry basket.

'That's just Molly,' said Andy, rolling over. 'Now, darling, get back down here. Pronto!'

Worse was to follow. While Evelyn's instinct would have been to sneak out of the front door, Andy insisted that she stay for breakfast. Margaret was waiting for them at the table. She was not dressed in one of the stylish business suits in which Evelyn was used to seeing her but in her dressing-gown, with a mud pack applied to her face.

This is wrong, thought Evelyn. Yes, I get on very well with Margaret and the two of us will always, as it were, 'have Manchester'. But the fact remains that she is my boss. And that last night I was doing several slightly sordid things with her son.

What was even more unnerving was how normal Margaret acted, like she was talking to one of the family. Prompted by the face mask, she launched into an enthusiastic discussion of wrinkles. Then which cosmetics promised how much anti-ageing effect. Then her upcoming birthday dinner.

This is absolutely nothing like home, thought Evelyn, as Andy wandered into the kitchen and asked someone unseen to make them each a full Irish. If a boyfriend needed to stay over for whatever reason my mother wouldn't hear of us sharing a bedroom. In fact, our rooms would be on separate floors. And if I dared bring a boy down to the breakfast table unannounced, well, there'd be war. Or total silence. One or the other. Not here, though. Margaret is amazingly open-minded.

'Darling, how do you like your eggs?' shouted Andy through the hatch.

Evelyn thought about her reply for a moment. It was all 'darling' from the boyfriend and 'I'm your best friend' from the mother/boss. Just for one insane moment she felt like popping this perfect bubble of harmony by answering, 'Unfertilized!' Instead she simply said, 'Hard.'

And so Evelyn's perfect new life continued and Margaret Leamy gathered her ever closer to her bosom. And Andy too. As springtime gave way to the hottest Irish summer in years, the gifts became more elaborate and her standing at work kept climbing. Evelyn felt uneasy. Something would have to give. A day of reckoning was coming down the tracks.

Those same few months saw John in very different circumstances and it wasn't just because the seasons in Australia felt so topsy-turvy. On an overcast autumn day, by checking the registers of all eight hostels, he established that Sophie was definitely not in Coff's Harbour. The search took a whole day, by which time he had missed the last bus north. Without any thought of exploring the town or even taking a stroll on the lovely beach, he stayed in a hostel near the bus stop and moved on again in the morning. The next likely place she could have gone was Byron Bay.

This town was much bigger, much more vibrant, and searching it proved a much harder task. There were dozens of hostels and hotels scattered over quite a radius. Nevertheless, John tramped around them as quickly as he could. Neither was the task of checking the registers entirely straightforward. John had no specific right to inspect them and in several hostels he received a cool response to his request.

'Who are you and why do you want to know?'

'John Fallon. Because I'm looking for a girl called Sophie.'

'Better you go down to Cocomanga's nightclub, mate. Bet you'll find plenty of babes called Sophie.'

Not everyone was sympathetic to a young man tracking down the most beautiful girl he'd ever seen.

Eventually John satisfied himself that Sophie was not in Byron Bay but it took several days and spared him not a moment to enjoy its delights. Scuba-diving or snorkelling were not on his agenda, not even so much as a simple horse-ride along the shore. As for Cocomanga's nightclub and each of its many rivals, John spent some time in every one, but he didn't notice the girls wearing very short dresses or even the bikini-clad babes.

On along the Gold Coast went John, alighting from the bus in Coolangatta, Burleigh Heads and a town by the name of Surfer's Paradise. Apparently, the waves there were something special, and fellow travellers said the bungee jump couldn't be missed. Still, John refused to partake in anything that even smelt of fun, and instead put his heart and soul into searching every kind of tourist accommodation the entire length of Cavill Avenue.

Eventually, after several further stops, he got to Brisbane, about halfway up the east coast of Australia and a thousand kilometres from where he'd started. It was when he got off the bus that it finally happened. He looked around himself and took in the fact that Brisbane is no kind of town. It is a city. With hotels and hostels too many to count, let alone for any one man to search, Brisbane was the end of the line. He fell to his knees and let out a low moan of despair.

*

In a rooftop room at the Palace hostel, John looked through his finances and counted the extent of his poverty. By this stage, all his traveller's cheques had been used up, his account was overdrawn and his credit card was very much in the red. The decision to walk away from a good job in Sydney was coming home to roost. He went outside and over to the edge of the roof to survey the traffic eight storeys below. It was a long way down.

After thinking things over, he galloped down the sixteen flights of stairs to the bar and ordered a big jug of beer. He might as well acknowledge defeat, if not in style, then at least drunk. As he sat up on to a high stool, though, John had his first piece of luck in weeks. The girl beside him was one he vaguely recognized.

'Excuse me,' he said, tapping her on the shoulder, 'but are you by any chance a friend of Sophie Joyce?'

She was. Hail hallelujah! She turned out to be a very friendly and helpful girl. She had been travelling with Sophie until just three days before when they had taken different paths. Sophie had decided to skip Brisbane and head for Noosa, a town just a hundred kilometres north. In addition, the girl was able to explain why John hadn't found Sophie so far. Their tour group had at one stage travelled off the beaten path of the coastal towns and into the outback.

She took a battered copy of the *Rough Guide to Australia* from her backpack and traced for John the places where Sophie had said she intended to go. Noosa, Hervey Bay, Frazer Island, the Whitsundays and all the way to Cape York. Sophie, it emerged, was set on taking a leisurely tour of every attraction from the bottom to the top of Queensland. Exactly how long she was going to spend in each place could not be known and, now that the weather had cooled and the backpackers' funds were low, there was even a strong possibility that she would settle down in some town if short-term work was available. One thing was certain, though: Sophie had a flight booked, leaving Cairns on 3 September for Perth on the other side of the country.

But that's months away, thought John.

Nevertheless he now had hope. Back in his room, after assessing his finances one more time and having a long, hard look at the calendar, he decided to take a new approach. He would head north, following Sophie's itinerary but no longer with the sole focus of finding her. There were just too many possible detours, too many islands along the way. It was just too big a bloody continent for one man to search every nook and cranny. It was also high time he had a go at snorkelling, scuba-diving and all the rest, and the only way he could do it was by maxing out his credit card over a six-week trip to Cairns. Once there, he would hopefully get another pharmacy job. Maybe, oh, please, please, maybe, he would run into Sophie somewhere along the way. If all else failed though, he knew that Cairns airport on 3 September was the absolute last resort. There and then he was definitely guaranteed to find her.

22

Dublin
4/9/95

Greetings, Johnny,

So you were asking after things with me and Andy. Well, c'mere till I tell you what happened between us just yesterday. I made the classic mistake of opening his sock drawer . . . and what did I find? About twenty or thirty pairs of socks, obviously! What was strange was the way they were arranged. Not in a jumble, but in orderly little rows according to colour. It was a bit weird but not all that surprising given the way he obsesses over having everything perfect.

I shut the drawer quickly in case he'd catch me snooping but then he switched on the electric shower and I knew I had another few minutes.

The next drawer down was full of underwear and again they were very carefully organized. Then I opened his wardrobe and found more of the same. His shirts were hung according to a system, as were his trousers and even his T-shirts. At the bottom were ten pairs of footwear. Shoe, runner, boot and slipper: each sat beside his matcher in a line that might have been drawn with a ruler.

Anyway, I had more or less finished but something was bugging me about the sock drawer. Something small that I now realized was out of place. In a room where nothing was out of place. I opened it once more and, as I thought, one pair of socks was not quite as it should have been. I picked it up. Underneath there was a small red box. I reached in and opened it. Inside there was a ring. A big shiny sparkly diamond engagement ring.

I took it out and stared at it with my mouth open. Oh, sweet Jesus! As I realized what it meant I stopped breathing for a few seconds and my heart began to beat faster. Then I heard the key turned in the door of the en-suite bathroom. Feck! I slapped the drawer closed just as he emerged. Thankfully I had my back turned so he hadn't seen what I had been up to. Or that I was holding the ring. As I made straight for the bathroom he'd just vacated, he asked what was wrong.

I didn't answer. I couldn't answer. I needed a few minutes alone . . .

Cairns,
4/9/95

Hey, Ev,

There has been a change of plan! Having replenished my finances, I should, in theory, be getting back on the tourist trail. I had pencilled in a hike around New Zealand and then Hawaii, California and New York. Due to certain events yesterday, though, those are places I'm no longer bothered with.

Perhaps you will recall me telling you about this girl Sophie who I first met back in Sydney. Well, I did indeed continue the search for her up along the east coast, but the chance meeting I'd been hoping for never did happen. Nevertheless I knew for certain that she'd be passing through Cairns airport on 3 September so that's why I put down roots here. Got a job, got an apartment and settled down to wait. The winter days crept by slowly but I knew for certain we'd be together again, and lo and behold! Yesterday the day finally came. I had already checked the flights out to Perth and there was only one, at eight thirty p.m.

I set off to the airport with a bouquet of twelve red roses but was first delayed when standing in line to buy a bus ticket. It was one of those automated machines, y'know? Anyway, there was no big queue, just one guy in front of me, so I was sure I'd make it. Unfortunately this one guy turned out to be an awful ditherer. For a whole minute he didn't touch the screen but stared at it like 'twas written in hieroglyphics. When he did finally complete his transaction, I leapt into action and typed in my request. As my ticket began to print, the guy who'd delayed me stepped on to the bus. By the time that ticket fell into my hot little hand, the door of the bus had closed and it pulled out of the station.

For feck sake! A glance at the timetable confirmed that the next shuttle out to the airport would be in an hour. I didn't have an hour. Not if I wanted to be on time to meet the love of my life and hand her the bouquet of roses. I wasn't unduly put out, however. All it meant was that I'd have to take a taxi . . .

As members of the last generation routinely to send letters to one another, Evelyn and John both tended towards missives that ran to several pages. Evelyn's, for instance, went on to describe in detail what had gone on after she'd got locked into the en-suite bathroom at the Leamys' house:

- The pressure she put herself under to decide there and then whether or not to say yes to Andy's marriage proposal.
- The difficulty in thinking straight while coming out in goose pimples, dressed in nothing but a skimpy bra and knickers without so much as a towel to fashion into a sarong.
- How Andy's impatient streak manifested itself in shouting down telephones and several attempts to barge down the door.
- How he had also fetched his mother.
- She had continually pondered the question of whether to say yes. After all, Andy was handsome, intelligent, ambitious and strong. He ticked an awful lot of boxes. And yet . . . and yet . . .
- And then the eventual arrival of the locksmith.
- Just in time to prevent any delay or inconvenience to Margaret Leamy's birthday dinner.

John's letter was also a long one and gave a blow-by-blow account of his trip to the airport to meet Sophie:

- Of how twilight was descending and he could see the bright lights from planes and runways getting closer until, all of a sudden, his taxi was pulled over to the side of the road.
- The single bead of sweat on his driver's forehead. The female cop who was unhappy about something.
- The realization that this taxi was going nowhere and

he might miss his rendezvous. The decision to get out and walk.

- How he discovered a dirt-track shortcut across the mangrove scrubland. And then an abandoned old bicycle.
- The slight problem of his attire, a cream suit and pinstripe tie. Not ideal cycling gear.
- How he had gathered up his trouser legs and tucked them inside his socks, then balanced his roses on the handlebars.
- But how the chain had fallen off. Not once, but four times. The repair was difficult because the chain was greasy and had become jammed between the cog and frame. In yanking it loose, he'd got black smudges on his sleeves.
- How eventually he had thrown the bike into the mangrove bushes, clutched the roses tightly to his chest, and broken into a mad gallop.
- And duly made it on time. No sooner had he walked into the airport than he had seen Sophie in the distance.

. . . Good God! I saw her and my heart skipped a beat. Possibly several. Lying down across three seats in the waiting area. She was still truly and totally the most beautiful girl I'd ever seen. I took a deep breath and walked across the tiled floor.

But, Ev, I ask you! Does anything ever turn out the way you imagined it? Anything ever??! Far from her noticing me and getting up and crossing the floor in a run, arms outstretched to greet me halfway, Sophie was actually asleep. I went right up and woke her.

'Oh!' she said, rubbing her bleary eyes. 'Hiya, ahmm . . .'

And it became apparent that although she recognized me as someone she'd met before, my name escaped her. I told her.

'Yes, John! Of course,' she said. 'You were nice.'

NICE?! I was nice*?*

'Sorry to be unsociable,' she said, 'but I'm absolutely wrecked. It was lovely to see you again . . . ahmm . . . John.' With that she lay back down and put her head on the fleece she was using as a pillow. She closed her eyes and within a few seconds was asleep once more.

I stayed right where I was, absolutely gobsmacked. My mind raced to consider what to do next.

. . . I needed a sign.

Get married to Andy. Yes or no.

If only I had had a coin I would have flipped it. If only I had had dice I would have rolled them. If only I had had a Ouija board or a tarot deck or a crystal ball, I'd have given any of them a go.

But no. I had none. I knelt down and squinted through the keyhole. Andy and Margaret were sitting on the end of the bed. They were talking quietly, which suggested that I wasn't supposed to hear. I cupped my ear to the hole and realized that he was apologizing to her for all the inconvenience. On this the very morning of her birthday.

At which point I had an idea. Without further ado, I stood up and walked over to the toilet. I dropped the ring down into it.

'Okay!' I whispered and put my hand on the flushing lever. 'If this flush carries the ring away, then that is a sign!'

I pulled.

When the cascading waterfalls had run dry and the swirling eddies receded, the ring was . . . still there. Faithful and true, it just awaited my rescuing hand. All I had to do was reach in and . . .

I went back over to the keyhole and heard the distant sound of the locksmith stomping up the stairs. Then I heard Andy greet him and explain the situation. 'It really is urgent,' he said. 'My mother's birthday dinner is in just a few hours.'

Unconsciously, my hand reached again for the toilet lever and I flushed, thinking, Okay, best of three!

The ring finally disappeared, carrying a month of Andy's salary into the city's sewer. He was a pretty decent guy, I reflected, but NOT my Prince Charming.

Outside I could hear the locksmith jangling a set of keys. I knew I had just seconds before he found the correct one and put it in the lock.

I wondered if there was any point in attempting to hide behind the door.

Or in the shower.

Or . . .

Or under the bathmat?

Or . . .

And then it hit me. In a blinding flash, I knew exactly what I must do.

. . . Do? I must do nothing. I could do nothing. Painful as it was to realize, I had just spent seven months of my life labouring under a vast misunderstanding. I had assumed that my three wonderful days with Sophie had meant as much to her as they did to me. I had assumed that the only obstacle in my path was finding her, that on meeting again we'd get right back to the perfection of a long-lost Sunday we'd spent together in a hotel room.

But in the meantime Sophie had been touring Australia – I mean, really touring it! Not like me, who was just passing through. She'd probably forged loads of friendships since then, had dozens of deep and meaningful conversations. She had most likely, it pained me to think, had other lovers too. For her, I was just another guy from way down the track.

. . . Thankfully, it was quite a large bathmat. Also fortunate was the fact that it was black, to match my bra. I pulled it up from the floor, tried it as a skirt and found that, yes, it covered the essentials pretty well . . . And so it came to pass, my dear Johnny, that your correspondent found herself making her escape out of the bathroom window. It opened on to a flat roof, which I scampered across. Then I stepped down on to a wall (no easy task when one hand must be constantly employed holding your 'skirt' together!). From there it was a case of walking along (showing the balance and poise of a supermodel) until I got to the end and hopped down into the mews lane. I made my way (along a street of funny looks) to a taxi rank and hence home to Cowper.

Naturally all this means that I will have to tender my resignation to Leamy's. So it really was an idiotic thing to do. Still, though, I suppose it says something about my relationship with Andy that I feel sorrier about breaking up with Margaret than with him.

Yours as always

Evelyn

. . . I kissed Sophie on the forehead without waking her. Then I left the airport, went straight past the taxi rank and gritted my teeth for a long walk back to my apartment. I noticed that the dozen red roses were still in my hand. I plucked off each of the flowers and put them in the pocket of my jacket. I threw away the stems. Then I picked out the first rose and started to peel it petal by petal. The idea was, like Hansel, to leave a little trail of red all the way home.

John

23

He hadn't the stomach for more travelling in New Zealand and America as planned. John just worked out his two weeks' notice at the pharmacy in Cairns and flew home to Dublin airport where he was collected by Evelyn.

'First things first,' said Evelyn, as they walked out to the Corsa. 'A piece of scandalous gossip which doesn't involve either of us for a change! Or not exactly . . .'

'Go on,' said John, with a smile, amazed at how quickly their conversation had slipped back into a certain groove.

'It concerns my wonderful flatmate, Michelle. I think you may have met her once or twice.'

John laughed.

'Well, she's got a new boyfriend and who could it be? Only a certain lad called Gary, whom I seem to dimly recall from my own murky past.'

'Get off!' said John. 'Michelle and Gary? An item? Flamin' heck!'

'Less of the flaming, mate! What with your tan and the crazy lingo, you sound like an extra on *Home and Away*.'

'That's as may be, but answer me this: does he still have bright yellow bootlaces?'

'No, Johnny. Afraid not. Fashion waits for no man. It was brown desert boots with purple laces that I found under the table this morning.'

*

They went back to Evelyn's apartment in Cowper Downs, arriving as the evening turned to dusk. The entire hall area was chock-a-block with cardboard boxes.

'Courtesy of my beloved mother,' said Evelyn. 'Despite my protests she has finally insisted on redecorating my old bedroom – in some tasteful shade of pink, no doubt. The upshot is that most of my stuff had to be moved out. I haven't sorted through it yet.'

'Well, it does make the place a little cosy.' John was weaving a path towards the living room. 'I hope you still have room for me. I could easily stay with Brian instead.'

'No way,' said Evelyn, 'because the other news is that Michelle has gone off to Kerry with Gary for a week doing a yachting course. Cliona, meanwhile, has been sent by her company to a job in Italy. All of which means that you and I, and the boxes, have the place to ourselves. The bad news is that, when they heard you were coming, the girls both locked their bedroom doors so you'll still have to kip on the couch.'

'Afraid I'll rummage through their stuff?' said John, with one eyebrow raised.

'Yes,' said Evelyn, 'especially their knicker drawers. But honestly, John, you really are welcome and can stay as long as you like.'

'Thanks, Ev,' he said, putting his backpack down. 'I'm sure I'll find myself a new place fairly quickly.'

From the top flap of his bag he pulled out a copy of the *Herald* he'd bought in the airport. It had an extensive listing of available accommodation.

'Put away that paper, lanky boy!' cried Evelyn, from the kitchen. 'Tonight is a night for talking about everything that's happened since we last met. And figuring out what it all means. And drinking, too. And if you're hungry enough then maybe you'll even eat my dodgy spag Bol.'

'All the many frogs I've kissed,' said Evelyn, 'they all had one thing in common.'

'Stop! Let me guess,' said John, mischievously. 'Green skin.'

'No,' said Evelyn. 'You know well what I mean. All the unsuitable men. All of them had one thing in common.'

'They each had a penis!'

'No!'

'What? They didn't? Well, then, Ev, I'm afraid you may have inadvertently gone out with some women. Did any of these so-called men of yours speak in a high-pitched voice?'

'Ha-bloody-ha. Feck off, Johnny. They all had something in common besides being male.'

'Oh . . . I see now . . . Was it sweaty armpits?'

'Ick, John Fallon!'

'But I was in love with her!' he explained.

'Pah! Love? What do you know about love, you eejit? You say, "I love you," far too cheaply. Those are words that should be kept under lock and key in a special corner of your brain. Only to be used on a special occasion for a special person. You, John Fallon, throw them around like confetti.'

'I think some of the blame has to go to John Walton,' said Evelyn, as she filled up their glasses for the fourth time.

'John Walton? Was he in the year ahead of us?'

'No! I'm talking about television. The head of the Walton family. You remember him, surely.'

'Yeah, got him now. But how is it his fault?'

'I was seven when I first saw him. That's an impressionable age, and there he was, as close to perfect as you could hope to get. Strong, manly, with the rough hands of a sawmill worker and burning blue eyes. Also, he was kind, intelligent, faithful and plainly quite useful in the sack, judging by the brood he produced. There was absolutely no sign of his wife Olivia looking dissatisfied with her lot, was there?'

'Indeed!'

'And that's the perfect unattainable man I've been searching for ever since.'

'Didn't he use to wear dungarees?'

'Yes. Like I've said. The man was totally perfect!'

'Okay! I admit it. Yes! Sophie did have big breasts. That was not, however, as you seem to be suggesting, the entire basis of our relationship.'

'Hmm. I wonder, Johnny, were you breastfed for too long by your mother? Or perhaps not long enough?'

'Stop that, Ev. My mother's breasts are not an image I wish to dwell on!'

They finally retired for the night, Evelyn to her bed and John to the couch in the front room. Both doors were left open.

'It's good to be back,' John called out.

'And good to have you back,' replied Evelyn. 'Now goodnight . . . John-Boy.'

'Goodnight, Mary Ellen.'

'Goodnight, Jim-Bob.'

'Goodnight, Elizabeth . . .'

24

John and Evelyn lived alone together for a week, beginning their mornings with a perusal of the newspaper classified section. Evelyn had been looking for a new job since her bathmat exploits, and John for a job and an apartment. Neither saw anything enticing advertised, though, and once they had scanned the paper, they gleefully went for breakfast in the Billboard Café and took the rest of the day off.

They talked on several occasions about Evelyn's relationship with her mother, the cardboard boxes providing the trigger for Evelyn's theories on the subject. Like the fact that Evelyn's sister and brother were eight and nine years older than her: the perfect family in the minimum number of moves – which strongly suggested that Evelyn had been somewhat 'unplanned'.

Also, despite a comfortable middle-class existence, her mother was never quite satisfied, specifically with her role as a stay-at-home housewife. She always gave the impression that she was wasted in it and could have done so much more, if only . . . She generally vented her frustration at Evelyn, whose older brother and sister, too, had suffered their share of unfair criticism. Was it a coincidence that they both lived safely far away in Surrey and Florida?

And why didn't she get a job now her three children were reared? The answer was that, although she was a very capable woman, she had no qualifications. Thus she would need to start in an entry-level position. And take orders from some younger person. Something she could not possibly endure.

And so to her renovation of the house. Adding on a conservatory and tearing up the garden in the name of landscaping. All on her husband's, by no means huge, teacher's salary.

And, most laughable of all, Evelyn spoke of the little sign hung in her mother's kitchen . . .

My children are my masterpieces

John, too, thought about his family on a few occasions during the week. In his case, though, the issue was whether he should go home and visit them in Cappataggle. He had promised he'd be back from his travels in time to help out with tagging the sheep. The way things had worked out with Sophie, however, meant that he was back in Ireland a month ahead of schedule. Early or not, though, John knew from experience that if he went home his father would certainly find work for him. And plenty of it.

Thus he decided to say nothing about the change of plans. Instead he made a call home from one of the phone boxes on Rathmines Road and pretended to his mother that he was in Auckland. Evelyn waited for him outside on the street and was unable to stop herself laughing.

Whether at the cinema or the theatre, whether taking walks in the park or playing pitch 'n' putt near Johnny Fox's in the Dublin mountains, Evelyn and John ate lots of ice-cream and enjoyed the last few days of an Indian summer. Tension was growing between them, though – tension of the sexual variety. On the sixth day there was an incident in the afternoon. Evelyn was gone to the shop on Highfield and John had a shower without closing the bathroom door. When she came back early, she saw him drying his hair with a towel. He was naked and facing her. Tanned all over, bar a triangle halfway down. She stared.

It wasn't until he began moving the towel down to his chest that she stepped away into the front room. She was out of sight by the time he looked up. Hearing sounds from the kitchen, he pushed the door closed. Nevertheless, she had seen him. He hadn't seen her see him.

'I'm sorry to leave you alone, John,' said Evelyn, that evening, as she applied the last of her mascara. 'But I just have to go to this thing tonight.'

The annual engineering awards were being held in the Burlington. It would be a glamorous and formal occasion. Yes, there would be the probable embarrassment of running into Margaret and Andy Leamy. On the other hand, the cream of Evelyn's profession would be there and it was a brilliant opportunity to network and possibly persuade someone to give her a new job, preferably at associate level but anything above junior would do.

Almost ready, all that remained before Evelyn could go was to zip up the back of her dress, a classy silver number from Quin and Donnelly. Without really thinking what she was about, she walked into the hall and asked John to help her.

He took hold of the zipper with one hand and placed his other palm flat against her lower back. Evelyn's breath froze and her lips parted. The intimacy of it. The firm strength of that hand on her back. The close proximity of his warmth behind her.

Sweet, sweet Jesus! she thought. She stood stock still. I want to turn around and face him but if I do it's inevitable we'll kiss. Then pretty soon this dress will come off and be thrown on the floor. I'll miss the bloody engineering awards.

I must not turn around, she told herself.

And she didn't.

The awards are only on tonight, and this can wait until tomorrow, she thought. Or even just until I get home . . . Yes, that's it! . . . Whatever time it is, one a.m. or two, I'll go in and wake him up and ask him to pull the zip back down . . . and then surely . . .

Yes, that was a good plan.

'Thanks, Johnny,' she said, a little too loudly, and pulled away as soon as the zip was at the top. 'I have to go. Do wait up!'

When Evelyn came home, having secured an interview with Michael Newcombe, it was just half past midnight. John was not on the couch. In fact, he was not in the apartment.

It took a while, but Evelyn managed eventually to wriggle out of the dress.

On her own.

Frog 9

25

'Once upon a time,' said Michelle, 'there was a princess who got lost in the forest. Eventually she came across an evil witch sitting beside a pond. The witch cast a spell on the princess and gave her a terrible choice. "In this pond," cackled the witch, "there are a hundred frogs. One of them is your perfect Prince Charming. Over the next while they will jump out one at a time. You must kiss each one and when you do a little number will light up on the top of its head. The prince has the highest number, but what that is, I will not tell. Hint, it is not one hundred! That would be too obvious. Based on the numbers, you must decide which frog to take home. If you turn a frog down, then he will jump back in the pond never to be seen again. If you decide to take him home, then you must carry the frog back to your castle and marry him immediately. Only then will you find out whether or not he's the prince . . ."'

It was autumn 1999. After completing her master's, Michelle Neylon had gone on to do a PhD and was now employed as a lecturer by the Trinity maths department. Her specialist fields were applied probability, statistics, and decision theory.

This particular lecture owed quite a bit to conversations she'd had with Evelyn years before. Unlike back then, however, Michelle now knew that mathematics could provide an answer to any dilemma. Including one's choice of life partner.

'So, any suggestions as to her best strategy?'

'Dr Neylon,' said a skinny girl, 'why can't the princess just kiss every one of the frogs? See which has the highest number.'

'I already told you,' said Michelle. 'Because she only gets one chance. By the time she figures out for absolutely definite which was the highest frog, he'll be back in the pond never to be seen again.'

'She'll be stuck with the very last frog, the hundredth,' said the cute boy with the fringe. 'Or else she'll get a one-way trip to the nunnery.'

'Exactly,' said Michelle. He was smart as well as cute.

'Well, then, it's impossible, Dr Neylon,' said the girl dressed top to toe in Benetton. 'She may as well pick any frog at random.'

'Tut, tut,' said Michelle, shaking her head at Ms Benetton. 'That's no kind of attitude to take. Thankfully, unlike you, this particular princess happened to be quite good at maths . . . So, the first frog jumped out and when the princess kissed it, the number forty-three lit up on his head. She kicked him back into the pond. The second frog approached and this time his number was forty-seven. Still though, our princess rejected him. And so on through frogs numbered twenty-four, fifteen, sixty-one and again twenty-four. There was one puny specimen whose number was three-quarters and a particularly repulsive fellow numbered minus one. Eventually though the thirty-seventh frog jumped out. That was the point when the princess requested a little break and sat on a tree stump to consider what she had learned. By this stage she had a pretty good feel for what numbers were available. She also knew that the highest she'd ever seen was sixty-one.

Though her strategy before had been to reject every frog out of hand, from now on she determined that she would definitely accept the next frog to come out with a number higher than sixty-one.'

'Did it work?' asked the skinny girl.

'It did,' said Michelle. 'After another few frogs, one came out numbered sixty-two and she took him home and married him. On the very next morning she woke up beside a prince.'

'That's just a fairytale,' said Ms Benetton, 'where happy endings don't have to make any sense.'

'Oh, but it does make sense,' said Michelle, smiling wryly to think how cocky first-years had become since her day, even when they knew diddly-squat. 'And the whole point of this exercise is to show you how maths can be applied not just to fairytales but to real life. It's ten years since a colleague of mine, who is no maths genius, stated this problem in terms of finding her optimal marriage partner.'

'But why did the princess reject the first thirty-seven frogs out of hand?' asked cute boy.

'Well,' said Michelle, 'what else could she do? When the first frog came out she knew absolutely nothing about how his number ranked. The same was true for the second frog and the third. She needed to see a fair selection of frogs before knowing what sort of number might be the highest.'

'But why after thirty-seven per cent?' said the boy.

'Well, that's where the pure maths comes in,' said Michelle, and she swept over to the blackboard to explain with chalk. 'For that number we have to thank Merrill Flood.'

Where N is the number of frogs
And k is the number rejected out of hand
And j is the position of the best frog in the sequence
Then the probability of choosing the best based on an optimal stopping strategy may be expressed

$$P_k\{N, j\} = \frac{k}{N} \sum_{j=k+1}^{N} \left(\frac{1}{j-1} \right)$$

'But how does this apply –' asked Ms Benetton.

Michelle cut her off. 'To real life? Come on, it's simple. The way people should choose their life partner is to date a few girls or guys to see what's available. Somewhere along the line, though, there comes a time when kissing frogs must stop. At that point you choose the next best one that comes along.'

26

On the night that Evelyn went to the engineering awards, John had intended to stay in and watch television. Then the phone rang. It was Brian, inviting him out to a house party on Whitworth Road, being held by one of Aoife's old school-friends.

Three hours later, John was first in the queue for the toilet when a girl crawled up the stairs and looked at him mournfully. She smelt distinctly as if she'd brought too much peach schnapps to the party. Chivalry demanded he let her go in first, while his trembling bladder made competing suggestions. Her hair and face swung it: short and raven black, pretty and pale. He nodded his assent and she scuttled in, past the vacating tenant.

Through the closed door came a sound that might have been retching. The toilet flushed and taps were turned on. There was a clatter of something falling, then silence.

Time fidgeted by. The crossed-legs queue behind John conveyed their disapproval at him for letting her in.

'It's been fully nine minutes,' declared the guy with the goatee beard and a digital watch.

'Bitch should've had to wait just like everyone else,' said the girl with three nose studs.

'That's right.'

'Yeah.'

'We're all bursting!' said a chorus of agreement.

The queue shifted from a line into a semicircle around

John. He tried to keep his head down. The goatee beard had to shout to be heard.

'That's fully eleven minutes now!'

Just then the bathroom door opened and there was a chaotic push of bodies to stake a claim. As three or four of them scrummaged in the doorway, some lad bellowed, 'Well, I bags the sink anyway. 'Twill do me grand.'

His hand was already at his zipper.

Looking none the worse for her illness, the black-haired girl was gamely sucking a Polo mint with a smile. 'Name's Carmel,' she told John. Without further ado she took him by the hand and led him downstairs to the music. There they slow-danced to a fast song and then snogged.

And what of John's bladder? It stretched and expanded heroically.

Later, about the time that Evelyn was arriving back to Cowper with a dress that needed to be unzipped, John found himself in an apartment in Ringsend. He was making love to Carmel on a blanket that she'd laid out on the carpet of her front room. This arrangement, pushing the coffee-table into the kitchen, making sure the door was locked, was necessary because it was only a one-bedroom and her flatmate was asleep in there. Carmel was clearly too much of a lady to contemplate having sex in a room with a third party present. She was an excellent lover, exhausting John with exhilaration before finally retiring to the bathroom to put on her pyjamas. (They were decorated with hundreds of little penguins wearing pink scarves and hats.) Then, without waking her flatmate, she pulled out the quilt from her bedroom and arranged it over the blanket. John and she cuddled in together beneath.

Long after Carmel had fallen asleep, John stayed awake, looking at the ceiling and listening to the night. They were lying beside the chimney, and because they were near the railway he could hear the trains rolling by, bound for Howth, Bray or stations he did not know.

It's only when things are totally right that you see the extent to which they were previously totally wrong. It's true that John had had some fabulous girlfriends before, most notably Michelle and Sophie. It's even true that, in each case, he'd fallen madly in love. To that extent the situation which developed with Carmel (very quickly, certainly inside three weeks of their first meeting) was not so very new. The difference, though – such an obvious and crucial one – was that this time the girlfriend loved him back with an intensity equal to his own.

He loved her.

She loved him.

And suddenly the missing piece of the jigsaw slotted into place. Suddenly the stars in outer space aligned to throw this small planet on to an entirely new orbit.

It was, for instance, a month into their relationship before they finally spent their first night apart. Even this short separation prompted them to exchange a pair of typically zealous love letters:

> . . . . feel that this is a love that's going to last until the End of our Lives. Most likely until the End of Time itself when God will appear from out behind a black hole and offer us each a handshake in congratulation at the infinite fidelity of our souls.

. . . convinced our Love is on an entirely different level from whatever the rest of this World chooses to call Love. Our feelings have about them a depth and a height, a strength and a power, an intensity and a concentration, a force, a dimension, an extent, a scale, a size, a degree, a magnitude, an enormity, an infinity . . . You get the gist? And the rest of the world, to the extent they claim to be in love? The rest of the world is only pretending!

There was no cliché about the greatness and perfection of love that couldn't describe the relationship of John and Carmel. They spent every evening and weekend together, walking and talking on the pier at Dun Laoghaire, having picnics on Dollymount Strand. If the opportunity arose, they made love between the sand-dunes. If not, they went home to her apartment in Ringsend and renounced comfortable slumber for the romance of sleeping on the floor of her front room. In addition to the sound of trains going by, their trysts were often accompanied by the hum of the washing-machine in the adjoining kitchen. Carmel's flatmate was a stickler for utilizing the night-saver electricity and insisted on putting on her laundry at midnight.

They even devised little private nicknames for one another: Catkin for her, and Cuddlebug for him. While out shopping they bought each other matching gifts: tiny troll dolls. The girl one had pink hair and the boy one had blue.

And they were quite explicit in planning the rest of their lives together. How many children they'd like to have. And their names. Where they'd best like to build their little cottage. What colour they'd paint each room.

Marriage inevitably was on the cards. There was just

one small stumbling block: the fact that Carmel was in college. Although she was the same age as John, she was in college, a mature student just beginning her third year in UCD medicine. It wasn't practical to get married when she wasn't earning any money. In only a few years, however, she'd begin her internship, which would be a paid position. The plan was to book a church as soon as she got that far.

Not that marriage mattered. It was just a slip of paper. What they had as a couple went way past something that could be reduced to ink on a page. Everyone they knew could see it. Whether at parties or pub quizzes, they were the kind of couple who all their contemporaries could see were meant for one another. Even John's parents understood this very early on when he brought Carmel home to meet them. Well, his mother did anyway. The thoughts of John's father were harder to read.

Meeting them off the train he gestured that Carmel should sit beside him in the passenger seat. Then he set about making conversation.

'Tell me. Are you anything at all to the Harringtons from outside Claremorris? Because if you are then –'

'No. Not as far as I know.'

'Right, right . . .' he said, his voice trailing off in disappointment. 'Or did you know Niall Sheedy who hurled with the Tubber Junior Bs for a spell?'

No, Carmel didn't know Niall Sheedy. Nor, it soon emerged, did she know Ian Moore, Fergus Tobin or Maura Callinan. And yet John's father persisted with the line of questioning, trying to establish some person who connected them. But there was no such person (other than John, obviously) and Carmel was mightily relieved when they finally got to John's home. His mother's greeting was warm and welcoming. In her usual style, she dished up helping after helping of hospitality until Carmel was so full she had to go to the guest room for a lie-down.

Later, John had to go out and help his father with the evening foddering. He offered Carmel a pair of wellies but she had already decided to take a bath. As he was hauling hay bales and buckets of spilling water to sheep in their pens, his mother came out to the farmyard and joined him. She told him how lovely Carmel was and how much she approved.

27

There was one observer who refused to see what everyone else could see. Who simply could not hear the happiness and would choke rather than join in the chorus of people saying, 'John and Carmel are so good together.'

Obviously there was the fact that John was not at home on the night Evelyn had rushed home specifically so he could pull down the zip of her dress. But that wasn't the only reason.

No – honestly! It wasn't!

'I agree wholeheartedly,' she said to Michelle, as they surveyed the state of their front room. 'Something will have to be done.'

The cause of their disapproval was the pair of empty wine glasses on the coffee-table, which had not been placed on the coasters provided. And the sleeping bag was still rolled out on the couch and had not yet been tidied away. Also, the two people who should have politely tidied away every trace of their existence, John and Carmel, were currently in the shower. Together! Both! At the same time, if you don't mind!

'I only ever agreed that he could stay for a week,' Evelyn continued. 'I had no idea it would turn into a month and counting.'

'Nor, presumably,' chipped in Michelle, wryly, 'that he'd be inviting a "special" guest.'

'No,' said Evelyn, more quietly. 'That certainly was a bolt from the blue.'

'And what,' asked Michelle, leaning down a little closer, 'is the nature of this stain on the carpet?'

Neither – leaving aside the matter of whether he had outstayed his welcome – was Evelyn convinced when John raved to her about his new love.

'I'm sorry, Johnny, but haven't I heard all this before? I thought it was Michelle who was the love of your life. Or was it Sophie? Or Valerie? Goddamn, I get so confused . . .'

'This girl really is different, Ev.'

'Different how? Has she got three breasts?'

'No. She . . . I'm embarrassed to be saying this . . . but I think she's my soul-mate.'

'Oh, sweet Jesus, Johnny. You sound like a character in a really bad movie!'

'Well . . . yes, I suppose. But I was reading about the theory of it recently and I think it fits exactly with what I'm feeling.'

'Go on. This should be good.'

'It's a Greek thing. Yer man, Plato. He told this story about how all humans originally consisted of four arms, four legs, and a single head made of two faces. We could walk upright, backwards or forwards, and also roll over and over at high speed. We were mighty and strong, so much so that we posed a threat to the gods themselves. Zeus thought first to kill us all, as he had the giants, but he had a little bit of mercy. He simply split us in half, condemning us to spend our lives searching for our other half.'

'Which will make us feel *complete*?' asked Evelyn, eyes wide, sarcastically.

'Exactly.'

'Oh, John Fallon, you really have gone soft.'

It was amazing how little time Evelyn had for this kind of philosophizing when it was about John's love-life rather than her own. Currently non-existent.

But there was something else, too. Evelyn did not actually like Carmel as a person. She found her a bit too eager to please, a bit sickly sweet. The way she never missed a chance to mention that she'd been to boarding school and had won a load of bloody hockey medals. Who the feck cared? Then there was the whole I-am-a-little-lady aspect to her personality. The slowness and exaggerated grace with which she walked downstairs, for instance. And that bloody Isla St Clair hairstyle, like it was 1982 on *The Generation Game*. And that ridiculously measured accent, impossible to place, certainly not that of her native County Clare. And, oh, several hundred other small annoyances.

The bottom line was that she was not good enough. She wasn't good enough to be the lifelong soul-mate of one of Evelyn's dearest friends.

There was tension on the other side too. When John had started going out with Carmel he found it perfectly natural to tell Evelyn a lot of the details, as he had done about previous girlfriends. Evelyn, over the years, had always been his special confidante and often his best adviser in dealings with the opposite sex.

After a few weeks with Carmel, however, he began to recognize that things could not continue in this vein. To discuss anything of consequence with Evelyn felt like a betrayal of Carmel. In any case, he didn't feel the same need to confide in her now that he had Carmel to bounce ideas off.

The upshot was that when he talked to Evelyn he was much more guarded than before. She noticed and asked him what was wrong.

'Nothing. Absolutely nothing,' he said firmly.

Which was true. But for how much longer?

28

It could never happen, Evelyn was often heard to say, that she would ever find a modern band that meant as much to her as the Smiths had in 1986. Or the Cure, or Joy Division or Echo & the Bunnymen. There was an intensity to those bands and to the way she'd listened to them (lying on her bed with the lights switched off and the curtains drawn) that could never be replicated. After that era of giants, of faultless albums like *Closer*, *Faith* and *Ocean Rain*, had come a time for musical pygmies. Like Blur and Oasis. The once quite decent R.E.M. had sold out to the mass market, and as for the relentless rise of bloody U2 – aaaargh!

Nevertheless, despite her protestations, Evelyn had never really given up on finding a wonderful new band and was still in the habit of reading the NME and checking out Dave Fanning for an hour most evenings. On the odd night she'd even take a stroll down to Whelan's to see what she might see. Which was what happened one evening in mid-November. Whereas previously she might have cajoled John into accompanying her, that was no longer an option, and Michelle and Cliona were busy, so she decided to go on her own.

The first band she saw, called Brando, was just more of the same old same – a throaty singer obviously in thrall to Kurt Cobain. Next, please!

The second act was a wee girl with acoustic guitar and a

Spanish flamenco style. But with lyrics about being raped. And child abuse. And suicide by hanging. Evelyn took the opportunity for a long trip to the Ladies to fix her tights.

The third and last act of the night was a band called Trousers On Fire, and here at last was something that Evelyn could get into. Their music was tuneful with memorable hooks, like the Cure in their middle period. The lyrics were not quite so good, their meaning perhaps a little like sixth-class poetry. The singer of those lyrics, though, was the icing on the proverbial cake. He was the main focus of Evelyn's attention, and not just because of what came out of his mouth. There was also the shape of that mouth. And every other inch of his gorgeously attractive body. And the moves he made, shifting around the stage with a determined strut.

Strut . . .

Strut . . .

Strut . . .

Evelyn found she wasn't even listening to the music any more.

She had never been backstage before at any venue, let alone the fabled Whelan's. It was surprisingly small.

'So, which song did you like best?' asked the singer.

'Oh, I don't know their names yet,' said Evelyn, 'but the slow one about quicksand.'

'"Cynicism With A Smile", it's called.'

'Yeah, I think the music is really brooding and threatening, y'know?'

'And what about the lyrics? Don't you like them?'

What could Evelyn say to the singer? That in fact she was not very excited by the lyrics but was excited by *him*?

'God, yeah, I love the lyrics. They really get inside the mind of the twisted character.'

'Thanks. I wrote that one about an ex-girlfriend who was unfaithful.'

'Fascinating . . .'

'So, you want to see a bit more, yeah?'

Of what? His mouth? His body? Stripped naked and strutting like . . .

'Of my lyrics, yeah? They're back at my flat in Rathmines.'

'Excellent,' said Evelyn. 'Lead the way!'

Cynicism With A Smile

Painted Lovers, we would never have lost E-G-Am
Till you said it wasn't worth the cost E-G-Am-C
Still it shimmered like a piece of broken glass E-G-Am
While scarlet moon shone, every night we passed E-G-Am-C

It was like a crowded neon street on fire
Like a strange trip taking us higher and higher
Like the warm glow inside your blanket brings
Was it any, or all, or none of these things?

Chorus
I built my altar to love up on quicksand E-G-Am-C
Of the ground, around, I soon lost control E-G-D
I love to love to love, love to love to love,
love to love to love, love it E-G-Am-C
Your cynicism with a smile Am-E
Oh, such a smile! Am-E

I walked away with a broken stare, still I fall
Cursing myself at every scene that I recall

In shock, right after, on the beach, like a shell
Hearing seagulls scream, the tolling of the bell

Did you lie to your diary as you betrayed yourself?
Hide from really feeling how you felt?
Is all that we have said now made meaningless,
Your every gesture just a cobweb caress?

By Shane Cullen 12/3/95

God, though, Shane was good in bed, with a long, slowly climbing fervour that Evelyn now realized had been entirely lacking in the wham-bam style practised by Andy. Once they had finally done the deed he hopped out of bed and grabbed his guitar. There followed a sweet little serenade as he sang her a beautiful version of the Smiths' 'I Won't Share You'. Listening to him, Evelyn was struck once more by his strong deep voice, and his physical grace. Yes, his lyric writing could use a little work. But truly, genuinely, this lad had the talent to become a star.

And she wasn't just thinking that because she'd had six screaming orgasms.

29

When the falling-out between Evelyn and John finally came, Brian played a part and so did Michelle. But, with or without their help, a parting of the ways had probably become inevitable. The trouble dated back to the day John had finally moved out from Cowper Downs, vacating the couch after six weeks of unofficial tenantship. He was no sooner out the door than Brian rang up, looking for him. Evelyn answered. 'Gone,' she said drily, 'dragging his sweaty socks behind him.'

'And was he with Carmel?' asked Brian.

'Oh, yes,' said Evelyn. 'Little Miss Jolly Hockeysticks is in tow bringing tweeness and wetness wherever she goes. Like a saccharine cloud.'

'Okaaaay . . .' said Brian, and left it at that.

But, of course, he didn't leave it at that. He gave a slightly exaggerated synopsis of the exchange when he met John a week later for a house-warming drink in the Hill pub, Ranelagh.

'Feck, that was bitchy!' said John. 'In the first place I kept all my sweaty socks in a specially designated plastic bag . . . for the most part . . . and as for Carmel she has never been anything other than completely friendly to Evelyn. What the feck is her problem?'

'So you're saying,' said Michelle, when she ran into Brian and Aoife in early December at a very drunken soirée in Terenure, 'that he called her a total feckin' bitch?'

'More or less, Shell, but he was well within his rights,' said Brian, pulling out twenty Marlboro and offering her one. 'She called his girlf –'

'Are you saying that John Fallon, who recently abused our hospitality for six bloody weeks, called my oldest friend a total feckin' bitch?'

'Pretty much,' said Brian, stroking his beard thoughtfully. 'I suppose so, yeah.'

Which Michelle fed back to Evelyn and then a showdown became inevitable. It happened on a Saturday morning in December when the trains were on strike. John needed to get home to help with the sheep (their hoofs needed paring) and was never too enthusiastic about the bus, which tended to take ages, stopping in every town and village. Evelyn, who was also heading west, offered to give him a lift in her Corsa. She had no sooner collected him, though, than she said, 'We need to talk, John.'

So, as she drove out of Dublin, they talked.

About whether he had actually called her a 'total feckin' bitch' in those exact words.

About Brian and the reliability of his utterances when drink had been consumed.

About Carmel and whether or not she was good enough.

About Shane, on whom John had no opinion one way or the other, having only met the guy twice and not had much of a chance to talk.

About how long was meant when one said, 'You can stay in my apartment for as long as you want.'

About growing apart.

About whether or not the motorway bypass of Kinnegad would ever be completed.

About Carmel and whether or not she was good enough.

About why the car in front of you is invariably driven by an imbecile that should never be let out on the public road.

About Carmel and whether or not she was good enough.

Each time they returned to the topic, Evelyn's criticism of Carmel was more scathing until John lost his cool: 'Feckin' give it a rest, will you?' he shouted. 'You're way over the top. She's a nice person and I'm sick of listening to your sniping.'

'But, John, I only say these things because I –'

'Because you what?'

Because of how she still felt about him. Despite how well she was getting on with Shane, John was still the most important man in her life. Give or take her father. She didn't know how to explain, and began, 'Because –'

'Because,' he interrupted, again shouting far louder than was necessary in the small confines of an Opel Corsa, 'whatever your crappy reason, I don't want to listen to it any more, Evelyn. I've had enough of your crap to last me a lifetime. Several lifetimes in fact.'

'Really?' said Evelyn, now getting equally mad. 'Well, if listening to me is such a chore then I wonder why you're even in my car right now.'

'As do I! Believe me, as do bloody I!'

Evelyn was very calm. She put on her left indicator and eased a little pressure on to the brake. Within thirty seconds she had pulled her car on to the hard shoulder and come to a complete stop. 'Right then,' she said.

'Right then, what?'

'You don't want to listen to me. You don't want to be in my car. So don't!'

John turned towards her but neither could look the other in the eye. Several weeks of built-up irritation was boiling inside.

Then John reached into the back seat, grabbed his baggage and stepped out on to the N6.

'So that's it, then?' she called after him.

John leaned back into the car one more time. 'Yes,' he said. 'Over and out.'

Evelyn was sad as she drove away. John was sad too (not least because it was freezing cold and the nearest town was miles away), but also blazing with anger. Evelyn's running down of Carmel had been really hurtful.

1996 is just around the corner, he thought, as he stuck out a thumb into the traffic. New Year, new life, and to fuck with Evelyn Creed.

30

New lives indeed.

Several years passed in which Evelyn and John had no dealings with one another and were none the worse for it. Dublin is small, as cities go, so there was the odd occasion when one or the other was spied in the distance but they never came face to face. Likewise they shared several friends and acquaintances, but both Evelyn and John made a point of never asking them questions about how the other was doing. Their friendship was something that no longer fitted with the present situation and needed to be put in the past.

Nor did either pine for the bond that had been lost. Both had found the love of their lives and acted accordingly. By being very, very happy, most of the time.

John got a job in Meagher's pharmacy on Baggot Street. Though the work still caused the same mixture of boredom and stress, pharmacists were in short supply so salaries soon began to go up very rapidly. Which eased John's pain considerably. Meanwhile, his 'little Catkin' progressed steadily through college, getting a first in most exams (bar the extremely tricky cardiac module). She gave a lot of the credit to her Cuddlebug for being such a help with the revision. Night after night he had given her little tests from the textbook until he was so familiar with the material he might even have passed the exam himself.

Meanwhile John and Carmel enjoyed a near endless

round of dinner parties held by friends in their first semi-decent accommodation. And they generally went on at least two foreign holidays each year. Skiing in Andorra during the winter break and maybe Turkey or Corfu during summer. They took lots of photos of horizons. They also brought their two little troll dolls, the pink- and blue-haired ones, to each destination and took a photo of the pair standing in some implausible place for a jokey souvenir. It was, Carmel used to say, *soooooooooo* cute!

Evelyn, too, was living the life, if not quite so conventionally. By day she carried on a regular existence working as senior engineer for Michael Newcombe, but by night she was a fully fledged rock chick. Whether attending the ever more popular gigs of Trousers On Fire, making the coffee during rehearsals or simply spending her nights with a gorgeous hunk of strutting rock god, her life was all about the Music.

A particular source of pleasure was that her relationship with Shane had spurred him into writing what many regarded as his best ever song, 'Love On A Dying Planet'. Its intertwining of romance with ecological issues was a quantum leap forward in songwriting sophistication.

Love On A Dying Planet

If we go down to the woods today, we're in for
a big surprise, E-G-A-B
Deforestation strips bare, naked before our eyes. E-G-A-F#
Darkness falls around us, wakes the animal inside, G-B-C-D
We feel the loss of the Last Ones, who had no
place to hide. G-B-C-D

Chorus

Because we're in love on a dying planet, C-B-C-B
A tide of death is rising everywhere, B-A-B-A
So we close our eyes and kiss, C-B-C-B
And the truth is, we don't care. B-A-B-A

If we go down to the beach today, guess we'll get a shock.
Sandcastles turn to purple, scum upon the rocks.
But run to the water, lose ourselves to the sea,
We'll enter depths containing, who knows what may be?

Don't go out in the world today, better we stay in bed,
Because everywhere's a scar wound that Earth Mother bled.
There's a hole in the southern sky, an ozone cyst,
Rains of the future taste of Goodbye Kiss . . .

By Shane Cullen 3/2/96

And was there anything at all amiss during that period of young love's bliss? Not really, but if we must scratch around, there was quite a lot of jealousy in John's case. Carmel had a few ex-boyfriends who popped up socially now and then. The thought of them with her in the past, let alone in the present or future, made his blood boil. Thus he tended to be hypersensitive whenever they were about. Like, for instance, at a fancy-dress party they went to about eighteen months into their relationship. John was dressed as a lion, Carmel as Dorothy from *The Wizard of Oz*. An ex-boyfriend, done up as the Tin Man, approached Carmel, and John overheard his syrupy opening line: 'I've come looking for my heart, Dorothy. The one you stole when I first laid eyes on you!'

She laughed dismissively but chatted to him nonetheless, smiling in a way that John didn't like. He was enraged and quickly determined that the Tin Man was a few inches shorter than himself. The only worry was his replica axe. When Tin Man left it against the bar and headed for the Gents, John followed.

Tin Man was at a urinal when John shoved him in the shoulder and growled, 'Who do you think you are, coming on to my girlfriend?'

Tin Man's reflex reaction was to turn around and defend himself, raising both his hands, resulting in a hot wet slash across John's brown furry knees. Incensed, John punched him, aiming at his nose. Instead he connected with his left ear.

Afterwards everyone fussed about Tin Man's superficial injury with not a thought for John's fractured knuckle. Even Carmel was not all that sympathetic.

Perhaps Evelyn, too, could detect one very small fly in her ointment. In that same year, Shane decided to kick the bass player out of Trousers On Fire. In Evelyn's mind this was a big mistake, not just because the lad was a decent musician but also because he was a good guy. As a person. As a friend. It disturbed her slightly to watch how Shane could just discard him once he'd decided that the bass sound was getting between him and his goal: making it in the music business.

'Your focus must be totally on the music, yeah,' he explained, 'if you want to be a success.'

Still, apart from these minor hiccups, in every other way things trundled along nicely. Evelyn had at last found her prince. And John daydreamed about where to build a castle with his princess.

The days turned to weeks, the weeks to months and the year unto 1999.

31

John's shop was quiet so he was keeping himself busy by chopping up sheets of tablets into twos, when he had the pleasant surprise of a visit from a man who had once had a beard. But no more. He did, however, still have long hair. It was tied back in a tidy ponytail and was in much better condition than heretofore. He bore only a very slight resemblance to Jim Morrison.

John called him into the dispensary and Brian explained that he was just coming from the airport. He'd been on holiday in Rome.

'You lucky fecker,' said John. 'With Aoife, I suppose.'

'But of course,' said Brian, looking a little nervous as he reached into his jacket pocket for his cigarettes and lighter. They weren't there. 'Oh, feck, I keep forgetting I'm off them.'

'Good man. Hope you manage to stay off this time. Do you want to try the patches?'

'No, John. That's not why I'm here . . . Listen, the thing is . . . The reason I called in is because I need a bit of a favour.'

'Okaaay . . . What sort of favour?'

'The big kind. The kind you did for me before.'

'You're not serious!'

'Deadly serious.'

'But why, Brian? Surely at this stage . . .'

'Of course, John. I know. We're not kids messing around

any more. It's just that . . . well . . . Aoife had a bout of gastritis. She threw up her pill for a few days in a row and then while we were in Rome we ran out of condoms and –'

'That's enough detail, Brian. I think you should just advise Aoife to go to the doctor this time. Get all the proper medical checks on BP and bloods. It's too dangerous for me to just hand out the pill.'

'But that's just it, John. She did go to her doctor.'

'And?'

'And was refused.'

'On what grounds?'

'That it was too long since the deed was done. Monday night.'

'Brian! That's at least . . . eighty hours ago. There's no way she can take the pill now. It's called the morning-after pill! At worst it has to be taken within seventy-two hours.'

Brian mulled that over, his hand again rummaging in the jacket pocket. 'That's like three days. But we only did it four days ago. C'mon, Aoife might as well take it anyway. Can't hurt.'

'No, Brian. No.'

'Please.'

'But it can hurt, Brian! It can!' John whispered, as a customer approached the counter at the worst possible time. 'It's too late. To take the pill now probably won't stop a pregnancy. Instead, if there is a foetus, it might just damage it. Not kill it, just increase the risk of it being born with congenital defects.'

Brian looked at him in stunned silence. 'It!' he mumbled under his breath. 'It!'

'There's nothing to be done,' said John, 'but wait for

whenever Aoife's period is next due. Then everything will be much clearer . . .'

He went out to serve the customer, who was in urgent need of something for a runny nose. When he concluded the transaction and came back into the dispensary, Brian was taking deep breaths. John gave him a consolatory pat on the shoulder. 'So, now, what do you think?' he asked.

'I think,' said Brian, putting on a wry smile, 'that I picked a bad week to give up cigarettes.'

That evening John came home to the apartment in Ranelagh he shared with Carmel.

'Did you see?' she said. 'I left it out on the table. We got yet another wedding invite. This time it's Audrey and Martin on October the ninth.'

'Oh, yeah.'

'Did you like the unusual insignia on the card? Quite nice, isn't it? I've noticed most couples get them designed and printed up by Lantz these days . . .'

'I did. Is that a fact?'

And then after a slight pause . . . the actual point of the conversation.

'So, Cuddlebug, when do you think we'll be the ones getting married? My intern year is almost finished, you know! Soon I'll be made an SHO at the hospital.'

Whoa.

How the time had flown.

John closed his eyes and wondered how honest he could be. Should he tell Carmel that somehow, gradually, without him even realizing the change, he was no longer so sure that marriage was their destiny? How had that happened? It was almost an outrage! When he thought back to his earlier unshakeable conviction, any kind of doubts seemed sacrilegious. And yet, and yet . . . Somewhere along the line, that manic love energy had faded. Somewhere the momentum had been lost. Arguments over trivial things. Plus one important thing – to him, at least. Oh, God, how shameful it was to admit! How could he be so shallow – such a Neanderthal?

The thing was sex. Or, rather, the lack thereof.

They had thought maybe living together would relight the spark. It hadn't. They had found this two-bedroom apartment in Willbrook (it had to have two bedrooms for her parents' sake: she was their eldest daughter and couldn't possibly be sharing a bed with a man), but her work at the hospital was very hard and the hours long. She was, quite understandably, often tired. She started going to bed absurdly early, like nine o'clock, just when John was watching something decent on TV. Even though he hurried to the master bedroom at the credits, the lights were off. She was snoring.

He learned his lesson and started going to bed early too, only to find there was some crime drama involving a troubled pathologist that Carmel desperately wanted to stay up and watch, 'for research'. Determined, he'd wait in bed until midnight, grimly fighting off the temptation of sleep. Sometimes he conked out. Sometimes he held on and she would eventually arrive yawning and saying, 'Oh, no, Cuddlebug, I'm much too tired for any of that.'

But the less that they had 'any of that' the more he thought about 'any of that'. And where once he had had eyes only for Carmel, now . . . well, now he was noticing other women . . . everywhere.

The world was full of them. Millions – nay, billions – of eligible women. It wasn't like in centuries gone by when maybe a few dozen people were in the tribe or the village and that represented the known universe. It must have been relatively easy to choose a partner and remain fairly content with them for a (much shorter) lifetime. Now he lived in an age of travel, with literally the whole world of women potentially available. The level of choice was bewildering, like a supermarket with seventeen kinds of ice-cream – only much, much worse.

Yes, he had turned into a Neanderthal.

And yet, in every other respect, Carmel was an excellent woman. Pretty, clever, funny and kind, she was liked by everyone who ever met her (with the sole exception of Evelyn, obviously). Now that Evelyn came to mind, what was it she had said to him a long, long time ago? Something about the percentage of compatibility that's acceptable, that's as good as it gets? Probably things with Carmel were about 90 per cent right. What if he split up with her, shooting for 100, and didn't find anyone better? What if next time around he wound up with a girl with whom he was even less compatible?

Everyone always said how lucky he was to have found Carmel. She was a gem. Everyone always asked, 'How long more until ye make an announcement?' And, yes, it was time. Everyone they knew was getting married or engaged or having their first kid. It was the thing. It was the time . . .

But John needed more time.

It wasn't that he didn't want to get married as such. Just that he'd rather wait until things between them improved.

Then he could pop the question with the fullest of enthusiasm. Yes, that would be wonderful.

Just a little more time.

So . . .

How should he answer?

'I suppose . . .' He trailed off as her face took on an angry complexion.

'Oh, here we go,' she said. 'For Chrissakes! You've got your rabbit face on.'

'I haven't!'

'You have! That little face you make when you're thinking one thing and saying another. Let me guess, you're thinking about sex again, aren't you? You're being so unreasonable. We do have sex! As much sex as any couple who've been together a few years could expect to have.'

Carmel paused for breath and switched deftly from defence to attack.

'And it's not just me who's slowed down a little, Cuddlebug! You used to be so romantic – where has all that gone? You used to buy me flowers for no particular reason, but you nearly forgot them last Valentine's Day. It took the girls at work to remind you.'

She walked away towards the master bedroom before turning back with a final remark.

'Last weekend my friend Jacintha's fella just whisked her off to Venice for a surprise romantic weekend. What are the chances of that ever happening to me? We both know. Nil!'

Which was true. Sad, but absolutely true. Once upon a time John was always doing romantic things. But not any more. And yet . . . in those days, even his most generous gestures never actually cost him any effort at all. They seemed so natural and right and true. That was love, wasn't it?

Now, a few years later, he'd have to force himself to do things that no longer just naturally occurred to him. Such behaviour is generally called 'Working At Your Relationship'.

If you replace joy with effort, wondered John, is that still love?

And how exactly is 'working' at love any different from pretending?

Evelyn's problem with Shane was quite different. The difficulty was . . . well, something almost as unmentionable as sex. Namely, money.

The thing about Shane Cullen was that although he was a deeply talented songwriter and performer, these talents did not necessarily translate into great earning potential. Yes, there was income from gigs and from the sale of the three CD singles he had released (to considerable acclaim from the Irish press, who tipped Trousers On Fire to go on to greater things very soon). But the amounts involved were tiny, and were always eaten up by the costs of management, promotion and maintenance of the rusty old tour van.

So Shane's vocation was very much subsidized by the dole. And to the extent that he lived with Evelyn, but paid no rent, paid for no groceries, or electricity, or bills of any kind, then it could be said that he was subsidized even more by her.

One thing that money did not go on was the payment of other band members. Over the years, one by one, Shane had kicked them all out of the group as time-wasters. He alone was properly focused on success. Trousers On Fire now had but one member and, in consequence, Shane had turned to modern technology, replacing each musician in turn with keyboards and computers.

He no longer lived in the bedsit at the top of an old house in Rathmines, but still kept it rented, having kitted it out as a recording studio. This investment was another instance in which Evelyn had been extremely helpful, in so far as she had paid for almost everything in the place. Everywhere you looked now there were microphones, speakers and miscellaneous black boxes. There were electric leads underfoot, some even sprouting from an overloaded socket in the kitchenette. The leads all led eventually to a laptop, on a table plainly never intended for dining at. The couch and both chairs were taken up with piles of books, all music-related. In fact, the only place to sit, tucked into the corner, was on his old (single) bed.

'Does it not drive you mad that your hard work as a junior associate in Newcombe's is bankrolling Shane to pursue his hopeless, self-indulgent dreams?' demanded Michelle, when visiting one Saturday.

The musical genius himself was not at home. He had rushed off earlier to his lair in Rathmines after the muse hit him and he had to lay down an idea.

This was a question that Michelle had asked Evelyn several times over the past few years. And indeed Evelyn's mother had also made enquiries along similar lines. Evelyn's reply on every occasion had always been the same: 'Honestly, it doesn't,' she said firmly. 'I've always been a believer in Music with a capital M, and Shane's music in particular. The stuff he's doing right now is really trance-y, but with clever lyrics, way better than anything you'd ever hear on the radio.'

This was the first time that the reply was not completely true. Evelyn was indeed starting to feel just a little short-changed. She was beginning to doubt that Trousers On Fire was ever going to hit the big-time, or even the level just-above-cult-status-in-a-small-town-time. Assuming it didn't, would all practical financial matters be left up to her indefinitely? She'd been happy to take up the slack for a few years, but for ever? That was a worrying prospect.

It was a relief when Michelle did not probe further but changed the subject to show Evelyn something she'd bought to celebrate the new lecturing position in the maths department: her very first mobile phone.

'It's nice,' said Evelyn, 'but I can't imagine I'll ever get one.'

Then they talked about Michelle's new job and her love-life, which in Michelle's case was only ever a sex-life. Since Gary, she'd been through quite a few men. The current squeeze was a solicitor, although she admitted to finding one of her students attractive too.

'Michelle! That's awful. He must be ten years younger than you.'

'True,' smiled Michelle. 'I'm just saying, is all. It's not like I'd actually seduce him or anything.'

'Well, see that you don't!'

'He even carries a skateboard into class . . . Maybe when he's a little older . . .'

'Oh, Michelle Neylon!'

32

Those were strange days indeed as everyone talked of the approaching new millennium. And the Y2K bug. The theory had it that in the new year every electrical device in the world was going to be confused by a date reading 00. They were all going to short-circuit and generally go haywire, causing bank accounts to zero out, computers to wipe their hard drives and planes to fall from the sky. Everyone and everything had to be rendered Y2K compliant, and there was a lot of money to be made by IT consultants.

People also wondered what they would do on the night of Friday, 31 December 1999. It wasn't just any old New Year's Eve but the End of the Millennium and the dawn of the 2000s. Somehow that seemed like an incredibly important thing, and people made plans months in advance. Some would fly to London to greet midnight with the crowds in Trafalgar Square. Others travelled towards the International Date Line in order to be first to the party. A few more spiritual souls rented cottages in Connemara to face the clock in solitude.

In Dublin, there were formal champagne dinners advertised for three hundred pounds a ticket and churches holding vigils (for free) where you could kneel and pray during the final countdown. Whichever way one picked to ring in the new year, however, it was clear that it had to be weighted with enormous significance.

One such end-of-the-millennium morning John was at

work, arguing with a trainee about the spelling of 'millennium' when Brian rang.

'So anyway,' he said, and it was apparent, even over the phone, that he was pausing to drag on a cigarette, 'I've got a bit of news for you.'

'Oh, yeah?'

'Yeah,' said Brian, and took another heavy drag. 'I've got a bun in the oven.'

Throughout that autumn, John became increasingly tetchy in his dealings with Carmel. His doubts about marriage and craving for more sex combined to make him a less than wonderful partner. Until one day, at Hallowe'en, Carmel turned the tables on him spectacularly.

'Right then, mister,' she said, when he had 'forgotten' to do the washing-up for the umpteenth time because he was too busy brooding. 'I've had enough. Since you plainly don't want this to work, I can't hold everything together alone. I think we need to take a break. You need to use the time to decide if you're in for the long haul or out.'

Take a break? That was not something John had been contemplating. He was purely fixated on not getting married. 'What?' he said.

'You heard me. Now get out. If you're not back in a week then don't come back at all.'

John was stunned.

John was in turmoil.

Nevertheless, after moving some of his stuff to Brian's temporarily, he didn't let the opportunity go to waste. That very night John went to Copper Face Jacks, well known as the disco where you couldn't fail to score. Overly eager, he arrived when the place was empty. When at last it began to fill, he decided not to make a fool of himself on the dance floor. Rather, he perched on a stool strategically placed so that every woman in the place must pass through his radar. Two yards from the door of the ladies' toilet.

In the next few hours, he indeed saw them all. Skimpiness and transparency were the order of the day, fashion-wise. He saw several acres of naked midriff, thigh and cleavage. Though he wasn't specifically checking, the girls probably had faces too. The DJ announced that they were into the final hour of the night and it was time to make a move. John eyed the most gorgeous girls as they emerged from the toilet but the supermodels did not reciprocate, bustling past, oblivious to his warm and interesting personality. He set his sights lower and finally managed to get a second glance from a girl. She smiled shyly and pushed past in the direction of the dance floor. John followed without finishing his drink.

Never the most natural dancer, John waved his arms vaguely and flexed his knees over and back. He manoeuvred to within two feet of the girl who'd smiled at him and gazed at her as one song finished and another began. They exchanged more shy smiles and again a minute later. The songs kept coming, but it was just like his days touring around the world: John had forgotten how to be cool. He was scared to make the leap of just twenty-four inches between him and the girl. He stared at her, hoping it would somehow get easier.

The moment evaporated. Her friend received her silent signals and came between them, turning her back to wall John off. When the song finished they trooped off the floor and beat a hasty retreat to some dark corner where John couldn't find them.

On the next night, John tried a different nightclub with similar results.

And the next.

He went back to Carmel well before the week-long break was up.

Which was about the time that Evelyn got pregnant.

Unplanned, obviously.

'YOU'RE WHAT?' shouted Shane, in the time-honoured fashion of less than supportive young men.

In the weeks afterwards, though, he recovered his good humour and managed to come to some sort of accommodation with this new reality. By ignoring it entirely.

'So, have you written a new song about it yet?' asked Evelyn, playfully, one day while flicking through *What to Expect When You're Expecting*.

'About what?' he said blankly. 'Oh, the millennium. No, it's already too much of a cliché.'

'No. Not the bloody millennium. The little thing that will soon be playing havoc with our lives.'

'Huh? The Y2K bug?'

She threw the book at his head.

33

'It really was a lovely ceremony.'

'Yes, lovely.'

'I thought the vows were very sweet.'

'Sweet vows, yes.'

'And as for the bump, it was hardly noticeable.'

'Bump, not noticeable, indeed.'

'Cuddlebug!'

'Yes?'

'Cuddlebug, are you listening to a word I'm saying?'

'Of course!'

'Well, it doesn't feel like it. You seem distracted.'

'Distracted, seem, yes.'

'CUDDLEBUG!'

John and Carmel were lying side by side in bed in their room at the Grand Hotel, Malahide. It was 31 December and the morning after the wedding of Aoife Hennessy and Brian O'Grady. It had been arranged in a fairly hasty – some would say shotgun – manner, but was none the worse for that. The bridesmaids had looked beautiful in cerise. The bridal gown had wowed one and all. And John, as best man, had given a marvellous mixture of the humorous and profound in his speech.

As well as being the morning after, it was also the dawn of Millennium Eve. So it was indeed true to say that John was distracted. For him more than most, the day had a life-changing feel. By midnight, he felt certain his life would be set irrevocably on a new path into the future.

On the other side of the city, Evelyn was awake too while Shane still snored on the pillow beside her. She had her hand under her nightie and was trying to work something out. Where exactly in her midriff was the pain?

Here? If so, it might mean a kidney infection.

Or was it over here, a bit lower, where it might be coming from her ovary?

Or here, a bit higher, where it might be just plain old indigestion?

She couldn't figure it out. She decided to get up and gave Shane a gentle poke in the ribs. The only thing for it was go to the doctor, millennium or no bloody millennium.

Head still stuck to the pillow, John cast his mind back over the previous few weeks. The way he had had to lose what he had in order to properly appreciate it. Or almost lose it, anyway.

Having peered into the abyss that was Dublin's midweek nightclub scene, he understood what life would be like without Carmel. His time living on Brian's floor had been short but thoroughly miserable. Now he was pushing thirty, such deprivations no longer seemed like fun. More importantly, he had been disabused of one key fantasy: that the only thing stopping him having oceans of sizzling sex with compliant young women was that he was stuck going out with someone. Now he knew different.

In any case, he had decided it was high time to think about growing up. Oddly enough, that had been prompted by a slew of calls from his bank. They weren't happy. His current account was well in the black, but that in itself was a new kind of problem.

'Why,' his bank adviser had asked, 'have you not begun making investments? Stocks and shares are where it's at right now. Our special managed fund is currently yielding annual growth of fifteen to twenty per cent, so you can't possibly lose.'

Then she had taken a look at the rest of his profile. And was aghast. 'You don't even have life insurance, or any kind of serious-illness cover. How can you possibly have left it this late to start a pension?'

John was left in no doubt that he needed to get his act together. Retirement age was only thirty-six years away and closing in fast. In order to guarantee income approximate to his final wage, he'd need to begin saving at least two hundred pounds a month right away. Index-linked!

Another thing that was increasingly looming on the horizon was for how much longer he and Carmel should continue renting the apartment. It was dead money after all. Absolute lunacy to be shovelling out nine hundred pounds a month purely to pay a landlord's mortgage. How much better to get one of your own, to get your foot on the property ladder, which was rising so fast it might soon disappear into the clouds.

Yes, indeed, it was high time to cop on about a lot of things. But where to start? On a bright sunny morning, just a fortnight earlier, he had walked through the door of McGowan's jeweller's on O'Connell Street and emerged clutching a small but extremely expensive green box. Inside was a large tear-shaped diamond mounted on a band of gold. He had decided to ask Carmel to marry him. He had decided he would pop said question on Millennium Eve.

Evelyn would have been quite prepared to go to the doctor on her own but nevertheless she was pleased when Shane said he was coming too. Not that he was very positive, constantly predicting that the surgery couldn't possibly be open on today of all days.

He was wrong, though: Dr Mulhall actually opened for two hours on the morning of the big day and insisted on taking Evelyn ahead of the queue.

'I can't be conclusive,' he said, having fiddled around with the stethoscope and tested her urine sample, 'but I feel your protein levels are not quite right. How many weeks are you along again?'

'Ten.'

'Okay. Well, by rights you wouldn't be due a scan until week twelve, but I think I'll send you a bit early. Can you go in today?'

When would be the best time to propose? John wondered.

It had been his preoccupation since the moment he'd opened his eyes that morning. Whether to do it over breakfast, lunch or dinner? Or perhaps later, at the party they were going to in Ballsbridge, right at the exact tolling of the bell for midnight. It would be nice to make the moment as special as possible, but he couldn't decide.

Carmel started getting all stressed about the fact that she'd forgotten to remove her makeup. And packing her case and worrying lest she leave anything behind in the hotel room. The mood wasn't right so John felt it best to wait until after they'd checked out. Then he suggested to her that they leave their cases in Left Luggage and stay for lunch at the Grand. The restaurant was always getting excellent reviews.

So that was what they did, and before the waitress had even arrived with the menus, John realized there was no point in waiting. It would be hanging over him until he got out the words. Moving out of his seat and going before her on one bended knee, he said, 'Carmel, would you marry me?'

'There's just something about seeing it, yeah? Actually seeing it with your own two eyes!'

'Yes, Shane. There really is.'

'God, I never realized how absolutely fuckin' fantastic it would be!'

'Yes, Shane. It is fantastic. I'm glad you've finally figured that out.'

Evelyn and Shane were walking down Merrion Square, away from the almost empty maternity hospital where they'd just seen the first ultrasound scan of their baby. Evelyn was relieved that all its movements and measurements were well within range. The pain in her abdomen and the high protein reading had been red herrings. The baby was fine and thriving. Thank God.

If Evelyn was relieved, though, Shane was absolutely ecstatic. He wasn't so much walking down the path as bouncing along it, like a huge ball of elastic bands.

'I never, ever knew,' he said.

'Yes,' said Evelyn, with a delighted smile. 'I had kind of gathered that.'

'But I know now, yeah?' he said firmly. 'And nothing can ever be the same again.'

*

'YES! Of course I will, Cuddlebug,' shrieked Carmel, and she leapt off her chair to get down on the floor beside him for the biggest of hugs.

There was a polite round of applause from the other diners in the restaurant as the cause of her outburst became apparent. Carmel tried on the ring, and not only did she like it, but it fitted perfectly. John had swiped another of her rings one day when she was in the shower and brought it with him to the jeweller's to make sure of the size.

'Congratulations to you both,' said the waitress. 'Perhaps you would like glasses of champagne?'

'Make it a bottle!' blurted Carmel.

'Make it two bottles!' said John, high on a mixture of relief and elation.

'There's something I want to say,' said Shane, when they were back in the apartment and lying together on the couch. 'I know I haven't really been very enthusiastic about the pregnancy, but today's changed that.'

'Hmm,' said Evelyn, purring contentedly.

'From now on, I'm going to be much better at helping you in every way that I can, yeah? I want the best for this baby and I want the best for you.'

'Hmm,' said Evelyn.

'And not just around the apartment but financially, too. I'm going to have to get myself a job. A paying job, I mean. Because, obviously, Trousers On Fire is very much a job. The point I'm making is that I do still have a degree in business, so maybe I can get some kind of regular job that brings in a bit of money.'

'Hmmmmm,' said Evelyn.

'Part-time obviously.'

John and Carmel were so happy that day. They didn't leave the restaurant for hours and then it was only to traipse across drunkenly to the hotel bar. Where they kept on drinking with other stragglers from Brian's wedding until it was way too late to contemplate crossing town for the millennium party they were supposed to attend. Some time after eleven, Carmel got a notion that they should go outside and walk down to the beach.

So off they went, both humming 'Here Comes The Bride'. Not surprisingly, it being midwinter and quite dark, the beach was deserted. More unpredictable, though, was the fact that when they got there, Carmel turned to John, reached for his belt and made it clear that she'd like to make love.

So they did, on a large flat rock just below the wall. Carmel was on top with her breasts exposed, kept warm enough, presumably, by the high level of alcohol in her blood. John was beneath her, inside her, eyes rolling in his head and the thought flickering through what was left of his mind that she was the sex goddess of a thousand years. What an eejit he was that time he'd thought of letting her go.

Towards the city centre, there was a loud ripping sound and fireworks began to light up the sky.

There was no millennium-night sex in Evelyn's apartment. She was content to sleep and Shane was content to lie by her side and rub her belly with gentle strokes.

34

Mr Brendan Fallon, John's father, pushed a sheep up against the wall of the outhouse. Then he crouched and held her there with his shoulder while reaching down to her underbelly. Finding a teat, he put a jug below it and began to squeeze out some milk.

This particular ewe had given birth to triplets just two days previously. The problem was that while two of the lambs were a decent size and thriving, the runt was getting very little milk. His mother had not really bonded with him and he was too weak to compete with his siblings. Mr Fallon was trying to redress the balance, trying to keep him alive until he could fight his own corner.

'God bless the work,' said his wife, and he looked up to see that her head had appeared in the doorway.

'How're things?'

'Actually I have big news,' said Nuala Fallon. 'I'm just off the phone with your son.'

'Big news?' gasped Mr Fallon, as the sheep made a wriggle to try to escape. He held her. 'Go on.'

'He's after getting engaged to that lovely girl he's been seeing. Carmel. You know, the one from Clare.'

'Is that right?' said Mr Fallon, as the sheep gave him a kick with her left hind hoof. He brushed it off.

'It is. And isn't it great? That wee girl is an absolute dote.'

'Right, yeah, a dote.'

Nuala pursed her lips as a huge smile threatened to overwhelm her face. She scrunched up her eyes but couldn't help shedding a tear. 'Brendan . . . you don't seem so happy.'

'I think I've enough to give him a taste anyway,' said Mr Fallon, as he pulled out the jug and held it up to the light. 'Is there any chance you could hand me in that bottle I left on the ground outside?'

Nuala did as he asked. It was an old whiskey bottle. Mr Fallon poured in the contents of the jug and fastened on a rubber teat. Then he went over to the smallest lamb. It was lying in the dark under a trough, looking none too lively. When Mr Fallon placed the teat in its mouth, it began to wake up.

'I said, you don't look too happy with the news,' said Nuala. 'Have you an objection of some kind?'

'He's sucking nicely now,' said Mr Fallon, keeping his eyes on the lamb. 'I'm starting to think he might just do.'

'Oh, fiddlesticks, Brendan. What do you think of your son's engagement?'

'I think,' said Mr Fallon, 'that I'm not so sure at all at all.'

'Whatever do you mean?'

But Mr Fallon only had a gut feeling and was never the type to explain himself.

'You haven't seen the tagger around, have you, by any chance, Nuala?' he asked. 'I had a look already in the workshop but there was no sign of it.'

Evelyn's parents, too, were in receipt of a momentous phone call. Now that a scan had confirmed the existence of a little head, two arms and two legs, Evelyn felt the time had come to break the news.

Evelyn's father told his wife the minute he got off the phone. Then they sat themselves down and had a cup of tea to recover. For a long while they were silent, digesting the news.

At last, Sarah Creed spoke: 'Well, Frank. I just can't believe she would do this to me!'

'What?'

'Make such a show of me by getting pregnant outside marriage. Go out of her way to hurt me.'

'Hurt you?'

'Absolutely. Though I don't know why I'm surprised. Since she was no size at all, there's been a pattern of this kind of behaviour.'

'Ah, now, in fairness –'

'When I think of all the education she's had,' said Sarah, 'yet she had to go and blow it like this. Let me tell you, if I'd had half the opportunities . . .'

'She told me,' said Frank, trying to be positive, 'that the fella, Shane, has got right interested since the pregnancy. A totally different man, I hear. Taking on responsibility. Obviously marriage must be just around the corner.'

'I very much doubt it,' said Sarah. 'Sure Evelyn doesn't give a flying feck about what I would want. Just to spite me, she'll probably go in for this common-law arrangement you read so much about in the papers, huh?'

'Maybe.' Frank nodded and let out a sigh. He took off his glasses to give them a polish on his shirt. 'Maybe you're right.'

They fell into silence again, pondering how the child they were so proud of, whom they both loved (despite Sarah's 'critical' tendencies) with the everyday but ferocious intensity of parents, was now in the situation of one of those girls they used to gossip about.

'And there isn't a damn thing,' said Frank, 'high up nor low down, that we can do about it.'

They could only watch from the sidelines. And worry.

'If only,' said Sarah, 'she had stayed with Fintan. Now there was a lovely lad. Such good manners. You may be sure he wouldn't have put the cart before the horse.'

'Or even,' said Frank, 'that other fellow she used to be great pals with . . . What was his name? We met him at her graduation.'

'I know the lad you mean. I can see his face.'

'Me too. But what was his name?'

John Fallon was sitting on a throne with his queen at his side. Before them were the long tables of a huge banqueting hall. 'This is impressive!' he said.

'Didn't I tell you?' said Carmel, gleefully. 'Isn't it everything I said it would be?'

'Indeed. It really is. Good call. This is definitely the place.'

'Since before I can remember, Cuddlebug, I've wanted to have my wedding here.'

They were in the Brian Boru Room at Dromoland Castle, a very posh hotel in County Clare that was soon to host their wedding reception.

'And isn't it just the best ever luck that we managed to get a date this year? Do you realize that normally there's a two-year waiting list?'

'Yes,' said John, with a smile. 'I think you might just have mentioned the fact once or twice.'

Carmel had chanced to make her phone enquiry on the very day there had been a cancellation. A slot was available on Sunday, 11 June. 'The day after my birthday, which makes it even more special! Brilliant!'

John leaned across his throne to hers and kissed her.

Naturally there had been a certain amount of surprise when they first laid eyes on the price list. Dinner would be a hefty twenty-five pounds per head, and if they wanted to offer a choice of main course, an additional five pounds. Multiply that by approximately 180 guests and it wouldn't be long adding up. The wine did not come cheap either, and if you wanted to supply your own, perhaps some nice but cheaper stuff that you brought over on the boat from France, the hotel had a service charge per bottle called 'corkage'. Offering all guests a drink of their choice for the toast was another cost, but the buck's fizz on arrival was actually provided for free, as was the man who would play the bagpipes while they walked in via the red carpet.

What clinched the deal was the courtesy and enthusiasm of the weddings manager. She left John and Carmel in no doubt that they would be pampered with silver service and they were quite happy to put down a deposit of a thousand pounds.

'Why don't we get a photo?' said John, retrieving a camera from the pocket of his jacket. 'The woman will do it, I'm sure. Me and my wife-to-be sitting on thrones like medieval royalty.'

'I've a better idea,' said Carmel, pulling the camera from him. 'How about we take a picture instead of these two little guys?' From her handbag, she produced the two little troll dolls, blue- and pink-haired. Then she stood them beside one another on the armrests of the thrones and took a shot. 'Now that,' she said, 'is just going to be the cutest photo EVER!'

*

Next stop on their trip to County Clare was the church in Cratloe, just eight miles away. ('Isn't it so quaint, Cuddle-bug?') There they met the priest, who agreed to celebrate the Mass and talked them through the various legal requirements.

'A letter of freedom from every single parish I've ever lived in?' John was boggled.

'Theoretically, yes,' said the priest, who seemed a very decent sort. 'But in practice your home parish will probably suffice.'

'And the pre-marital course,' said Carmel. 'Do we have to?'

'I'd strongly recommend it,' said the priest. 'You might find out this marriage lark is not such a bright idea after all!'

All three laughed heartily.

'Now then,' said Carmel, 'if there's nothing else, I'd love to just take a photo before we go.'

'Of course,' said the priest, reaching out to take the camera from her. 'Where would ye like to stand?'

'Oh, it's not of me and John,' said Carmel, keeping hold of the camera as she reached into her handbag once more.

These, thought Evelyn, are officially the happiest days of my life. So far!

Still working away in Michael Newcombe's, despite morning sickness that rumbled on for most of the day, Evelyn was irrepressible. She was attacking her job with renewed vigour because she didn't want to leave any of her projects hanging when the time came to go on maternity leave that summer. The due date had been fixed as 28 July, but she was planning to finish work three weeks before. Possibly earlier if there were any more difficulties with her blood pressure.

On the home front, too, she was full of the joys of approaching spring. For too long she had acted as if the apartment was just a temporary halting site. Now that there was a baby on the way, the time had come to accept that they were not going anywhere else for a while. As a consequence, she finally found the motivation to chase up the landlord about several items, like the loose tile in the bathroom and the gammy radiator. In addition, she and Shane made a few trips out to Atlantic Homestores to buy much-needed shelves, light shades and a proper cabinet for their CDs. Purchase of baby paraphernalia was something that good sense demanded be left closer to the time.

Shane was doing his bit, or certainly more than he used to, tidying up after himself, if not after Evelyn, recognizing that ironing was not really a fit occupation for a pregnant woman with dodgy blood pressure.

'So what about this business of you looking for a job?' she asked mildly, one evening.

'Oh, that,' he said. 'Perhaps I didn't explain myself clearly. I was thinking more in terms of leaving it until you were on maternity leave when we'd need the extra money, yeah?'

'Really?' said Evelyn. 'But I thought . . .' At that moment she felt a flicker of movement inside her bump and pressed her hand to the spot. Shane reached out and placed his hand there too.

'Oh, all right,' he said, with a sigh. 'If it's what you want. I suppose there's no time like the present. I'll just give it another few weeks, yeah? Finish up a few of the tracks I'm working on first.'

'That'd be just fine,' said Evelyn, genuinely glad of any move he made in the direction of paid employment. Even if only in inches.

35

John and Carmel's apartment was absolutely festooned with samples of dress material, catalogues of floral arrangements, prototypes of Mass booklets, planograms of seating arrangements, brochures from photographers and, more than anything else, bridal magazines. Carmel had gone into Eason's and simply bought a copy of every one available. Then several of her recently married friends had donated their collections, so there were easily thirty or forty strewn around on the coffee-table, the kitchen counter and every other available surface.

John leafed through one. 'I see here yet another article about wonderful weddings. And nowhere does it mention the need for the couple to . . . y'know . . . have a bit of fun together on the big day.'

'Pardon, Cuddlebug?' said Carmel, lost in concentration as she looked at a list provided by Dromoland of available local musicians. Obviously they were going to need an organist but she also had a strong hankering for a string quartet. She'd been to enough weddings herself to know that there was just something about that Gabriel's Oboe thingie, played, let's see . . . probably during Communion. Or perhaps while the register was being signed. Decisions, decisions!

'I said, nowhere does the article mention the need for the bride not to worry too much about everything being perfect. That maybe she should just set out to have fun with her fella.'

'What are you on about, Cuddlebug?' said Carmel, just a little cross now at being interrupted and still not having a clue what he was on about.

'Fun?' said John, trying to signify with his grin the concept in question.

'Fun *what*?'

'Oh, never mind. How is the search for an organist going?'

'Not too bad,' said Carmel, wondering why he was always interrupting when he didn't seem to have anything sensible to contribute, 'at least until I lost my train of thought.'

For a while they sat in silence as John scanned another bridal magazine. There was something else on his mind, though, and eventually he had to say, 'I heard an interesting thing today from one of the girls at work.'

'Did you? That's nice.'

'Something that might be of interest to both of us and relevant to the wedding.'

'I doubt it,' said Carmel, refusing to lift her eyes from the list of County Clare musicians.

'It's about our first dance. I wonder if you've got around to thinking of that yet?'

'Of course I've got around to it!' Carmel snapped, and glared at him. 'I made that decision a week ago, for Chrissakes! We're having "Wind Beneath My Wings" and then a follow-up with "My Lovely Rose of Clare". Like I said, it's sorted!'

'Great,' said John, flatly. 'They both sound lovely. But what I want to know is, have you thought about exactly *how* we'll dance to them?'

'What *are* you on about, John? We'll dance the way we've always danced. My hands around your neck, your arms around my waist and . . . well, that's it, basically. What more is there to it?'

'But that's just it! There could be a bit more to it. What the girl in work told me is that there's waltzing lessons starting tonight in Rathmines. Y'know? Every week for the next two months, proper one two-three waltzing. Wouldn't it be kinda fun to learn how to do it properly instead of just shuffling around the floor the way we usually do?'

'No, it would not be kinda fun.'

'It's just it's something I've always admired but never knew where to go to get lessons in this day and age.'

'That's nice for you, John, but as you can see, I'm a little bit busy at the moment.'

'With our big dance coming up, this seems like the perfect opportunity.'

'For you, John, but I'm not even slightly interested.'

'So that's a no, then.'

Carmel gave the matter a quick rethink. Anything that would get him out of her hair would be useful. 'I'll tell you what, John, why don't you go on your own tonight and check it out? See if it's as much . . . fun as you seem to imagine. Then maybe the next week, if I'm not up to my eyes in more important things, I might think about going.'

John had been to Rathmines church several times, back during his early days in Dublin when he still went to Mass every week. One thing he had never really noticed, though, was the rundown little hall nestled to the left of the chapel. A sign said the dancing lessons were within.

Inside, five minutes late for the start time advertised, John found an old-fashioned scene. The men were all at one end of the hall, the women at the other.

'You there,' said an elderly gent with a beard. He was a priest. 'Just fall in and copy.'

John took his place among the men who had formed three lines of five. Then the elderly priest stood in front with his back to them and the lesson began.

'*Sloooow* quick quick *sloooow* quick quick *sloooow* quick quick.'

Copying the old man's smooth and well-worn moves, they all stepped right, then they all stepped left. Next they all stepped forwards, and they all stepped back. You took one long step with the leading foot, then followed more quickly with the other foot, then stamped the leading foot quickly a second time. And that was waltzing, Viennese style, in a nutshell.

The priest left the men to practise and went down the other end to teach the women the same move. When he returned, he turned his attention to teaching them the basic step of quickstep and jive, which was similar but with an important difference.

'*Sloooow sloooow* quick quick *sloooow sloooow* quick quick *sloooow sloooow* quick quick.'

The next part of the lesson was where John deduced that the segregation of the two genders had nothing (or, at least, not too much) to do with stuffy old Catholic ways.

'If you're going to learn to waltz properly,' said the priest, 'you need to grasp a sequence of moves in which the woman's and man's parts are completely opposite of one another.'

'It was a light-bulb moment,' said John, triumphantly, when he got home to find Carmel sitting up in bed with an A4 pad. 'We'll be facing one another, of course, and the point is not just to one two-three over and back on the spot but to move about the room. Y'know? Like you see in those fabulous films where "The Blue Danube" is playing and they're all swirling around a ballroom.'

John had come home slightly sweaty, absolutely delighted with himself and everything he'd learned. He was extremely enthusiastic to go again the next week, preferably with Carmel. 'You'd love it!' he said. 'It was such good fun, and it's really designed for couples, so it would be better if we learned at the same time. Once we've mastered all the steps he'll be encouraging people to dance together from the third or fourth week.'

'Mmm,' said Carmel, though whether in reference to what John was saying or the list she was drawing up it was hard to know.

'And it's also in aid of charity,' John continued. 'The priest gave a short spiel at the end about this orphanage in Romania. That's where the money goes. Isn't that great?'

'Mmmm.'

'So, you start by doing your waltz in the shape of a diamond and then you do this little spin-around bit when you reverse the direction and it propels you down along the dance floor. Honestly, it's amazing when you see it done properly.'

'Mmm,' said Carmel, definitely referring this time to a problem with the list on her A4 pad.

> 'Because we're in love on a dying planet,
> A tide of death is rising everywhere,
> So we close our eyes and kiss,
> And the truth is, we don't care.'

'I think there's definitely fewer people,' said Michelle, 'at this gig than at the last one of his you dragged me to.'

'Ssh, Mizz Neylon,' said Evelyn, in her cross-school-teacher voice. 'Have a bit of respect. That's *my* song he's singing, I'll have you know.'

'And a very good one it is too,' said Michelle. 'What position did it reach in the charts again? Was it number one for long?'

'Ha bloody ha, Michelle! You're just jealous because nobody has ever written a love song for you. Certainly not one that includes a theme of impending ecological disaster.'

'Feckity-feck, Evelyn, how very true, and it makes me almost sick with envy.'

They both doubled over laughing. They were sitting upstairs on the balcony at Whelan's as Trousers On Fire (Shane plus various machines) played 'their' first gig of the year. The song 'Love On A Dying Planet' came to an end and, as always, there was a big round of applause. Though he might not have crossed over into mainstream commercial success – yet! – Shane still had a hardcore following that could almost fill Whelan's on any given night.

Almost.

And only Whelan's. Certainly not any of the bigger venues like the Olympia, the Stadium or Vicar Street, let alone The Point.

'And now I'd like to play a new one, hot off the press, as it were . . .'

'He doesn't seem to be strutting around as much as I remember,' mused Michelle.

'Oh, that's just on stage because he's manning so many instruments,' said Evelyn. 'Believe me, at home he still struts . . . sometimes twice in one night!'

They laughed again.

'So what's the story with him getting a proper job?' asked Michelle. 'Any chance of him paying a bit of rent anytime soon?'

'As a matter of fact,' said Evelyn, 'he applied for three jobs only the other day. I'm not sure if he'll get any of them, but it can only be a matter of time. Meanwhile he's got quite a few songs that he needs to finish working on. He's in the bedsit morning, noon and night, these days, trying to get them sorted so that he can devote himself fully to work, and then to the baby when it comes.'

'Doctors did not differ, these tests are rarely wrong.
The letter says it's positive, as you've been all along.'

'Good,' said Michelle. 'And, incidentally, when you say "baby", do you know yet if it's a boy or a girl?'

'Well, I'm not sure I want to know. In any case they can't tell until the scan at sixteen weeks. That's when it'll be big enough for them to see.'

'His teeny little willy!' laughed Michelle. 'Or lack thereof!'

'Michelle, such a thing to say!' said Evelyn. 'Speaking of teeny little willies, I hope you haven't been ogling any of your students recently.'

'Stare into different spaces and mouth the words oh damn,
And no we just can't turn it back.
And no we just can't turn it back.
Not now . . .'

'No, like I said before, there's a few who are very cute but I'm not quite that desperate yet. I had a falling-out with the solicitor fella but there's another one on the horizon, so I'm not stuck on the shelf yet.'

'Good girl,' said Evelyn. 'I'd hate to see you done for abusing your position over nineteen-year-olds with skateboards.'

There was a round of applause from the floor as the song ended.

'So, can I get you another drink?' asked Michelle, raising her glass.

'Ballygowan, please,' said Evelyn.

'Nothing stronger? I'm sure one wouldn't hurt.'

'Oh, all right, then,' said Evelyn. 'Feck it, you've twisted my arm. Something stronger it is. Get me . . . a double Ballygowan.'

Michelle laughed.

'Honestly, I'd love a glass of red,' said Evelyn, 'but apparently it affects the baby's ability to retain information and I don't need this little critter having me to blame when it does crap in the Leaving Cert.'

As Michelle went up to the bar, Shane introduced another new song. Evelyn listened, as she sucked ice from her glass.

'This next one's called "It's All Just Fine".'

'You often ask me what I'm thinking,
You want to know what's on my mind,
You think the truth it must be helpful,
I know what I know's not so kind.

'So then I go and then I go and then I say it's all just fine,
So then I go and then I go and then I say it's all just fine,
But it's not.

‘I have a deep and digging craving
For something not allowed to say,
I have a thirsty hungry yearning,
YOU are what is in my way.

‘So then I go and then I go and then I say it’s all just fine,
So then I go and then I go and then I say it’s all just fine,
But it’s not.
But it’s not.’

It was very good: a memorable tune propelled along by a stiff martial drumbeat and dark, brooding synths. When it was finished there was another big round of applause. Evelyn, however, was looking down into the bottom of her glass and did not join in.

Is there a more wonderful dance in the world than the jive? John wondered.

Answer: no. Just look at the whirl of it, the movement, the absolute exuberance of the in, out, spin and counterspin. And while I’m sure there’s a lot to be said for the tango, salsa, rumba and foxtrot, the jive has something that I’m sure none of those others has . . . the fact that it seems to have been designed with the shy, non-demonstrative Irish male in mind. Feck! I remember even my father used to be really good at it – and why wouldn’t he? All he really has to do is move in and out, *sloooow slooow* quick quick, and keep his hand in the air. The woman does most of the work. The man just stands there for the most part like a toddler with a spinning top. And yet for a minimum of input he gets to take part in this wonderful choreography. I’ll bet all those strange foreign dances make the man work a lot harder for his bread.

It was a nice theory, just a pity that he had nobody with whom to share it, or that he wasn't out on the floor, putting the theory into practice. Instead, he was sitting on the bench in Rathmines church hall, watching his fellow dancing students as they lit up the floor on the fourth week of lessons. In couples.

Naturally, the priest had tried to pair him up with someone, but John wouldn't go along with it. There was too much intimacy in it, he felt, for a man who was just a few months away from getting married. A vertical version of something horizontal – though he didn't say that to the priest. He still did all the solo lessons, learning about hesitation and box steps, spiral, pendulum and weaving, but sat it out whenever they tried anything two by two.

Carmel, meanwhile, was doing some late-night shopping in the Powerscourt with Gwen, one of her friends from boarding school. They were scouting for ideas as to what little favours might be placed on the tables at the wedding reception. Eventually Carmel almost shrieked with delight when the answer came to her. His and hers trolls for all the guests! A little pink-haired one and a little blue-haired one on every second place setting!

'Oh, my God,' said Gwen. 'That will be *sooooo* cute!'

36

Obviously, the lyrics to 'It's All Just Fine' could have been about anything: some former girlfriend of Shane's from years ago or an old band mate who had particularly annoyed him. Perhaps it was a coded critique of the Fianna Fáil/PD government – or not. Still, as Shane drove her to the doctor (in the old Corsa) for another check-up, Evelyn couldn't help feeling that it was about her. And, worse, that it was about the baby. Shane clearly felt resentful about being forced to get a proper job, resentment that he had been keeping pent up inside until the muse came a-calling with an idea for his new song.

There had been a very welcome development (for Evelyn, but not so much for Shane) on the job front that very morning when Shane had received an offer. It was as a data-entry operative and, as such, was probably not the world's most fulfilling role. Nevertheless, Evelyn was confident it could be a starting point for greater things. Shane, not so much. His initiation was to begin on Monday, 21 February, a date he had pencilled on to the calendar and decorated with skull and crossbones.

Evelyn had asked him for a copy of his new song lyric. As he switched lanes on Wellington Road, she studied the wording carefully.

'It's been a long time since you were so interested in my lyrics, yeah?' said Shane, rolling down his window to dangle his arm outside. He liked the feeling of air blowing past. The feeling of freedom.

'Yeah,' said Evelyn. 'I wonder why?'

'What do you mean?'

'Well, because it's so obviously about me and the bump.'

'No, it isn't. I can't believe you're falling into that trap, Evelyn. Surely you're with me for long enough that you know I write about a few things at any one time. That's what makes the songs so . . . universal.'

'Universal? This one seems very specific, Shane.'

'Specifically about you? Don't be paranoid. Where are you mentioned in it? Show me the line.'

'There's no line as such. It's just pretty clear that someone is stopping you doing what you want to do. If that's indeed the case then maybe it's something we ought to discuss openly, rather than me hearing your true feelings for the first time in Whelan's along with a hundred other people.'

'Actually, there were almost two hundred at that gig, yeah? But in any case the song is nothing to do with you or the bump. Like I said, the songs are all designed to be universal.'

'Universal, eh?' said Evelyn. 'How well have they done in the charts? How many of these universal songs made number one?'

Shane made no reply but pursed his lips grimly. He pulled his arm in, rolled up the window and drove the rest of the way with his shoulders hunched.

Evelyn leaned back in her seat and put her hand on the bump. There was just the faintest of kicks as the baby shifted within her. Hello, little person. She mouthed the words and felt the overwhelming sense of well-being that the baby always stirred in her. It didn't matter if Shane was having a big sulk. It didn't matter about the lyrics of his song. The important thing was inside her, its cells multiplying and body parts forming. I love you, I love you, I love you.

'You've got your rabbit face on again!'

'No, Carmel, honestly I haven't.'

'Yes, Cuddlebug, you do. I know that look. Tell me what's really on your mind.'

'Nothing. Honestly. I was just thinking about my chat with Brian last night. He told me a joke and I was trying to remember the punch-line.'

They were in Black Tie to scout for John's wedding attire.

'Tell it, then. I love a good joke.'

'That's just it. I've forgotten the last line so I really can't.'

'Okaaaay,' said Carmel. 'Whatever!' and she turned away as the shop assistant came over to serve them. 'I am marrying this guy,' she said, pointing at John, 'and I want you to make him look adorable.'

John did indeed have his rabbit face on and knew damn well what the punch-line of the joke was. That was precisely the problem. It preyed on his mind as he went into the dressing room with the first suit Carmel had picked out.

On the previous evening he had met Brian for drinks at the Hairy Lemon pub. The purpose of the get-together was to ask Brian to be his best man. Brian was honoured to be asked and immediately agreed. Later on in the evening, however, after they'd both had four pints, Brian said, 'Oh, I have a joke but I'm afraid it's a bit . . .'

'Go on.'

'It's in quite poor taste. I'm warning you!'

'Go *on*!'

'Okay. Why does the bride smile at the groom as they're walking down the aisle?'

'I don't know. Why?'

'Because she knows she'll never, ever, ever have to give him a blowjob again.'

John didn't laugh. And he wasn't laughing now.

There were so many levels on which it just wasn't funny. The fact that it was in poor taste. And horribly crude. But most of all because it totally rang true with regards to Carmel.

It wasn't just that type of sex, but lovemaking of any kind. And it wasn't just lovemaking, but intimacy. And it wasn't just intimacy, but time spent together. All of the above had deteriorated since the day after they'd got engaged, as if Carmel had previously been making an effort but no longer felt it necessary now that he was in the bag, the diamond ring on her finger. How much more sterile would their relationship become once the marriage certificate had been signed and stamped and sworn?

'You look *soooooo* cute!' said Carmel, when John emerged from the dressing room for the fourth time. 'That is definitely the one.'

'But the green waistcoat?' said John. 'I'm just not sure. Doesn't it make me look like an eejit? A bit like a leprechaun?'

'No, not at all, sir,' said the shop assistant, blankly.

'You're sure?'

'Yes, sir.'

'And what do you think, Carmel?'

'I can't see the problem, John. I don't know about eejits but leprechauns are so cute!'

John and Carmel's next stop was Lantz printers on Charlemont Street, to sort out the invitations. Carmel was in a quandary over the exact wording. Tradition dictated something like . . .

Mr & Mrs James Harrington
request the pleasure of your company
on the occasion of the marriage of their daughter

Carmel
to Mr John Fallon,

at Saint John the Baptist Church, Cratloe, Co. Clare
on Sunday, 11 June 2000
at 3 p.m.

and afterwards at Dromoland Castle
RSVP

But this form was predicated on the custom whereby the bride's parents paid for the event – which, much to her great annoyance, Carmel's parents were not prepared to do. The misers! The tightwads! The absolutely most embarrassing parents in the world ever. As she and John began to look through brochures full of different designs, Carmel kept chewing over the wording issue.

'It's all tied up in foreign property,' her mother had

wailed. 'The chalet in France and the apartment in Dubai. We can only contribute five hundred pounds.'

Pah! By Carmel's calculation the wedding was going to come to nine or ten K, and that was before you factored in the price of the honeymoon. So by any logic her parents had forfeited the right to be mentioned on the invitation.

On the other hand, their omission would be noted. People would deduce that her parents were mean-spirited Philistine skinflints, sorely lacking in any appreciation of their duties to a daughter who had always done her utmost to please, which in turn would reflect badly on Carmel herself, to be associated with such slobs.

So, which should she do? As usual, John didn't mind either way, which might be an example of his laid-back nature or another sign of what was becoming increasingly apparent: in lots of important matters, John was no help at all.

'Do you see any design you like?' John said, after they'd been browsing for half an hour.

'No, Cuddlebug. Nothing that really jumps out at me,' she said sadly. Yet almost as soon as the words were out of her mouth, Carmel was struck by a moment of inspiration. She reached into her handbag and took out the two little troll dolls.

After consulting with the manager it emerged that they did indeed have the facility to produce an invitation to individual specifications – for a very modest extra fee. Carmel knew exactly what she wanted: a line drawing of the boy troll and the girl troll, with a dash of colour for their pink and blue hair. 'What do you think, Cuddlebug?'

'Ahmm . . .' he said, wondering how to put it diplomatically. 'I don't really –'

'Mind?' said Carmel. 'What's bloody new?'

Then she turned back to the manager. 'Go ahead. Put the order through for two hundred cards.'

When they left the store they went down Harcourt Street together holding hands. It was a nice, simple, romantic gesture, perfectly fitting for a couple who had just ordered their wedding invitations. As they strolled, however, John couldn't help feeling that they were not holding hands because of the high emotion of the moment. Rather they were doing it because it felt like what a happy, passionately in-love couple should do. They were pretending. After a while John's hand got a bit sweaty, so Carmel let go.

John wasn't too disappointed. He was thinking instead that he was sick to the teeth of the fecking trolls and far from enthusiastic about having them plastered all over the invitations.

He was thinking also that he was sick to the teeth of being called 'Cuddlebug'.

If the truth be known (and it must eventually) he was also thinking that he was no longer in love with Carmel.

37

John spent the next few days in turmoil. For feck sake! What sort of a man would do such a thing? he wondered. What kind of man have I become?

He was disillusioned with everything: work, love, life, but most of all with himself. It was a long way from the kind of passionately romantic feelings he'd had in the past to where he was now, actively contemplating how to end his engagement to be married. He was ashamed when he thought back to the hundreds of times that he'd told Carmel he loved her, snuggled under a quilt as they planned their life together.

What does all that mean now? I certainly wasn't lying, but I don't feel like that any more. So what happened? How has the boy become such a man?

It just didn't fit with how John thought of himself. As a reasonably good guy. Breaking an engagement was the kind of thing that other men did. Not him. Never him. Until now.

He was lying on the couch on an evening after work. His eyes were closed, not just because he was wrecked from a particularly busy day with prescriptions but because he didn't want to open them and see what was right in front of him.

Carmel.

Carmel buzzing around.

Carmel making yet more plans for the wedding.

Carmel buzzing around, making wedding plans and wearing leggings.

John detested leggings. Why couldn't she ever wear a nice skirt or jeans around the apartment any more?

'Y'know, Cuddlebug, don't you,' Carmel said, putting down her clipboard, 'that tonight's the night I'm going for a drink with my old classmate David?'

John nodded and she wandered off into the bedroom. And this, too, was another indication of something dead under the floorboards of their relationship. John remembered the days when he had been filled with jealousy at her spending an evening alone with another man, when just the thought of her being unfaithful brought him out in a sweat. If she gave some guy too lingering a glance, he'd rant in the streets later as they walked home. He had been desperately insecure, immature and stupid. But no longer. Now he knew his worries about her fidelity were unfounded. Carmel really was genuinely reliable and honest to the core. She would never be unfaithful.

Sadly that realization had coincided with him ceasing to care. In fact, it was even worse than that. In his darkest, most perverse thoughts, John wished that Carmel would get drunk and have a fling with her old classmate David. John wouldn't be all that hurt, and it would be the perfect pretext for breaking up in that it would be NOT HIS FAULT.

Because a big consideration for John as he pondered the break-up was how others would take the news. Almost everyone agreed that he and Carmel made a lovely couple, so if the wedding were called off, there'd be a serious inquest into whose decision it had been and why. Nobody would buy the 'by mutual consent' routine. There would be interrogation of both parties, especially Carmel, until something juicy was unearthed.

Such as? The fact that he'd been wanting more sex. He would look like a complete Neanderthal. Which he was not! He was well able to empty and fill a dishwasher, put on a wash of colourfast clothes, cook a rudimentary curry. He was ever-vigilant about replacing the toilet seat in the down position.

What else could be drummed up against him? The fact that he had taken an irrational dislike to troll dolls, which were so cute and harmless. Was it Carmel's fault if she was fond of such little things? Not really. She was just being herself, and as much as it irritated him, she wasn't actually committing a crime. That John person, they would all say, was ridiculously petty.

Or . . . because they had somehow grown apart in terms of spending time together and having fun. This was the truth of it, really, the kernel of the problem. But it was also the reason least worthy of gossip and thus most likely to be discounted immediately.

No. If they broke up now John would not be cast in a good light, which was why he craved the perfect pretext, one in which the break-up would be NOT HIS FAULT. He even rolled the phrase around in his mind and on his tongue: the perfect pretext. The perfect pretext. The perfect pretext.

He couldn't pull the trigger without one. So much so that he had begun to daydream implausible scenarios where the pretext would fall into his lap. Example . . . Carmel is down in County Clare driving along a country road when she has to pass a truck laden with huge round bales of hay. As she overtakes, the yellow rope holding them snaps and several bales fall on to her car. She is killed instantly. With absolutely no pain, such is the instantaneousness of this tragic, tragic event. Afterwards at the funeral everyone is sympathetic to John for the catastrophic calamity that has ripped his intended future life to shreds. People are nice to him. Men shake his hand and women give him kisses. Absolutely nobody calls him a sex-crazed Neanderthal. But the bottom line is this. He no longer has to marry Carmel and it is not his fault!

The perfect pretext never did arrive and thankfully Carmel never fell victim to any agricultural accident on the roads of County Clare. Nevertheless John did eventually break the engagement in April. There was no single night when it happened. Rather, the break-up was a drawn-out affair that took a month of on again/off again before the final severance was completed. Many tears were shed on both sides and, indeed, many of their wedding deposits were lost.

Each of them found somewhere new to live: Carmel, an apartment in Islandbridge with her friend Gwen; John, a dingy bedsit on Synge Street. (He could certainly have afforded somewhere nicer but chose it because it felt like penance.) They spent a week traipsing back and forth from the apartment they had shared, moving their stuff. For the most part this was straightforward, but some items were tricky. The joint purchases. Things that they'd bought and paid for fifty:fifty in the days when they couldn't imagine not always being together. The CD collection could be divided into two piles, but when it came to their bed linen, was there any point in one person taking the quilt cover while the other took pillowcases and sheet?

And how could you halve a television? Ditto the laundry basket, clothes horse, bookshelf, radio alarm, tin opener and sugar bowl. John, feeling guilty as hell, wanted Carmel to take the lot but she wouldn't hear of it. She made careful calculations as to the value of each item and divvied them up accordingly.

They met for the last time at the apartment, now looking very empty, on the day that the lease ran out. They were due to return the keys to the letting agent and hopefully get their deposits back. To ensure that that happened, it was necessary to give the place a thorough cleaning so they both set to work. John vacuumed all the carpeted areas while Carmel mopped the kitchen tiles. John moved on to cleaning the windows while Carmel wiped the skirting boards. While she was in the bathroom, she noticed that there were two last (jointly purchased) items that neither of them had yet taken away: the bathmat and the toilet brush.

'Any preferences?' she asked John.

'No, Carmel. Take them both.'

'I will not take them both,' she said firmly. 'But, to be honest, Gwen and I already have a toilet brush. Do you have one in wherever it is you've moved to?'

'No,' said John. In fact he didn't even have his own toilet, only the use of a shared one down the hall from his bedsit.

'Well, that settles it. You have it, and I'll take the bathmat.'

At that point the letting agent arrived. They handed him their keys. As regards the deposit, he barely glanced around the apartment before agreeing that everything looked fine. From his folder he produced two cheques, one for each of them made out for £450. Then, just as quickly as he had come, he was gone.

John and Carmel stood in their apartment alone.

'Maybe . . .' said John.

'Maybe . . . what?' she replied, and they looked one another in the eye.

He wanted to say more but couldn't figure what. Now that the final separation was just seconds away from becoming a reality he was thinking all sorts of jumbled thoughts. Like that he was sorry for what he had done. That Carmel really was a very nice person and that this could well be the biggest mistake of his life. That maybe . . . maybe . . . was there any way, even at this late stage, that things could be different, that the few little problems they'd been having could be ironed out, with a bit more effort, with a bit more give and take, for the sake of all the good times? Would it hurt to have one more try?

'Maybe. I'm leaving now,' said Carmel, and she leaned down to place something at his feet.

Before John could respond she was already going out of the door. He remained rooted to the spot as she trotted down the staircase. Then the door slammed in the lobby. After a minute or two of staring into space he bent down and picked up his toilet brush.

When 11 June rolled around, the day the wedding should have taken place, both Carmel and John sought distraction. Carmel took a holiday in Greece and John told his employer he needed a week off. He didn't travel too far, only home to Cappataggle. His mother, well aware of the significance of the date, was all questions about how he was coping – and how did he feel? John didn't spend much time inside the home. He went out to his father and, without any explanation, fell to working beside him. It was the time of year for shearing the sheep and dipping them to protect against flies. They had an occasional conversation about hurling or soccer.

38

Everyone knows that really awful things happen occasionally. Like, say, your computer crashing and deleting all your files. However, we generally imagine such things will never happen to us. Or if they do, that before the crash there'll be a little period of warning when you'll know it's impending and use the opportunity to save everything on to disk. But this notion is totally false. One day, sooner or later, bad things do indeed happen to each of us and there is no warning. You wake up and switch on your computer to find everything is deleted and gone. Your car hits the wall before you have time to cry out, 'Stop – let me take that corner again more slowly.' Your grandfather collapses with a heart attack and you do not get to tell him you love him. You wake up on the morning of 12 February 2000 and you immediately sense that something is very wrong. There are spots of blood in your knickers. And the most desperate cramps imaginable are wrestling just below your guts.

At some level, Evelyn knew immediately that it was all over. The pregnancy. The half-life of her tiny, almost sixteen-week-old foetus. And yet she clung to hope, putting on a sanitary pad, rousing Shane and getting on the road to Holles Street Hospital. Once there, the midwife immediately checked for a foetal heartbeat. And was not sure that she could find one. After that Evelyn was taken for a full scan and the result was the same. Except more certain. There was no foetal heartbeat.

At which point Evelyn felt an overwhelming need to go to the toilet. When she got there the pad was saturated, and there was much more to come. On and on in a river of much more than you could possibly believe had been in there. The pain was brutal, but her sense of devastation and loss was more piercing still.

Evelyn cried.

Afterwards they had to do a D and C.

Afterwards she was in a lot of pain but was now perfectly free to take painkillers because she was no longer pregnant.

Afterwards they told her that it wasn't remotely her fault. That it wasn't the glass of wine she'd had last Sunday. Nor was it the fact that she hadn't bothered to do her pelvic-floor exercises. That 20 per cent of all pregnancies end in miscarriage. That often there's a chromosomal defect. That these things just happen.

Afterwards she lay on her hospital bed and, although she was awake, spent a very long time with her eyes tightly shut.

She had spread the news of her pregnancy after she'd passed the supposed twelve-week safety line so didn't have the option of keeping the loss to herself. Parents, her sister in Florida and her brother in the UK, aunts, work colleagues and all her friends had known that she was having a baby and would have to be told that she was now no longer having a baby.

A baby . . .

A child . . .

Or just a mass of developing cells?

No.

And another thing struck Evelyn. How often in her life she'd heard of this aunt or that friend of her mother having had a miscarriage. And the tone in which it was always said suggested that this was a fairly minor inconvenience. Mrs X had five children, with one miscarriage between child number two and child number three. No big deal. Just a ball that had been dropped.

But it was a big deal. It was terrible. It put into perspective every other thing that she had ever thought was awful: whether or not to split up with Gary, and the lyrics of Shane's silly song.

This miscarriage was not a statistic. The number had been ONE and was now erased to ZERO.

Evelyn was discharged on the Monday morning, 14 February, Valentine's Day. When Shane collected her, he brought a bunch of flowers for the nurses, who had been so caring, and another for Evelyn. They drove home, and Shane did all the talking. What did he say? Evelyn didn't know because she wasn't listening.

There was no question of going out for any kind of Valentine's celebration, of course, but as the day progressed Evelyn came gradually out of her shell. Shane could not have been more understanding or attentive, and by the evening, they were lying on the couch in one another's arms. Clinging tightly to what remained.

'I have something for you, yeah?' he said eventually. 'It's not really a Valentine's gift. You may or may not want it.'

'Go on,' said Evelyn, trying her best. 'Go and get it. I'm intrigued.'

Shane went to the bedroom and returned bearing a little

red box. From which he produced a gold ring. 'Evelyn Creed,' he said, kneeling beside where her head lay on the couch, 'would you please do me the great honour of granting me your hand in marriage?'

So this was it, finally it, the moment Evelyn had been anticipating and yet avoiding for years. The moment when she had definitively to decide whether her man was a prince. Whether all the boxes on the checklist were ticked. Whether pretty good was good enough. Whether she had kissed enough frogs to know the right answer.

'Yes, I will, of course,' she said, and reached out her arms to pull him close and hug him. There was no need to let her horoscope decide or play any games.

When you know, you know, and she just knew.

39

It was exactly a week later that Evelyn again woke up in the morning with a vague feeling that something was not right. It concerned work, she sensed, but what was it? She couldn't immediately figure it out. After all, she was on extended sick leave from Michael Newcombe's and they'd been very sympathetic, so why should she be uneasy? Fully a minute later, the answer dawned on her. Something she'd completely forgotten about in all the commotion of the previous ten days. It was Monday, 21 February, the day of Shane's initiation into his new job as a data-entry operative. Yet according to the clock radio it was eight thirty-two a.m. and he was still snoring in the bed beside her.

'Shane – Shane!'

'Uh.'

'Wake up!'

'Uh?'

'You've got work in twenty-eight minutes.'

'Uh-uh.'

On closer questioning it was confirmed that Shane did not, in fact, have work in twenty-eight minutes or twenty-seven or at all, in fact.

'I resigned, yeah? Didn't I tell you?'

'You resigned before you even started?'

'Well, there didn't seem to be any point.'

'What do you mean?' said Evelyn, her eyes narrowing. She suspected exactly what he meant.

'Well . . . y'know, yeah?'

'No, I don't. Tell me.'

'The whole reason why I agreed to do it had sort of –'

'Miscarried? Is that the word you're looking for?'

'Well . . . yeah. Yeah, it is.'

Which made Evelyn absolutely livid. The logic of his position was in one sense perfectly rational but in every other way seemed like a total betrayal. He had used the miscarriage as an excuse to back out of taking his share of financial responsibility.

'What's the plan, then, Shane?' she asked bitterly. 'Were you hoping we could just go back to the way it was before the pregnancy, with you noodling away in your recording studio while I slave to bring home the bacon?'

'Of course not,' said Shane. 'Things have to be different. They need to be shaken up and, as a matter of fact, I have another idea about how we might make a fresh start, yeah?'

'You do?'

'Yeah,' he said, and took a deep breath before laying out his proposition. 'Y'know you've often mentioned you were born in New York when your parents were over there working, back in the day?'

'Yes.'

'So, by my reckoning, you could apply for a US passport, if you wanted, yeah?'

'Yes. Theoretically. It's not something I've ever wanted to do, though,' said Evelyn. 'I only lived there for three months when I was a baby, so it's not like I feel any connection to the place.'

'Okay . . . but what if, maybe, we could move there after we get married? If we did, and you had a US passport, the two of us could get green cards and stay for a few years at least, yeah?'

'What? Where is this coming from? Why do you want to go to America?'

'It would just be so new and different,' said Shane. 'I've reached the stage where I think my writing needs exposure to some fresh inspiration if I'm to push on to the next level, yeah?'

He got out of bed and stumbled sleepily in the direction of the bathroom. He didn't bother to close the door and Evelyn could hear the strong jet of his urine hitting the toilet bowl. She smiled.

She lay back on the pillow, closed her eyes and actually started to laugh. Not because she was happy but because she had witnessed the final straw floating into place and the camel's back was well and truly broken. There was nothing now that the world could throw at her to make things any worse.

As she lay there perfectly still, Evelyn finalized her decision on several important matters without any wavering or hesitation.

Under no circumstances was she going to get a US passport.

Or move to America.

Or marry Shane.

It was time to throw this particular frog back into the dark green pond where he belonged.

Frog 10

40

'Two children, abandoned by their parents, are lured into captivity by a homicidal maniac . . .'

'Bawbaw.'

'An awkward youngster, who never quite fits in, is rejected and laughed at wherever she goes. Ultimately she winds up all alone as the weather begins to turn cold . . .'

'Bawbaw!'

'Porridge pours out over the brim of a cooking pot until it fills the kitchen, then the house and eventually perhaps the whole world . . .'

'DADA, BAWBAW!'

'A whole family struggle to pull up a turnip so enormous that it seems they will never manage to drag it out of the ground . . .'

'DADA, MY WANT . . .'

'With her granny missing, presumed dead, a young girl is attacked by a wolf . . .'

'. . . A BAWBAW!'

With a heavy sigh, Brian stood up from where he'd been sitting on a chair beside the cot. 'Okay, okay, I'll get you a bawbaw.' Eyes half closed with exhaustion, he shuffled out on to the landing and down the stairs. It was five thirty a.m. The little blighter, his two-year-old son James, had already had a wakening at two ten, which Brian had managed to sort out. Now, however, the cute little blondie-haired toddler was convinced it was morning, that it was time to get up, which made him a bit less cute.

Monday to Friday, this would have been Aoife's problem, but weekends were Brian's shift. It was the least he could do now that Aoife was only a month away from having their second child.

Plan A in these situations was to go in and talk soothingly to James about something, anything at all. Often he was comforted by just the tone of a parent's voice and would settle again. Other times he demanded a bottle of milk, after which he might possibly settle or, much more likely, would be thoroughly refreshed and ready to start the day.

It being 4 May, there was just enough dawn for Brian to think he didn't need to switch on any light. Barefoot, he stepped on an abandoned Dora the Explorer and stumbled into the kitchen, cursing. He flicked on the kettle, put six scoops of powder into a bottle of cold water and waited for the spout of boiling water, which would help it dissolve. In another life, he would have lit a cigarette, or perhaps fiddled with his ponytail. Neither option being available, he resumed his train of thought. There was a book of fairytales that an aunt had recently given James.

They must be pretty frightening for children, he thought. In every one of them there comes a point where it seems that all is lost.

'BAWBAW!' came a shout from upstairs.

But, on the other hand, no matter how hopeless the situation, no matter what the threat of violence, cruelty or natural disaster, somehow everything works out okay in the end.

'DADA, MY WANT BAWBAW.'

But how? How does the happy-ever-after always happen? Is there meant to be some kind of moral message in those tales or what?

Brian started back up the stairs with the warm bottle.

Let's see . . . *Hansel and Gretel*? Saved by bravery and wit. That's a very positive lesson for kids.

James's rising volume made it apparent that he must now be standing up in the cot.

The Enormous Turnip? Pulled from the ground by sheer dogged persistence from every last member of the team. Again, that's good.

Brian entered the bedroom just as James put one leg on the rail of the cot in an attempt to climb out.

The Ugly Duckling? A revealing transformation, making apparent the magnificence that was inside all along.

Brian handed James the bottle and the child lay back down.

The Magic Porridge Pot? Finding the right formula of words. And what about *Little Red Riding Hood*?

'Ta ta, Dada,' said James, before closing his eyes and sticking the teat into his mouth.

Her story doesn't have a moral, really, thought Brian, smiling despite himself at the little boy's politeness. Just pure dumb luck and coincidence. Little Red Riding Hood and the granny are saved by some guy who was never mentioned previously in the story but just happened to be walking by the cottage at the exact right moment. And happened to be carrying an axe. And happened to be capable of using said axe in a very precise surgical fashion to cut the wolf open and get them out.

'Dada?' said James, his eyes flicking open once more.

'Yes, sonny boy?'

'Uppa?'

There was no point in further efforts to get him back to sleep. Best just admit defeat, accept that the new day had begun and bring him downstairs.

'C'mon so,' said Brian, and put out his arms. 'Maybe you might watch Nick Junior on the telly and let me doze off on the couch.'

'Uppa! Uppa!'

'Because if you don't, sonny boy, if you don't . . .'

'Bawbaw! Dada! Ta ta!' said James, wrapping his arms around Brian's neck.

'. . . I'm going to sell you to a man I know called Rumpelstiltskin.'

41

Far from Brian's three-bed semi-d in the outer suburb of Ratoath was John's city-centre bachelor pad on Stephen's Street. John was not at home on this particular Saturday morning but at his girlfriend's place, also in the city centre, down at the IFSC. They did not wake up as early as five thirty but neither did they sleep in. Some time before seven John fumbled to shut off the alarm. He had barely found the right button when his girlfriend put one hand on his shoulder and pulled him back towards her.

'Just like clockwork.' She chuckled, pulling his shorts out of the way.

My God, this is good, to be finally with the girl I was meant for right from the start, thought John, in the small part of his conscious brain not overwhelmed by hormones.

It had taken thirteen years since they first met, of wrong roads and paths not taken. Thirteen years of learning what was possible in life and what were just the crazy dreams of youth. Thirteen long years before they had finally ended up together.

Well, sort of, anyway.

The period after he had broken his engagement to Carmel had been the longest dark period of John's life. Lonely times he had endured before, but added to that now was the guilt at what he had done – to Carmel, obviously, but also to himself and his whole way of seeing himself.

After observing the date of his cancelled wedding at his parents' place, John had gradually re-entered the world, but he wasn't quite the same. He was a bit more cautious when expressing his opinion on any subject, a lot more cynical when the subject was love or relationships. Though disappointed that his romantic notions of love had collapsed, he nevertheless embraced the new reality as he saw it. That there is no love, only biological need. And there is no relationship, only the coming together of two individuals on a temporary basis for the purpose of satisfying said biological need.

With that in mind he visited the nightclub Copper Face Jacks once more. Though it was the scene of several previous failures, this time around he approached women with just the right air of couldn't-give-a-damn casualness. Which is (at least in a disco setting) so much more attractive than sincerity. He scored.

And did so again the following week and the week after that. In fact, there followed a period when John managed to get laid at least once or twice a month with a series of interchangeable girls. Or almost interchangeable. There was one young woman who was destined always to stick in his mind, not so much because he ever got to know her properly but because she had two belly-buttons – the result of a childhood operation on her left kidney, she told him.

But still John was not happy. Despite extolling to Brian the ecstasies of his new lifestyle he very quickly grew weary of waking up to post-coital reality. Because there was always a huge difference between the scenes before and after sex. Once the deed was done, usually at a frenetic pace, there was a long, slow aftermath of awkwardness. When hormones were no longer part of the equation, and the rush had passed, when the girl was no longer primarily a sex object but rather an actual person, it could go one of two ways. Sometimes it became apparent that the girl was falling for him and he felt nothing in return. Other times it was John who felt the first stirrings of an affection that had nothing to do with lust. Whether or which, the end result was the same: phone numbers were exchanged and one of them was false. They kissed goodbye but one set of eyes were closed and the other resolutely open. There was a promise to see one another again but they did no such thing – unless many months later by chance among the shoppers on Grafton Street.

It wasn't nice. It wasn't wonderful. It wasn't what he wanted at all.

So John was ready for something different on the night when he saw a girl at Kehoe's bar who was familiar from many years before.

'Hey, you,' he said, tapping her on the shoulder. 'Still drinking Ritz?'

'Is anyone . . . John?' She had taken just a beat to recognize him.

'Nice to see you again,' he said, and it really was. Aged – what? Maybe thirty-two or so, she was now even more beautiful than he remembered. Her hair still long, brown and curly. Her figure a perfect ten.

'I was trying to get a Bacardi and Coke,' she said, 'but I can't catch the barmaid's attention.'

'Let me order,' said John. 'It really is great to see you again, Michelle.'

'A little lower,' said Michelle.

'There?' asked John.

'Ooooooh . . .'

'Faster?'

'No! Slower.'

'Stop?'

'No, never stop.'

And then all hell broke loose. If before Michelle had been moaning, now she began to cry out in little yelps. Then the yelps turned to squeals. And the squeals to shrieks. And then finally, after several waves of shrieking, there was one last blood-curdling scream. Then silence. She and John collapsed on the bed.

'That wasn't too bad,' she whispered, shuddering as another aftershock pulsed through her.

John, struggling to catch his breath, agreed. Indeed, unlike their student days, this time around Michelle and his sex-life left nothing to be desired.

Unfortunately, becoming attuned beneath the sheets did not turn John and Michelle into a couple. Michelle in particular didn't want ties or to be referred to as anyone's girlfriend.

'We can be friends with benefits,' she had told John matter-of-factly, on the very first morning after their reunion.

'What does that mean?' he had asked, not having heard the term before.

'Sex without strings,' she replied.

'Without strings?' he said, still not really getting it. 'I presume that extends to handcuffs and leather straps and all that. Fine by me. I've never really wanted to try that S and M stuff.'

'No, John. It means that I'd like us to have sex again.

Possibly many times. But I'm never going to get a key cut for you.'

'Sorry, I still don't –'

'It means friends, you eejit,' she said impatiently, 'who have a sexual relationship without being emotionally involved or any kind of commitment. I'm not going to be your girlfriend.'

'Okaaaaay,' said John, uncertainly, not so much because he agreed but because it was obvious Michelle would not be persuaded otherwise. Over the following weeks, though, he became more convinced that it was an excellent and eminently practical arrangement, particularly now that he had lost his silly illusions about love, now that he no longer believed in relationships, let alone marriage. Now that he was realistic and sensible and wise.

Even now when they had been 'together' for almost a year there was no question of John thinking, for instance, about buying an engagement ring. Likewise there had been no exchange of Valentine's cards in February. And they never, ever said, even when drunk and/or in the throes of sexual passion, 'I love you.'

On the contrary, Michelle had recently been stressing that their arrangement did not preclude having other sexual partners from time to time. 'You should definitely have another girl, if you want,' she had said.

Which was, John guessed, a signal that Michelle wanted to 'have' some other boy. Quite possibly a student of hers to whom she often referred. A black-haired one with gorgeous brown eyes. And the body of a male model. And a skateboard.

On the other hand there were also some practical

benefits to the friends part of friends-with-benefits. For Michelle, at least. Now that she was quite senior in the Trinity maths department, she was moving in the upper circle of the college hierarchy. It entailed quite a few formal dinners and attendance at various conventions. On some of those occasions, one was expected to bring one's wife/husband/partner. Through bitter experience, Michelle had learned that turning up to such events solo was not appreciated, and certainly not if you were a young woman with Michelle's good looks. Far too many men tended to drift away from their wives and form a semicircle around her. This was flattering, of course, but put quite a few well-placed female noses out of joint thereby threatening Michelle's career prospects. Having learned her lesson, she was now in the habit of bringing John along when such occasions arose.

This fine May morning was one.

'So, John, I won't see you again until early tomorrow at the airport, okay?' said Michelle, as she switched off the hairdryer.

There was a conference in Brighton on the Mathematics of Behavioural Operations. John had taken a few days off work and was going along especially for the gala dinner on the Tuesday night. Michelle crossed her bedroom to the wardrobe and took out the dress she was intending to wear – designed by Paul Costelloe, lime green with yellow splashes and little purple flecks. Gorgeous.

'Oh!' she exclaimed. 'There's a great big Guinness stain. Some fecker must have spilled it on me that last day we were at the Curragh.'

'You'd hardly notice it,' said John, still lying in bed.

'No, John, *you*'d hardly notice it. Every other woman in

the place will detect it a mile off. And I don't have time to wash it now. I'm already running late.'

'Why is that again? How come you're going in on a Saturday?'

'For the tutorial,' said Michelle. 'I told you. There's a student who needs a little extra help. I have to get in early to set up a PowerPoint presentation.'

'Fair enough,' said John. 'Then why don't I throw the dress into the washing-machine for you? I can even hang around until the cycle is done and transfer it to the dryer, if you like?'

'You will do no such thing,' said Michelle, her eyes wide with disbelief at his ignorance. 'It's designer! It needs to be hand-washed and certainly never let near a tumble-dryer. I'll wash it myself this evening and it should drip dry in time.'

'Oh. Okay. Just trying to be helpful.'

'The biggest way you could help me now, John, is by getting out of that bed so I can make it. Anyway, don't you have to go and count some tablets?'

'No, actually. I've taken the day off. But you're right. I do have to get out of bed. There's something else I have to do.'

42

'Are you sure you don't need to go to the toilet?'

'What?'

'I said, are you sure you don't need to go to the toilet?'

'Yes, Evelyn.'

'Because we have plenty of time. If you want to go back inside. Or if you think you might have forgotten anything.'

'Yes, Evelyn. So you've already said. I'm fine, so let's get going, shall we?'

'Mobile phone . . . and charger?'

'Yes.'

'The letter and your number?'

'Yes.'

'Nightie, dressing-gown and slippers?'

'Yes, yes and obviously yes. Can we go now? Mother of God!'

'If you're quite sure?'

'Quite sure.'

'Okay then . . .'

Evelyn turned the key in the ignition. Still the same old blue Corsa she'd had since years ago. In the passenger seat was her mother, Sarah. Evelyn steered out of their driveway on to the road to Athlone. Once there she would take the bypass to the N6. Then onwards, via Moate, Horseleap, Tyrrellspass, Kinnegad, to their ultimate destination, a place where Evelyn had not been for almost two years: Dublin.

*

After her miscarriage and the subsequent break-up with Shane, Evelyn was an emotional wreck but limped along with her life as before. The final straw came a few months later when her father died. He was only sixty-two when he was diagnosed with stomach cancer, and the speed with which he had deteriorated had come as a desperate shock to Evelyn, her siblings and, most of all, her mother. Before the end, Evelyn decided it was her duty to quit her job and move home to Ballymahon. By the time Frank Creed was admitted to the hospice, she had worked out her notice at Newcombe's, wound up the lease on her apartment and put all her things into cardboard boxes.

Evelyn's older brother and sister both brought their families home to Ireland for that final week. They were all around, too, for the funeral and immediate aftermath. Ultimately, however, they had jobs to return to and children who were missing school. A fortnight after her father's death Evelyn hugged her sister goodbye. Then there were two. Evelyn and her mother. Left all alone together.

The next few months were an awful time for them both, but it was the daughter who held things together. As her mother spent her days wandering around the house in a dressing-gown and a haze of grief, Evelyn handled all the arrangements. Inheritance, life assurance, bank accounts and bills: all that Sarah had to do was sign wherever Evelyn indicated. Cooking, grocery shopping and laundry were also taken care of. In fact, there were only two small signs of Evelyn's pain. One was the moulting of her hair: every time she took a shower, there was a clump to be removed from around the plughole. The second was her habit of eating quite a lot of chocolate spread. Straight from the jar. Something she had last been known to do when aged nine.

It was almost two months before Evelyn had time to undertake a task entirely for her own benefit: to haul a certain cardboard box down from the attic. Inside were various posters of melancholy young men with floppy fringes. She put them on the wall in the room now known as the spare bedroom.

Then she put on an old cassette of the album *Faith* by the Cure.

As a scratchy sinister bass line filled the room, she lay on the bed.

And she thought about her dad.

Her (dare she admit it) favourite parent by far.

Who had only ever loved her and hugged her and praised her and played with her and laughed with her.

Who had never sought to change her or demand an explanation.

Who had said it all without ever saying a word.

Who, in her memories, was always smiling.

Evelyn cried. And cried and cried.

After a desperately unhappy Christmas, Sarah Creed gradually began to come back to life, doing her share of the household chores, shopping for bread and milk in the Centra, answering the phone when it rang, a prospect that for a long time had filled her with inexplicable dread. By the first anniversary of Frank's death she had started on a regime of going for a swim every morning and was as stable and content as any woman could be who'd lost her husband well ahead of schedule.

'Evelyn,' she said, after the anniversary service, 'you've

been an absolute rock, but it's time now that you got on with your own life. Get back to work and whatnot. I suppose you'll be going back to Dublin soon?'

But Evelyn didn't answer. For the previous year she had poured her energies into the project of minding her mother. Doing something positive for someone else. Now that the focus was back on herself, she was not so sure what to do next. Certainly the obvious thing, a resumption of her life in Dublin, held no attraction. In fact she felt intimidated and exhausted by the idea of setting up again. Of searching for a new job and a new apartment. Then there was the prospect of searching for a new . . . life.

Back at home she had got used to having no social life whatsoever. She never went out to a pub or disco and had no desire to. Neither had she made any effort to remain in touch with her friends in Dublin. For a few months after the death, Michelle and Cliona had rung her at regular intervals but already those intervals were lengthening. She had nothing to say to these people and wasn't particularly interested in what they were up to either. The idea of trying to reconnect with them didn't seem worth the effort. The thought of trying to pick up all those threads was too daunting.

'I got a job,' Evelyn announced to her mother, a week later, but it was not quite what Sarah Creed had had in mind. It was as a shop assistant in Shanaher's, the smaller of the two local newsagents. Slightly decrepit, very much old school in layout and decor, the shop had only a smattering of loyal customers so it was generally very quiet. Evelyn soon settled into the rhythm there. When there was a customer in the shop she chatted with them. When there wasn't she picked up a magazine from the shelf and read it. *Hello!*, *Bella*, *Best* and even *Cosmopolitan*, she often managed to get through them all in a single day. For free.

Another development in Evelyn's life during her second year at home was perhaps more disturbing, involving something she would previously have said was unthinkable. She began to listen to country music. 'Not the mainstream crap,' she tried to explain to her mother, 'made by idiots in hats like Garth Brooks and Alan Jackson and Toby Keith.'

But her mother didn't understand – never could, never would, when it came to subtle but significant distinctions between types of music. 'I always loved that "Friends in Low Places" song! Put that one on!'

'I told you, Mum. I despise the man!'

'How about "Achy Breaky Heart"? I loved that one too.'

'Mum!'

Evelyn's taste was for the older, more gritty and authentic stuff. Hank Williams's *40 Greatest Hits* was the first one she ordered from Amazon and she immediately fell for tracks like 'Long Gone Lonesome Blues', 'Lost Highway' and 'Cold, Cold Heart'. Once that was digested she worked her way through the back catalogues of Waylon Jennings, Joe Ely, Townes Van Zandt and the Carter Family.

'Turn that bloody racket down,' her mother shouted up the stairs one evening. As she gradually recovered from her husband's death, so, too, she was regaining her capacity for finding fault with Evelyn. 'You're giving me a pain in the ear. I thought those Smiths were bad. At least they weren't all the same bloody tune.'

The pain in Sarah Creed's ear, however, proved to have very little to do with the fact that 'Wildwood Flower' was blaring at a ridiculous volume. After a painful night without sleep, her doctor confirmed that she had an ear infection. He prescribed an antibiotic, which solved the problem, but it was only three weeks later that the disease returned. And again a fortnight later. And again and again over the following months, until it became apparent that there must be some underlying problem. Sarah was referred to an ENT specialist in Athlone, who diagnosed a perforation of the eardrum. An operation, called a myringoplasty, was required. The consultant wrote a letter to the Royal Victoria Eye and Ear Hospital in Dublin to seek a date for surgery. There being quite a waiting list, the earliest available was the first Saturday in May.

'We'll definitely make it by half nine as planned,' said Evelyn.

No response. Sarah Creed was staring straight ahead through the windscreen.

'I said, there's no need to worry, Mum. We're definitely on schedule to be there in time.'

Still no response. The problem was that Sarah's good ear, the one with a fully functioning eardrum, was on the other side from Evelyn. If she only knew that her daughter was talking she would have cocked her head sideways to hear.

'It doesn't matter,' said Evelyn.

'That's in euro,' said her mother, turning to her suddenly, with an impatient expression. 'But what is it really? In pounds?'

43

Because the proper car park was miles down from the platform, John took a chance and parked illegally on the path opposite the taxi rank. Fortunately, his father's train was bang on time so he was back before it could be clamped. The relief he felt was soon dispelled when he took a good look at the face of Brendan Fallon. Specifically the awful thing on his eyelid. John couldn't bear to look at it but neither could he resist stealing another glance. Then another. Until his father noticed what he was doing and turned his face away.

'Jaysus, what a hellhole!' said Mr Fallon, pointing out of the window. 'Would you look at this traffic. Where in the name of God are they all going anyway? Will you tell me?'

'I don't know, Dad.'

'But look over there, John! There's a whole lane free on your left.'

'That's a bus lane, Dad.'

'Right, right . . . but look now . . . why is that car in it so?'

'That's a taxi, Dad. They're allowed to use it too.'

'Are they now? Jaysus, they make the rules to suit themselves. I don't know how you can put up with it.'

'Yes, Dad.'

'And those lights have gone red again. It beats me how anyone can live here!'

'It isn't easy, Dad . . .'

'And is that a Garda car up ahead? Why don't they –'

But John interrupted him. He was tired of talking about the traffic. He needed to ask his father if his eyelid hurt as badly as it looked. 'So how is it anyway, Dad? The cyst. Are you in much pain?'

'That little thing? It's fine. No pain,' said Mr Fallon.

At last the traffic light went green.

When John pulled into the eye and ear hospital he was surprised to find that there were no car spaces, except a few for the disabled. A porter advised him to park out on Adelaide Road, which was what he would have done if the last available spot hadn't disappeared just as he came upon it. A small blue car swung in just as he was about to indicate. After a bit of circling the area, he got a spot up on Harcourt Terrace.

The walk back to the hospital was not so very long. Then they went in through the entrance (which was impressively nineteenth century, all stone columns and stained glass) and took their seats in the waiting area.

Which put them just a few feet away from Evelyn Creed and her mother.

Fecksake! thought John, startled by the apparition. Look who it bloody is! By the time he recognized Evelyn, however (in the seat right bloody opposite him!), his father had already sat down and there could be no moving him. John took the seat beside him with his head bowed and spent the next few minutes afraid to look up lest there be any eye contact.

No sooner had he done so than Evelyn chanced to look up from her copy of *Fast Food Nation*. 'John bloody

Fallon!' she just about managed to stop herself shouting out. Then she, too, lowered her eyes in case he might look up.

At which point John's eyes flicked upwards for just a second. He couldn't resist taking a better look at the woman who had been his close friend until . . . He looked back down.

Evelyn looked up, just as curious as John to get a better look at the lad she hadn't laid eyes on in – what? Six and a half years?

They could probably have gone on in this way for quite some time but the spell was broken when their two parents happened to look across and see someone vaguely familiar.

'Isn't that the lad you used to be great pals with in college?' asked Sarah Creed.

At the same moment, Mr Fallon was moved to observe, 'Do you see yer wan over? I know I've seen her before.'

Both John and Evelyn tried to ignore their parents but there was no escape. Sarah got up off her chair and walked right up to John.

'Are you John?'

He wondered if he could get away with lying but his father was already nodding. Then she introduced herself and insisted that Evelyn come over for a big session of shaking hands. Both of the parents were all smiles at such a happy coincidence. Their children were beaming as well, but less convincingly. There was a very brief moment of eye contact and then they all sat down into their seats.

'So what are you in for, ma'am?' asked Mr Fallon.

Sarah explained her condition and returned the question. Mr Fallon opined that his was a far more minor procedure. In the past year he had developed a cyst on his left eyelid. It had proven resistant to every type of antibiotic so it was now necessary to have it drained.

'They're just going to fold the eyelid inside out to make the incision,' said Mr Fallon who had a very strong stomach for discussing such details. 'I'll be in and out in a few hours.'

'Yes,' replied Sarah, who was not quite so enthusiastic about discussing the nitty-gritty of how they were going to cut some skin off one part of her ear to plug a hole in another part. 'Isn't it amazing that this pair of ours haven't met in so long when they used to be such great pals?'

Then she turned towards Evelyn and fired the inevitable question. 'Why was that? Did ye have a falling-out?'

'Mrs Creed?' shouted a nurse from the doorway. 'Mrs Sarah Creed?'

After a hurried goodbye, Sarah and Evelyn were led away in the direction of ENT-HN. Shortly afterwards, John and his father were shepherded down the corridor to the Day Ward.

Sarah Creed had specified that she wanted a private room. Otherwise what was the point in paying that hefty annual premium to the health-insurance company? It wasn't as if she was on the basic plan either: after Frank's death she had upgraded to the one that was supposed to guarantee a private bed in every hospital from the Blackrock Clinic down to Letterkenny General. And yet? When the day finally came that she actually needed to test their promises, they let her down.

'Bloody typical!' she told the nurse, with her most forbidding frown.

'I'm sorry, but it's all dependent on availability,' said the nurse, utterly unintimidated. 'The whole hospital is working extra shifts at the moment to get through a huge backlog of elective surgeries. I'm afraid we have to put you into semi-private. It's just with one other lady.'

Evelyn put a consoling hand to her mother's back but Sarah refused to stop scowling. 'I'll be making a complaint about this!' she muttered, as the nurse led them into the room in question. 'It's just not good enough.'

'That's what I said too,' said the lady who was already in the room. She was sitting up in her bed at the far corner wearing a pink nightie and a mischievous smile. 'And wait until you see the swill they serve us up at mealtimes!'

John and his father were also facing circumstances that were not quite what they had expected.

'You don't have a bag with you?' asked the nurse.

'No,' said Mr Fallon.

'Then where's your pyjamas?'

'But I thought . . .'

He'd thought that since it was a day procedure he wouldn't need anything. When his wife had suggested it might be otherwise he had not heeded her. It had also been stated clearly on the admission letter that had been posted out to him. That, however, had been stuffed into a pocket of his coat and lost somewhere in the upper fields of the farm.

'Not to worry,' said the nurse. 'This happens from time to time. I'm sure we have a spare pair.' Which they had. Mr Fallon disappeared with them into the toilet attached to the treatment room and John eyed the door apprehensively. He was struck by the fact that he hadn't seen his father in pyjamas for . . . what? Maybe twenty-five years? Not since very early childhood. The prospect of it was shocking and somehow inappropriate. It was like seeing the president in pyjamas. Or the Queen of England. Or God Himself.

The pyjamas in question were a few sizes too small. When Mr Fallon emerged from the bathroom a few minutes later, he was very snugly packaged indeed. John had to stifle a gasp and look away. Then the nurse handed Mr Fallon the surgical gown to wear over the top and something for his head, which resembled a shower cap. John bit his lip.

'I suppose I look like a big auld eejit now?' Mr Fallon asked his son gruffly.

'No, Dad. God, no. You look . . .'

'. . . like?'

'Like someone else.'

Sarah did not need to worry about the quality of the hospital food for lunch since she was fasting. The nurse said that hers was the sixth operation scheduled for theatre that day. They couldn't tell her the exact time they'd take her down. In the meantime she was to get into the surgical gown and hat provided and be ready. Once that was done she climbed into her bed. There was nothing for her and Evelyn to do but wait and grow nervous about what was to come. Or almost nothing. The roommate, without needing much encouragement, began to tell them a little about herself.

Her name was Angela Vaughan, a true blue Dub from Marino, aged seventy-one and, until her recent retirement, a chiropodist. She had five children, all grown-up, and fifteen grandchildren. Most likely with two more on the way. And so, on and on, she gave the broad outline of what seemed like an unexceptional life until she paused just long enough for Evelyn to fit a question in edgeways.

'About your career in chiropody?'

'Oh, youz are interested, are youz? Because most people aren't one bit interested, in anyways. Most people don't realize at all.'

'Realize what?'

'Well, like, that in fifty years of doing the job, of being, may I say, one of the best in Dublin, if not *the* best . . .' and her eyes twinkled as she said it '. . . that it was inevitable I should come across more than a few famous feet in my time.'

'Like whose?' asked Sarah, cocking her good ear to make sure she heard correctly, her nervousness temporarily forgotten.

'Ah, y'know. Lots of the big names. I wouldn't want to say who exactly because, like, of the whole client confidentiality palaver.'

'Who? Who? C'mon, you have to tell us!' Evelyn joined in.

'Oh, okay.' She smiled, not needing all that much persuasion to throw off the secrecy of her profession. 'I s'pose the most famous in this day and age would have to be Bono.'

'Bono?' gasped Sarah.

'Yeah, y'know the lad I mean, don't you? From Cabra. I knew his mother and all belonging to her. He used to be a singer of some kind. Now he's always on the telly wearing sunglasses even when it's not remotely sunny.'

'Of course we know him,' said Evelyn. 'I just find it hard to imagine him requiring the services of a chiropodist, that's all.'

'An' why wouldn't he, missy? Feet are feet. The feet of the famous are just as likely to give trouble as ordinary folk's. In anyways, things like a callus or a corn or a verruca don't give a twopenny damn how much money youz have.'

'Fair enough,' said Sarah. 'So when was this, ma'am, that you . . . chiropodized for Bono?'

'About '83, I think,' said the old woman. 'Himself and that gang of his were touring over and back across Europe something savage at that stage. And him wearing these boots with a two-inch heel! Something had to give. His feet were in bits by the time I got to treat them.'

Evelyn and Sarah both nodded as the conversation was interrupted by the nurse.

'Sarah, they're on their fourth procedure now,' she said, from the doorway. 'It won't be too much longer.'

'Great!'

'I see your roommate is in one of her quiet moods. That's probably for the best.'

Evelyn and Sarah turned back towards Angela and found to their surprise that she appeared to have fallen asleep, two seconds after she'd been talking to them.

'What the . . .' said Evelyn.

The nurse explained that, though Angela was there to be treated for a cataract, she was in the early stages of Alzheimer's, in addition to another complicating psychiatric disorder. One of the symptoms was her habit of falling asleep very abruptly. 'But she could wake up again just as quickly.' She also tended to confabulate things. Where there were gaps in her memory, her brain would create an imaginary account that it really believed to be true.

Sure enough, no sooner had the nurse continued on

her rounds than Angela returned to consciousness. 'And Michael Flatley was another one,' she said. 'Can youz imagine what would have happened if I hadn't had him shipshape in time for *Riverdance*?'

The first step was to put special anaesthetic drops into Mr Fallon's eye. When these had begun to work, they attached a brace to the skin at the side. Its purpose was to keep his top eyelid open. Then . . . Then John had to put his hand to his face and watch through his fingers.

The young doctor produced a syringe. It was tiny but, nevertheless, it was a syringe and it had a needle. He inserted it into Mr Fallon's lower eyelid and injected an anaesthetic more powerful than the drops. Then he moved a few millimetres along the lid and injected again. And again and again, five times in all along the length of the lid. By the end of it John was no longer watching through his fingers. His eyes were shut tight.

'Very good, Mr Fallon,' said the doctor. 'We'll let that sink in and I'll be back in about twenty minutes to make the incision. Once that's done we should have the cyst drained in a jiffy and you'll be right as rain.'

'Y'know what?' John said to his father, after they had been left alone once more. 'I think maybe now would be a good time for me to go and get a bit of lunch.'

Despite very strong doubts about the truthfulness of Angela's yarns, they certainly served to pass the time for Evelyn and Sarah as they waited for the operation. Brendan Behan, Patrick Kavanagh and Samuel Beckett had all apparently placed their naked feet before her back in the 1950s. It also emerged that she had pared hard skin from the heels of almost every senior politician since the era of Dev and Lemass. Then there was the time she had helped Muhammad Ali when he fought in Croke Park. And Mother Teresa when she was over here too. The athlete's foot from Calcutta was the most virulent strain Angela had ever encountered.

Then the nurse came and told Sarah it was her time.

44

The options for eating in the eye and ear hospital were not extensive. There was a pair of vending machines in the Accident and Emergency Department and a coffee shop. Hot food was not available, but rather a selection of sandwiches, scones, crisps and sweets.

Evelyn decided to fill the time while her mother was in theatre by getting a snack. Underwhelmed by the choice, she hummed and hawed for several minutes before eventually settling on a tuna and sweetcorn sandwich with a pot of tea. Then she carried them on a tray towards the seating area, only to find that every table was occupied and every seat taken. Except one.

For a moment she paused and seriously considered whether she might just eat standing up. Perhaps there was a window-ledge or something. But no. That would be silly. She sat down in the one remaining seat and John looked up.

'Hello,' he said, with a smile. 'You look familiar.'

'Surely not,' she said coolly, refusing to look him in the face. Instead she tried to get on with the business of unloading her tray.

'No, really, you do.'

'I can't think why,' said Evelyn, as she poured her tea. 'Because I must say that your face doesn't ring any bells at all.'

'No?'

'No.'

'No?'

'I said,' and at last Evelyn looked him in the eye, 'no!'

'Oh, well,' said John, still smiling, not in the least put out by her frostiness. 'Perhaps I'm getting mixed up. Perhaps I never met you.'

For a moment there was silence as John took a bite of his ham and egg bap. Evelyn put a sachet of sugar in her tea. As she poured the milk he started again.

'It's probably from television. Have I seen you on television maybe?'

Evelyn looked up from her tea and, for the first time, allowed herself a really long hard stare at him. He was still skinny, but not as skinny. His hair was still brown but a lot tidier than she remembered and with three or four strands of silver. All trace of acne had left his face, and it was only fair to admit that he was a little bit handsome. A little bit well dressed. He smiled that old smile of his.

'Yeah,' she said. 'That's how you know me. Television.'

'What programme was it again?'

'Ahmm . . . *Big Brother*. I came second in the series last year.'

'Did you really?'

'Yes, well, I'm trying not to let it change me. To remain humble. Just watch how I still eat horrible pre-packaged sandwiches like regular people.'

'Yum yum. They sure is tasty, ain't they?'

'Yeah. And also I was on *Pop Idol* a few months ago. I came fourth in that.'

'Talented girl! You live a busy life!'

'Don't I just,' said Evelyn, breaking out of character abruptly to say, 'As do you, mister, from what I've heard on the wire. So, how is Michelle anyway?'

'Michelle . . .' John was jolted by the sudden shift in conversational gear. 'Ahmm, she's fine. You know Michelle. Much as she always was.'

'Really? Then I wonder why ye're back together.'

'I . . . ahmm . . . I . . .'

'So are ye engaged yet or what?' Evelyn's eyes narrowed and the air grew just a shade chilly.

'God, no, Evelyn. We're long past the point of believing in any of that old romantic hogwash.'

'Really?' said Evelyn. 'Are ye? Are you? Or is that Michelle's point of view?'

'Both.'

Evelyn raised her eyebrows a fraction.

Before she could ask another awkward question, John tried to change the subject. 'The decor in this place is pretty naff, isn't it? Could really do with refurbishment.'

'That's true,' said Evelyn. 'In fact I'd call it twee. Almost as twee as that girl you used to go out with. What was her name? The one you left waiting at the altar . . .'

'That's not fair, Evelyn. I broke up with her a whole six weeks before the wedding.'

'Good for you. I'm sure she appreciated the difference.'

'I . . .' said John, startled and confused. 'She . . .'

'Yes? What is it, John?'

'Oh, give over, Evelyn! I've made some mistakes, that's true. Who hasn't? Except you, obviously.'

She had that look of long ago, thought John, the wicked smirk and raised eyebrows. Sort of playful but also deadly serious in the conviction that she was right and the rest of the world could learn a lot if we all just paid more attention to what she said.

Her hair, he noted, was long again, falling past the shoulder. Her top was a black fitted cotton blouse, not unlike what she had been wearing a decade before. In fact all of her clothes were black and beneath them . . . the curves, in, out, over . . . well, she was still a very good-looking woman. He focused on her lips, which had no lipstick, red or otherwise. It was the only substantial difference from way back when.

'So you're living with your mother, I've heard,' he said.

'That's right.'

'Well,' he said, 'I hope you're not leaving any sweaty socks lying around the place. Some hostesses can react very badly to such things.'

He had meant it as a joke. She didn't find it funny.

'No, John,' she said icily. 'That isn't a problem for me. I place all my laundry in the correct receptacle.'

'Okay . . . I'm sure you do.'

'Also, of course, I make it a rule never to call her a – what was the phrase again? – "a total feckin' bitch".'

'What?'

'Oh, look, is that the time?' said Evelyn, and suddenly pushed her chair away from the table. 'I'd really better be getting back.'

'Evelyn, I was only joking,' said John, and reached out to catch her wrist. 'Don't leave in a huff. I'm sorry if I offended you.'

But there was no stopping her. She left in such haste that she knocked against one of the other tables and nearly tripped over a big folder containing someone's X-rays. John took one last bite of his bap before letting out a sigh of exasperation. He got up and followed her. 'Come on, Evelyn,' he called out, when he finally caught sight of her again, fifty yards ahead of him on the main corridor. She ignored him.

Fine, he thought. I'll just follow her to her mother's room in the ENT ward and she'll have to listen to me then.

Evelyn had other plans, however. Without warning she veered sideways and headed up the staircase without looking back. John began to jog. By the time he made it to the top of the stairs, he was puffing slightly and Evelyn was barely visible, down past the nurses' station on the ophthalmology ward. She disappeared around a corner to the left.

John kept up the pursuit but a nurse stepped into his path, scowling. 'No running allowed on the corridor, young man,' she hissed.

'Yes, of course. Sorry,' he gasped.

The nurse didn't seem to be in any hurry to step aside so John had to go around her. 'What patient are you here to see?' she asked, but John pretended not to hear and kept on walking at a more sedate pace. He had the distinct sensation that the nurse's eyes were burning a hole in his back. It felt like an age until he made it to the corner where he'd last seen Evelyn. He turned left only to find a short stub of a corridor. And no sign of Evelyn. And three doors.

'Eeny meeny miney mo . . .'

John opened the first door, which led into some sort of meeting room. There was a table and some tubular chairs and an old A4 refill pad lying on the carpet. A poster on the wall said, 'Wash YOUR hands.'

He opened the second door and it turned out to be a walk-in linen cupboard. The wooden shelving was stacked with sheets, pillow cases and blankets. On the floor was a small vacuum cleaner.

Finally John opened the third door, just a crack, more or less certain that Evelyn had to be inside. What he found, however, was a semi-private room fully occupied by two patients. There was whispering as he craned inside to take a better look and a better listen.

> '. . . To thee do we cry,
> Poor banished children of Eve.
> To thee do we send up our sighs,
> Mourning and weeping in this valley of tears.
> Turn then, most gracious Advocate,
> Thine eyes of mercy towards us,
> And after this our exile show unto us
> The blessed fruit of thy womb,
> Jesus.'

The speaker was an old white-haired woman who showed no sign of noticing his intrusion. Her eyes were open but her glasses, with extremely thick lenses, lay on her bedside locker. Also vying for space on the small piece of furniture were grapes, liquorice allsorts, an open bottle of Lucozade and a copy of the *Sacred Heart Messenger*.

In the bed opposite there was another patient, whom John couldn't see because a screen blocked his view. As the prayer continued, the second patient could be heard moaning quietly, the victim of some chronic pain uncontrolled by their medication.

'What *do* you think you're doing?' said a voice from over John's shoulder. It was the nurse, looking more irate than before.

*

After John had been led away, Evelyn stayed in bed for another few minutes while her new roommate murmured through ten Hail Marys. Only when she was certain the coast was clear did she pull back the sheets. She had a huge smile on her face. As she swung her feet to the floor, she began to laugh. Louder and longer than she had for maybe two years or more.

Her roommate was startled and made a quick grab for her glasses. The bottle of Lucozade fell to the floor.

45

'Have you got my steroid drops?'

'Yes, Dad,' said John, rummaging in his right front pocket and pulling out a green bottle. As he replaced it, the questioning continued.

'And my antibiotic drops?'

'Yes.'

This time the bottle John pulled out was blue.

'And my appointment slip with the date of my next check-up?'

'Indeed.'

The slip had been lodged in one of John's back pockets. As were the next items his father requested.

'And the information leaflets?'

There were ten, all told. In order to fit them in, John had folded them once, twice, three times. They were a bit crumpled but definitely still intact.

When John had returned to the treatment room after a thorough dressing-down from the nurse, his father was finished having sharp objects stuck into his eyelid. The draining was done, and a decision made that stitches were not necessary. He came on the scene just as the doctor was affixing a bandage patch over the eye and explaining the importance of warding off further infection. While his father changed out of the tight-fitting pyjamas, John was entrusted with minding all the take-home medicines and paperwork.

'Okay, sir,' said the doctor. 'You are free to go.'

'Right you are . . .' said Mr Fallon. 'But, John, do you definitely have my steroid drops?'

Meanwhile, when Evelyn returned to her mother's room, she found only an empty bed. In the other, of course, was Angela Vaughan.

'Oh, youz are back,' she said, delighted to have company once more. 'C'mere till I show you something.'

She clambered half out of her bed and opened the door of her bedside locker. From within she drew out what Evelyn thought was a large book. In fact, it was a sort of scrapbook. Angela opened it and beckoned Evelyn closer to have a look. Evelyn gasped and her face froze in disbelief.

Each page was made of plastic and consisted of nine little pockets, intended to hold stamps or little cards. What these pockets held, however, were souvenirs from fifty years in the practice of chiropody. Mostly toenails . . .

All of them were labelled meticulously (with small handwriting) so it was quite clear which nail had once been attached to Bob Geldof and which to Pierce Brosnan. There was a specimen of hard skin pared from the heel of Pope John Paul II during his visit in 1979 and, even more amazingly, the grey shrivelled remains of a callus dating all the way back to 1963, harvested from the arch of an American president.

'After I'd treated him,' said Angela, 'the dirty little beggar wiggled his big toe at me and asked if I offered a more intimate service.'

'Really, Angela?' asked Evelyn, holding back giggles. She didn't know whether to believe what she was seeing and hearing, but it didn't really matter. 'And what did you say?'

'I said absolutely nothing! I picked up his sock and put it back on the randy article.'

'I can still see out of my right eye,' said Brendan Fallon, patting at the bandage patch on his left. 'Don't worry, I'll be grand.'

Yes, John thought (but obviously wouldn't dream of saying). Knowing your levels of resilience, Dad, I'm sure you will be grand. Still, though, there's no denying that all of a sudden, you're starting to look old . . .

As John drove his father back to the railway station he found himself thinking back to the time when he first conceived of not taking over the farm. He had been sixteen, in his fourth year of secondary school. Up to that point his academic career had always been fairly mediocre. He did the bare minimum of homework and never an ounce of study. For some reason, he abruptly started to try a bit harder and was duly rewarded with a report card of Bs and Cs. When the Inter results were issued, he managed to score three As.

The career-guidance teacher congratulated him and told him to keep it up for the Leaving Cert. He asked what course John was thinking of doing in college. Such a thing had never seemed like an option before. John said he didn't know.

To celebrate the results, they were given a half-day from school. When John got home early, his father was surprised, but thought of a job for him: mucking out some sheep cubicles. As he levered up layers of muck and straw with the four-pronged fork, John was muttering to himself,

'We farmers are the last people in Western Europe doing hard physical labour. There's a machine for everything else.'

He thought what a doss it must be to work just forty hours a week, forty-eight weeks of the year. After he was done, he went into the house and showed the result card to his mother. 'Mam,' he said, 'I think I want to go to college.'

She nodded, pursed her lips and said, 'Okay.'

So, the matter was never discussed directly between John and his father. Nuala presumably told him and/or persuaded him. For that, John was eternally grateful because he could never have said it to his father himself.

And to his father John was grateful too. He had never tried to change John's mind about college, though it must have been obvious where it would lead him. Away from the farmyard. Leaving Brendan Fallon, ultimately, with no option but to keep on keeping on for as long as he could.

When they arrived at Heuston, John got a proper parking spot and insisted on accompanying his one-eyed father on to the train. There, he ensured that Mr Fallon got a seat with a table, facing against the direction of travel, just how he liked it.

On the way back to his car, John rang his mother to confirm his father's arrival time and check that she would be there to collect him at the other end. No sooner had he hung up than a text message arrived from Michelle, reminding him of their rendezvous at Dublin airport the next morning at seven, and that he was to bring a suit so he'd look presentable at the gala conference dinner.

John replied that he was looking forward to their trip, got into his car and drove out of the car park. He headed along the quays as far as O'Connell Bridge and then up through the centre to Stephen's Green. He came to the point where he would usually turn down King Street towards his apartment but for some reason he didn't. He continued his circuit of the Green and headed up Earlsfort.

Right outside the gate of the eye and ear hospital there was a parking space so he pulled in. He took a deep breath and walked down the avenue back into the hospital.

When Sarah Creed arrived back from theatre she was unconscious but came to as she was being transferred from the trolley into her bed. She and Evelyn hugged and began to talk about how the ear felt, but Angela kept interrupting. Though the old woman could be wonderfully entertaining, Evelyn felt they needed a break from hearing about chiropody. She told Angela that Sarah was very tired and pulled the screen around the bed to give them some privacy. No sooner had she sat down than Sarah had fallen back to sleep. Evelyn didn't wake her.

After a while of just sitting in her chair, staring into space, Evelyn heard someone come into the room. The footsteps came closer, right up to the screen, and stopped. All she could see of the person was the footwear. Brown men's shoes. There was a long pause of indecision and then the shoes walked away.

A few minutes later, one of the nurses poked her head through the screen to enquire after the patient. When Evelyn explained that Sarah had fallen back to sleep, the nurse said that was quite normal. 'There's really no need to worry. The operation was a complete success,' she said. 'There's a good chance that your mother will sleep for several hours now. If you like, you should probably go and get yourself dinner.'

'I don't know,' said Evelyn. 'What if she wakes up while I'm gone? I want to be there in case she's upset or in pain.'

'Of course,' said the nurse, 'but I can take your phone number and ring to tell you when she wakes up.'

As the nurse spoke, Evelyn heard another set of footsteps arrive. Once more, the brown shoes appeared at the bottom of the screen. Then a familiar head poked through alongside the nurse's.

'That sounds like a good plan,' said John. 'Come on, Ev. I want to take you out to dinner.'

46

'And what about your tenth frog?'

'The one who shall become my Prince Charming? Oh, John, I have my doubts that he exists,' said Evelyn, with a sigh. 'I think he may have been run over while crossing the road.'

'Ouch!'

'Or perhaps he got married to some other princess in an unfortunate case of mistaken identity.'

'Tragic.'

'Or there's been a cosmic mix-up, and he's gay.'

John shook his head and took another bite of his Hawaiian pizza. They were halfway through a meal in Pasta Fresca and had already got on to the topic of their love-lives – or lack thereof. 'But you're hardly going to meet him living at home with your mother, now, are you?'

'I suppose not. It's just there were things that happened two years ago. I nearly –'

'Surely you must miss Dublin. Surely you can't be happy sitting at home every single evening watching *Coronation Street* with your mother?'

'I am happy, actually, mister!' said Evelyn, smiling but defiant. 'You haven't a clue what you're talking about. First, because I don't miss Dublin one little bit, and second, because I do not watch *Corrie* every single night. That would be impossible. For your information it isn't even *on* every night. So I sometimes watch *EastEnders* instead.'

'Fair enough,' laughed John, looking her in the eye. 'Still, though, you really should move back up to Dublin, Ev. The place isn't the same without you.'

Evelyn took a sip of her wine before switching the focus of conversation. 'And, anyway, I don't think I'm the only one who's lost faith. What about you, for instance?'

John looked down at his plate and said nothing.

'Tell me, John – tell me about this little arrangement you have with Michelle. This friends-with-benefits thing ye have going on.'

'Ahmm . . . well . . . there's not too much to say, Ev. Michelle and I . . . well . . . we're just past the point of having any illusions about love and romance. We get together fairly regularly but without any commitment or any long-term aspect. And y'know . . . we enjoy our time together.'

'Shagging,' said Evelyn, bluntly.

'Well, we do more than just shag . . . but yes. Basically that's it . . . yes. And we make no apology for it. It's an eminently sensible arrangement. It's facing up to reality.'

'Go on,' said Evelyn. 'Tell me about this reality.'

'Okaaaaay . . . Take the whole idea of everlasting true love and marriage. It's a lovely thought, but does it ever actually happen? Just look at it statistically for a moment.'

'Statistically?' said Evelyn, eyebrows raised. 'Why does this sound like something Michelle would say?'

'Ssh. It's my opinion too. Anyway, the fact is that an increasing number of marriages do end in divorce – in the US, for instance, which we always copy eventually, it's at fifty per cent. By definition, those are cases where the idea of lasting love was an illusion. Correct?'

'Fair enough.'

'Then, logically, about fifty per cent of the marriages

remain intact. But surely quite a lot of these cases must be held together by factors other than love. Like, for instance, there's a percentage of people who stay together for the sake of their children, and some who do it for financial reasons. Some just can't face the idea that they've invested so much emotion in something that's failed, and others are afraid of the disapproval of family and friends, or dread the unknown and fear they might end up alone. People who believe that having no companion is worse than having one they no longer love. And some . . . some just stay out of nothing more than habit.'

'That's a pretty gloomy picture you're painting.'

'Not gloomy, Ev, realistic! And after all those percentages are taken away, all those couples no longer in love, how many are left? How many marriages remain held together truly by love?'

'One. At least.'

'One?'

'Yeah, my one. The one I'll have if I ever find the right frog. You can twist the statistics any way you like, John, but I don't believe it's as bleak as all that. I do, however, believe that you've allowed yourself to be overly influenced by Michelle, which isn't healthy. Michelle has her own reasons, personal ones, for feeling the way she does.'

'Which are?'

'Oh. Didn't she tell you?' replied Evelyn, with a smirk.

'No. We don't really discuss –'

'Yes, I bloody know ye don't. That's the problem, isn't it? I can't tell you the details but suffice it to say that her parents' marriage wasn't great. They may have got married in 1970 but it was a bit 1950s in style. It gave Michelle the idea that it's an institution that makes a woman into a slave, a servant. A person whose role is to stay in the home permanently, cooking and cleaning for no pay, only bed and board.'

'Oh.'

'Which is obviously a ridiculously outdated view for Michelle to take,' said Evelyn. 'Things are much better for women nowadays. As well as doing all the cooking and cleaning, many of us are allowed to have paid employment outside the home too . . .'

After their meal they came out on to Chatham Street laughing and in high spirits. It seemed a shame not to continue their banter so they walked in through the very next door to Neary's pub.

'Just the one,' Evelyn insisted. 'I have to get back to the hospital soon.'

John ordered a round and two packets of peanuts.

'Whatever happened to Brian? Do you still keep in touch?'

'Oh, yes. On the phone mostly. He doesn't get out much now. He's married and has a kid. A boy . . . I think. And another on the way.'

'Wow. And does he still have the beard, the long hair?'

'God, no. Not in years.'

'Good. They didn't suit him, to be honest, but I couldn't say that at the time.'

'I thought they were cool.'

'They were not cool, John. They were ick.'

'Ick? How could you say that, Ev? Next you're going to claim that Gary's fluorescent yellow bootlaces weren't cool either.'

'True. They were ick too. In retrospect, I can see just

how misguided many people's notions of fashion really were.'

'Including your own?'

'Certainly not.' She smiled mischievously. 'Everybody's but my own. That Gothic gear I used to wear, the black clothes and red lips, has stood the test of time. So I wear more or less the same style today. Minus the cherry red lipstick, obviously, because I'm too old for such blatant sexual provocation. I have therefore been totally vindicated as a young woman who had impeccable dress sense.'

'Or maybe,' said John, in the same spirit, 'your mammy isn't giving you enough pocket money so you just can't afford new clothes.'

Evelyn chuckled. 'I admit it, John,' she said. 'That's exactly why.'

'Speaking of Gary,' said John, after a brief interlude to visit the Gents, 'have you any notion what became of him?'

'Last I heard he, too, was married with sprogs. Three, I think. After finally giving up on college and being dumped by Michelle, he spent a few years bumming around in a New Age community up in Donegal. Making art, I heard someone say.'

'What? Like painting and drawing?'

'God, no, Johnny. The only drawing Gary ever did was of the dole! Boom, boom!'

'So how, then?'

'He made it out of stuff that he found washed up on the beach. As one does . . . Anyway, eventually he went back and did night classes in accountancy.'

'Really? And what about Fintan, your mother's favourite son-in-law?'

'No idea.'

'And Andy?'

'That eejit? I used to see him occasionally, rushing around at engineering events, but since I moved home, there's been no sighting. Sadly he's not in the habit of popping into Shanaher's for a copy of *Cosmo*.'

'And Gerard and Manus and the tall guy and . . . ?'

'No, *nada* and nothing, John. It's been years since I heard from any of them. I don't know about their marital status or if they're still in Dublin – or even still alive for that matter.'

'You could look them up on the Internet. There's bound to be some info about them on it.'

'Why?' Evelyn laughed. 'I don't believe you, John! Is that what you've done with your ex-girlfriends?'

'Sure. Only last month, actually, and the results were pretty interesting.'

'Let me guess. You found out one of them lectures in maths at Trinity?'

'Besides Michelle. It was the others I checked up. Just like you said, I'd lost all contact and was curious to see where they were now.'

'So where did they end up?'

'Okay. Well, Valerie Hayes is now Valerie Meenaghan. She moved down to Killarney and has her own chemist's shop.'

'How are her bruises after that time you threw her on the ground? Are the scars still noticeable? Was the Internet able to tell you that?'

'Feck off, Ev. As to Avril, she's listed as the chairperson

of a residents' association in an estate in Clane, County Kildare.'

'Fascinating! And what about the lovely girl who won several medals for hockey?'

'Carmel finished studying medicine and is now a registrar in Beaumont. She's part of the renal-transplant team.'

'Wonderful. And the blonde you trailed all over a continent?'

'There was more to Sophie than blonde hair, Ev.'

'Oh, yes, that's right. I seem to recall that she also had big breasts.'

'Ha ha, Ev. Anyway, it seems she's back in England and, bizarrely, she's become a cop.'

'What?'

'Yeah. The thumbnail picture is pretty small but it's definitely her. She's a PC working in a Safer Neighbourhood team in South Yorkshire.'

'Jesus, John! I bet you're wishing you hadn't screwed things up with her now, eh? You could be doing all sorts of interesting things with handcuffs!'

'Oh, stick it up your blouse! Anyway, less about me. I forgot to ask about that other guy you were with. What was his name again? Y'know the one who was a singer in a band?'

'Shane, you mean,' said Evelyn, before taking a big sip of her Guinness. 'No, I haven't got the latest there. I did get a letter from him, though, about a year ago.'

'Which said . . . ?'

'Well, it said a lot of things. On matters you know nothing about. The way we came to split up and what happened around that time. I doubt that Michelle filled you in, did she?'

'About what?' asked John, genuinely ignorant of all that had occurred.

'About . . . Ah, listen. I'll tell you about all that another time, Johnny. It's a bit heavy. Suffice it to say, though, that the letter also contained a bit about the state of his musical career.'

'Go on . . .'

'Well, it wasn't good. He had finally come to the conclusion that his band Trousers On Fire was just too far ahead of its time to connect with the ordinary masses. Too edgy, too challenging. His cult following remained loyal, apparently, but he couldn't seem to write the breakthrough ditty that would move the band on to the next level.'

'So what? He gave it up and got a real job like Gary and the rest of us?'

'God, no. He decided to become a writer instead.'

'What kind of writer?'

'Fiction. Literary fiction. Except . . .' Evelyn took another big swig from her Guinness and was savouring the taste until John gestured impatiently for her to continue. 'Except it may not be totally fiction. The thing about Shane is that he's an . . . "artist", who likes to draw on real life in his creative works. He made it clear to me in his letter that he was planning a novel that would feature a scenario very like my relationship with him.'

'The sonofabitch!'

'He emphasized that he'd be changing all the names. He's recasting himself as Sean and me as Ellen.'

'Wow! An extremely creative sonofabitch!'

'And he ended the letter by asking for my blessing.'

'I presume you wrote back and told him to respect your privacy and not to be such an exploitative jerk.'

'No, I didn't,' said Evelyn. 'I didn't write back at all. There'd be no point since he'll write it no matter what I say. And also because . . .' she downed the last of her pint '. . . on previous form, I'm quietly confident that nothing the fecking eejit writes will ever see the inside of a bookshop.'

John clapped her on the shoulder and they laughed and laughed.

47

John walked back to the hospital with Evelyn and waited outside while she went to check on her mother. Sarah was still asleep and the nurse said again that she would text Evelyn whenever the patient awoke.

'That's great,' said John.

'Why is it great?'

'Because it means that you and I . . .' he changed his mind about how to finish the sentence '. . . because I have an idea for a little trip we might take.' He pointed at his car, which was still parked outside the gate. 'C'mon with me for a spin. It'll only take a few minutes.'

'But you've been drinking Guinness.'

'Only the two,' he smiled, 'and I sipped them very slowly. C'mon, Ev, it'll be grand.'

'Oh, all right,' she said, and walked over to the passenger door. 'Take me somewhere, anywhere.'

She should have known. John drove her to Marlborough Road, where neither of them had been for more than a decade. There were ramps, which hadn't been there before, including one right outside number 64. John parked and they got out for a look.

The house itself was still painted that old blue-grey colour and they could see into some of the flats that had their curtains open. They were brightly lit and showed signs of recent refurbishment. Neither Evelyn nor John was interested in the house, of course: what they wanted to see was the old prefab.

'Feck! I don't believe it. Look what they've done,' said John.

He had walked over to the lane by the side of the house only to find that it was inaccessible. A pair of black wrought-iron gates, which had always been there but had been open, were shut and chained together. The lane itself had changed too. Though still comprised of gravel, it was overgrown with grass and weeds. John stood on his tip-toes at the left pier to get a glimpse of the prefab, but it was too far down and he couldn't manage it.

Evelyn brazenly went into the neighbour's yard and peered through a gap in the hedge. From that angle she thought she could make out a corner of the prefab's roof, but she wasn't sure. 'I think it's still there,' she said, 'but I'd like to know for sure. And also to find out what state it's in. Whether it's being used as a garden shed. I somehow doubt that students nowadays would put up with living in an icebox like we did.'

'I think I could probably get over this gate,' said John.

No sooner had he said the words than a man came out of the house opposite. He went over to his car but his eyes were on John.

'He seems to think you look suspicious,' whispered Evelyn, as she came back around to the gate. 'He must recognize you from the CCTV footage on *Crimewatch*.'

'Ssh! I'll just wait until he's gone,' hissed John.

But the man was going nowhere. He sat into his car just up the street and stayed there. Checking his rear-view mirror.

'Plan B,' said Evelyn. 'Come this way.'

She led John a bit further up Marlborough Road, down a small side-street, then down an even smaller side-street. They found themselves very close to the back of a blue-grey house. Surely it was 64. The prefab, if it was still there, must be tantalizingly close. All that stood in their way now was a high wall – a very high wall.

They looked around for something to climb but there was nothing.

'C'mon,' said John, bending down and cupping his hands together. 'Put your foot in here and I'll hoist you up.'

'Are you mad?'

'It's the only way, Ev. Don't worry, I won't look up your skirt.'

But he was not entirely true to his word. As he was lifting her up the wall, John did sneak a peep up her legs but couldn't see much through thick cotton tights. Maybe there was a hint of gusset or a suggestion of knickers. Whatever happened, Evelyn's eyes were just coming level with the top of the wall when John lost concentration for a second and his right foot slipped sideways. Evelyn dropped a few inches and damn near knocked her chin on the brick. Then John lost his balance entirely and fell backwards on to the ground. Evelyn managed to land on her two feet and stumbled but didn't fall over. She took a long look at John, lying on the concrete rubbing the back of his head.

'Damn you, John Fallon!' She laughed. 'I was one inch away from seeing it.'

'Well, I'm sorry for your trouble, missus,' he replied defiantly, 'but now it's your turn to hoist me up.'

'The hell I will.'

'But I'm taller. You won't have to lift me very high.'

'You're also heavier, fat boy. I'd slip a disc.'

'Maybe you should work out more – you'd have more strength.'

'Maybe you should too. You wouldn't be so fat.'

John patted his belly. Which wasn't really very large at all (yet). 'How will we ever get to find out if the prefab is still there? Find out what it looks like now?'

'Hmm,' said Evelyn. 'I'll tell you what we'll do. Get up off your bum and come here.'

He did so.

Then she put out her two hands and gestured for him to take them in his. 'I want you to close your eyes and we'll both cast our minds back to those days in the prefab.'

He did. She did.

Evelyn could picture the interior exactly. In her mind's eye she could take a tour throughout every one of the rooms and remember precisely where everything was. The chairs, the sugar bowl, even the colour of her toothbrush sitting in a glass that needed washing, were still crystal clear.

John thought of his first ever time having sex. His attempt to propose marriage. Throwing pebbles on to the roof, and evenings spent around the kitchen table chatting with Michelle, Cliona and all the gang. About everything from the meaning of life to their favourite character on *Dallas*. But, most especially, he thought of times spent with Evelyn.

A minute passed in silence while they replayed their memories from inside that little wooden box.

'Got a mental picture?' asked Evelyn, eventually.

'Yes.'

'Then open your eyes.'

'Okay, Ev. Now what?'

They were still holding hands but it felt a bit embarrassing now that their eyes were open. They let go.

'Can you remember it pretty much perfectly? I can.'

'Indeed, yeah.'

'Then, Johnny, I tell you solemnly that it still exists.'

'But . . .'

Evelyn was already walking away, heading out of the side-street. 'That prefab still exists whether it actually exists or not.'

'Now that,' he said to himself, shaking his head, 'is deep. Truly, madly deep.'

He ran to catch her up.

48

John's apartment was in a block on Stephen's Street, right in the centre of Dublin. He parked nearby in the multi-storey, and they went inside so Evelyn could use the bathroom.

'Mind you don't climb out my window,' he said. 'We're on the fourth floor up here.'

'Got it, Johnny.'

'I promise not to be lurking outside the door waiting to propose marriage.'

'Thank God for that.'

But then they caught one another's eye and both felt a little awkward at this exchange. Evelyn hurried inside and locked the door. After piddling, she pulled down the toilet lid and sat for a minute.

Then another minute.

She needed time to think.

There was the fact that she really must be getting back to the hospital soon.

That she was a little bit drunk having not had much practice at drinking pints recently.

That the evening had been the most enjoyable she'd had in God knew how long.

That she felt like there was blood returning to whole parts of herself, which (after the miscarriage and the break-up and her father's death) she'd thought had been amputated.

'C'mon, Ev.' John knocked on the door. 'Don't fall asleep. The coffee is made and I've even got some biscuits. Chocolate ones.'

'The pulse quickens!'

'The pupils dilate.'

'Breathing deepens.'

'And from the nerve endings pour forth a cascade of chemical messages to the brain.'

'Suppressing rational thought.'

'Beneath a blanket of pleasure and desire.'

It was Evelyn's turn to say the next line but she took a fit of laughing and couldn't. She clicked on the window to close it.

'Yes, Johnny. Those certainly are the effects. When it's done correctly at least!' Halfway through their cup of tea, John had insisted on Googling a few of Evelyn's ex-boyfriends. Then they'd hopped around various sites before alighting on a scientific paper that dealt with the subject of kissing.

Afterwards they sat back on the couch, facing one another from opposite ends. They still had their cups in their hands and still had opinions of which the other needed to be convinced.

'Love!'

'Sex!'

'Love, I tell you! How can you have forgotten that?'

'Honestly, Ev? How have I forgotten it? You already know. You were there. You saw. Every girl I ever kissed, I fell in love with. Given the slightest bit of encouragement – or none! But they all dumped me, and when I finally found one who loved me back . . . I don't know how or why but it shrivelled up and died.'

'Boo-hoo.'

'I'm not looking for sympathy, Ev. In any case I now know that kissing is purely done for biological reasons. It's simply a prelude to sex and reproduction. Did you not read that bit on the screen? It explained that the purpose of kissing is to exploit the fact of the lips having the slimmest layer of skin on the body. Also the biggest concentration of nerve endings. Hence it's an ideal site for two potential partners to transmit pheromones to one another. Arousal is enhanced on both sides and the survival of the species is ensured.'

'Pshaw, John Fallon! Pheromones? The survival of the species? You make it sound like we're creatures in a zoo. There has to be more to it than that. Scientists can only deal with things that can be measured. Particles and electricity. But what about the things that can't be measured, like the emotional impact of a kiss? With what instrument would they quantify that? While you're in the midst of it and, indeed, for days, weeks, sometimes years afterwards.'

'I don't know.'

'And what about all the other kinds of kisses that don't involve mysterious sexual chemicals? What about kissing your mother goodbye, or a small boy on the head, or blowing a kiss, or somewhere in the air beside your American aunt's cheek, or on the page of a letter with a big fat X?'

'I suppose . . .'

'And returning to just man and woman, what about the fact that it's not just a matter of putting any two sets of lips together? That there are good kisses and bad? That sometimes it works and sometimes it doesn't?'

'Oh, here we go again, Ev. I can see where this is leading. You're going to go into fairytale mode and claim that a kiss can be a test, that it can tell you whether you've bagged your prince or not, aren't you?'

'Well . . . yes, I suppose, maybe.'

'You still believe?'

'I don't . . . *not* believe . . .'

'You didn't seem so sure when we began this conversation in Pasta Fresca a few hours ago. You were saying that you might never meet the perfect frog. I thought you might be getting some common sense!'

'No, my faith did wobble slightly, but for some reason it seems to be returning.'

'Probably the alcohol.'

'No doubt.'

'So . . .' said John, draining the last of his tea. He stood up and walked right over beside her.

'So?'

'So!'

'So?'

'So what'll we do next?'

'What'll we do?'

'Yeah, it's only ten o'clock. Where next on our magical mystery tour of Dublin?'

He put his hand on her shoulder. For just a flicker of a second Evelyn thought back to that same hand pressing against her back as he zipped up her dress. For a flicker of a second she thought to answer bluntly, 'Your bedroom, Johnny,' but she didn't.

'Take me . . . take me down Grafton Street, Johnny,' she said. 'I want to see Saturday night.'

There were only a few places open, most notably McDonald's and Burger King, at each end. But that was not what Grafton Street at night was about. It was about the feeling and the sound of thousands of people passing through to get somewhere else, people going up or down the pedestrianized thoroughfare. The buzz in the air from all those footsteps. The sum of all those conversations about who and when and where to go next. The occasional piercing shriek of laughter from a drunken hen party. And on top of all these the overlapping music of buskers.

The first one that Evelyn and John came across was nestled in the doorway of Laura Ashley. A young man of about twenty, with an acoustic guitar, was singing 'One' by U2.

'Oh, sweet Jesus,' muttered Evelyn. 'Is there no getting away from them?'

She walked on without adding to the meagre collection of coins in his guitar case. Next up, outside a darkened HMV, there was a really old guy with a weird guitar. It looked like his own creation, with keys attached to the strings. Instead of strumming, he pressed the keys. Strange and pretty cool. His fingers moved in a complicated blur. Evelyn and John stopped for a few minutes to watch him, then threw in two euro for his trouble.

Onward they strolled, taking the street very slowly, past a juggler throwing tomahawks, a middle-aged man in a business suit playing the saxophone, a poet reciting 'The Lake Isle of Innisfree' for tourists, two South American girls playing the Pan pipes, an artist spray-painting pictures of planets while-U-wait, and at the very end, hiding herself shyly inside the doorway of River Island, an old woman with a small keyboard. The backbeat was set to waltz time and, as they approached, she began to play and sing an old trad tune.

'Last night as I lay dreaming
Of pleasant days gone by . . .'

They stood and listened to her for a moment before John had a notion. 'May I?' he said, and offered Evelyn his hand with a flourish.

'May you what?'

'Have this dance?'

'Oh!' said Evelyn, taken by surprise. 'All right.'

She wasn't sure how to start, but John took charge and guided her into the classic waltz position.

'Hey!' she exclaimed as they began to move back and forth. 'I do believe you've had lessons, sir!'

'I beg your pardon, Ms Creed, I think you'll find I'm just a naturally talented gentleman.'

'On the contrary, sir,' she said, as he gently pushed her backwards and began to carve out a diamond pattern. 'You definitely exhibit the signs of formal training. Most tellingly, you've only stepped on my dainty feet but the once!'

'The young, the old, the brave and the bold
Their duty to fulfil . . .'

'Oh, damn it all, Ms Creed, I fear you have seen right through me. I confess it. I have indeed had lessons.'

'From a qualified dance instructor, was it, sir?'

'Yes, miss. From fair Vienna itself!'

'Well, then, sir, I am most jealous,' she said, as the diamond was completed and John began to twist her in the opposite direction. 'For mine own part, tuition in the art of dance came from a clown.'

'From a clown?'

'Yes. I met him at the circus.'

'And what were you doing at the circus?'

'I was running away from home and hoping to join it. Possibly as a tightrope walker. Or maybe a trapeze artist. Or, at the very least, I held ambitions to be the person charged with mucking out the elephant's cage.'

> 'She threw her arms around me
> And said . . .'

'Good Lord, miss. Such an escapade!'

'Yes. Well, my mama and papa were often quite beastly.'

'How so, Ms Creed?'

'They made me wear a purple dress with orange stripes.'

'Ye Gad!'

'And fed me naught but cauliflower.'

'That is most irregular.'

'And they . . . and they . . .'

It seemed that Evelyn ran out of inspiration, at least temporarily. Her mouth was open but the sentence was not yet composed. John looked down into that mouth, those lips . . . Then he raised his eyes to Evelyn's and they locked on.

> 'The cock he crew in the morning,
> He crew both loud and shrill,
> And I . . .'

The sexual tension, which had been simmering all day, finally reached boiling point. There was no need for any further verbal communication. Each of them sensed it. The moment had arrived. They tilted their heads slightly to the right and were about to close in . . .

Beep beep.

One of their mobile phones had just received a message. Evelyn assumed it was hers and that the message might be an urgent one concerning her mother. She stepped back from John and rummaged in her coat. The screen of her Nokia was still dark, which meant it had to be John's. He pulled it from his pocket.

Maybe he should have claimed it was a message from his father.

Or, better still, that there was no message.

Maybe he could have come up with some excuse: it was an alarm.

Or a low battery sound.

Or something . . .

. . . anything . . .

Anything other than blurt out that it was a message from Michelle.

'And what does it say?'

'It says,' said John, who was just starting to realize that this would not go down well, but could see no other option than telling the truth, '"Can you make that six forty-five?"'

'What does that mean?'

'It means . . .' John sighed.

He explained that he was supposed to be meeting Michelle at the airport the following morning. That he was supposed to be accompanying her to a conference in Brighton.

'Oh,' said Evelyn, staring intently at one of the orange paving bricks beneath her feet. 'I see.'

She felt as if she'd been slapped. Logically, of course, feeling betrayed made no sense. After all, she'd known that John and Michelle were sort of together.

'But, of course,' said John, 'I'm now thinking that maybe I should ring her up and cancel those plans if –'

'Don't bother,' Evelyn interrupted. 'Certainly not on my account.'

'But, Ev, only a minute ago you and I were about –'

Beep beep.

Again came the sound of a mobile message arriving. This time it was Evelyn's phone. It was the nurse. Her mother had just woken up and was asking for her.

'I have to go, John,' she snapped. 'Have a wonderful time in Brighton with your girlfriend.'

'Just a second, Ev –'

'And after that, have yourself a wonderful life.'

'C'mon, Evelyn, wait.'

But she would not, could not, stand there for a moment longer. Without further ado, she stomped away, back up Grafton Street towards the hospital.

49

'For fuck fuck fuck fuck fuck *fuck* sake,' muttered John to himself, all the way down past Trinity and on through Westmoreland Street to the bridge. He was in no mood to go home. He was furious about how things had ended with Evelyn. About how he'd been a second from kissing her only to screw it up, certainly for the present, quite possibly for ever. And all because of an ill-timed text message. No, scratch that: all because of the person who'd sent that text message. John strode into the IFSC, made straight for Spencer Dock and barely nodded at the concierge as he crossed to the lift.

There was no reply when he knocked on the door of number 56. He waited and knocked several more times before reaching into his pocket. He fished out a key.

It was a key that he was not supposed to have. Michelle had made it very clear that she would never give him one since they didn't have 'that kind of relationship'. Nevertheless John had borrowed her spare key briefly a month back and got a copy made. It was something he had had no right to do, but he had justified it to himself: he would use it only in an emergency. This, however, was not the kind of emergency he'd been envisaging (something more like Michelle collapsing and being in dire need of medical assistance). Nevertheless, he turned it in the lock and the door swung open.

Good, he thought. I'll tell her I found it ajar.

*

Because Michelle wasn't there, John couldn't vent his anger. He was hoping she'd come home shortly but she didn't. He couldn't sustain his rage but neither could he let it drain away. Instead, it soured into sadness and grief for how a magical evening with Evelyn had turned to dust. He switched on the television and half watched a film. He put on a CD of David Gray and half listened to that. He took a yoghurt from the fridge, because it was the only food available, and could stomach only half of the tub. He took two cans of beer out and guzzled every drop in a matter of minutes.

Hit by a wave of drunken exhaustion, he decided to lie down. The couch was only a two-seater and far from comfortable. He looked at Michelle's bed, the one he had shared with her only the night before. He would keep his clothes on, he told himself, because he needed to be up and on his feet instantly whenever she did eventually come home. He lay down on the quilt. Then he felt a bit cold. He took off his shoes and slipped under the quilt. That was nice, very nice indeed . . . until he felt something touching his feet. Something deep down under the quilt.

He reached down and pulled it out, already fearing what it must be.

It was.

A pair of men's underpants.

Sweaty.

He held them between his thumb and forefinger as far away from his face as possible.

But close enough to be quite certain: they were not his.

After lying on the bed for a few minutes, feeling sorry for himself, John's eyes alighted on the dress Michelle was intending to wear to the conference gala dinner. Designer, lime green, with yellow splashes, little purple flecks and a great big Guinness stain – the one that needed to be hand-washed.

Suddenly injected with a new lease of life, John leaped to his feet and grabbed the dress. He brought it to the washing-machine, balled it up and threw it into the drum, followed by the abandoned pair of underpants, which just happened to be jet black. He put them both on together for a long wash cycle at 95 degrees.

Then he walked out, leaving behind the key he should never have had cut.

Sarah Creed was fine. Perhaps still a little groggy after the anaesthetic, but happy that her myringoplasty had been a complete success. In fact, she quickly grew bored with the topic and told Evelyn there was something else she needed to discuss. It had come to her as she lay on the operating table waiting for the doctors to begin: the fact that the wooden flooring in the dining room at home was looking the worse for wear. Black tracks were appearing on the parts where there was most foot traffic. And why wouldn't they? It was fully ten years since those boards had been laid. The only question then was whether to have them stripped and revarnished or perhaps tear them all up and go for tiles instead.

'Nice terracotta porcelain ones, perhaps?' said Evelyn, managing to sound far more enthusiastic than she ever would have in the past.

They continued the debate for a while, whispering because it was well past the official visiting time and they didn't want to wake Angela in the bed opposite. When it got to eleven o'clock, the nurse came in and suggested it was time for Evelyn to go.

The walk to the Albany guesthouse, where she had booked a room for the night, was not long. Nevertheless, after collecting the overnight bag from the boot of her car, she began to run – down Adelaide Road and on to Harcourt Street, weaving through the throng of late-night revellers converging on nightclubs like the POD, Crawdaddy, Copper's and the Vatican. She ran up the steps, into Reception and up the stairs to her room on the third floor. She stopped. She threw down her bag and took off her clothes without much care for where they landed, collapsed into the bed and closed her eyes, not to sleep but to try to untangle the confusion in her mind.

She went through a checklist she'd made up many years before . . .

Was he a good person? Yes.

Intelligent? Yes, except occasionally when he could be very stupid.

Trustworthy? Yes, except when he received annoying text messages that shattered your faith in him utterly.

Sense of humour? Definitely. Tall, handsome but also kind of scruffy.

Unafraid of spiders? He was yet to be tested but definitely unafraid of sheep.

And had he a nice smile? Very much yes.

It wasn't a perfect score by any means, but that didn't really matter. Evelyn was feeling it, both in her head and in the pit of her stomach.

A longing – what one songwriter had called 'a deep and digging craving'.

For the frog who might just be her prince.

For John Fallon.

It was such a pity that he was in some sort of fecked-up relationship with someone else.

The bedside clock said 5:40 a.m.

Evelyn had eventually fallen asleep and awoke with a start. Other than the clock, the room was pitch dark and she took a second to realize where she was. And why she was there.

Suddenly it dawned on her that John was due at the airport for six forty-five. Considering how little traffic he'd meet on a Sunday morning, it might well be that he'd head off in his car at about six – that was in twenty minutes. Evelyn switched on the bedside lamp and began to look for her clothes.

By the time she got down to John's apartment on Stephen's Street, he had already left. Not for the airport, however. As far as he was concerned his little arrangement with Michelle was over. His alarm had still gone off that morning, though, and he had decided that since he was awake he might as well do something useful. Go to Cappataggle, where his one-eyed father could probably do with help for a few days. John had thrown a few clothes into a bag and set off to collect his car from the multi-storey.

Evelyn hit the buzzer several times.

'Feck!' she fumed. 'I suppose that's it, then.'

But that was not it.

Out of the corner of her eye, Evelyn noticed a car going past in the street outside and registered that it was

John's. She pulled open the door of the apartment block and went out, fearing the car would be gone from view. It was stopped at the nearby traffic lights.

'Hey!' she said, after trotting over and knocking on his window.

'Hey!' he said, looking startled. Then he leaned across to open the passenger door.

The traffic light turned green and, not sure what to do next, John continued with the plan. He drove on, taking them down a deserted Sunday-morning George's Street towards the river. There was a heavy silence between them, neither knowing what to say. The car radio was tuned to Today FM. '. . . and in sports, Juan Sebastián Verón will require a late fitness test before Wednesday night's Premiership game against Arsenal at Old Trafford . . .'

'So I never did get to ask how you felt yesterday . . .' said John, after taking a deep breath '. . . about the way Man U discarded Lee Sharpe. And now this Verón fellow is the latest to wear his jersey. Is he a fitting successor?'

'Pah!' said Evelyn, smiling at the brilliantly timed triviality of the question. 'Man U must be absolutely mad. Verón may get the odd goal for them but his legs are nowhere near as lovely as Lee's.'

'Absolutely mad.' John nodded, and again they both went quiet to listen to the forecast.

'So . . .' John eventually said, as they passed down along the bridges, 'this is a nice surprise. I . . . I got the impression last night that we wouldn't be seeing each other again so soon.'

'Yes, well, I had some time to think and I came to a different conclusion,' said Evelyn.

'Which is . . . ?'

'Which is –' Evelyn stopped short, realizing that they were already past Inchicore. John seemed to be taking an eccentric route but they'd still be at the airport in minutes. Her mind flashed back to the two or three moments over the years when she and he might have got together but somehow never had. She needed another chance, but it wasn't going to fall effortlessly into her lap. She must be bold and simply come out with it. Say the words! 'Which is that I would like you, Johnny, to pull the car over to the side and turn off the engine.'

'Em, okay.'

So he pulled the car over on the hard shoulder. His hand still on the key, he looked at her. Evelyn leaned over the handbrake and put her hand to his neck.

He moved towards her.

She parted her lips.

As did he.

They tilted their heads and pulled one another close.

50

John never did make it to Cappataggle or, indeed, to the airport. His father managed on the farm without him, and Michelle made several attempts to call him but his mobile phone was powered off. Deeply annoyed, she had to board the plane without him but vowed to have words on her return. He had promised to come with her, to support her, and hadn't. And all because of another man's underpants! What a ridiculous overreaction. Not to mention having broken into her apartment. Not to mention what he had done to her dress.

Michelle's list of grievances, however, was the furthest thing from John's mind. On that fateful morning, he and Evelyn had finally got together and so begun the happiest days of their lives. Over the weeks and months that followed, their every spare moment was spent together, in one another's arms. Kissing. Cuddling. Making love. Being in love. Laughing about the meaning of life. Taking seriously the telling of trivial things.

In August, only three months later, John went down on bended knee and Evelyn said, 'Yes.' This was something both of them had done before, of course, with other partners. There was no backing out this time, and in January they were married in Evelyn's local church near Ballymahon. Brian was best man and gave a witty speech about sleep deprivation. Cliona was bridesmaid and saved the day by pinning up Evelyn's train when it threatened to fall apart. Even Michelle was there, along with her (extremely good-looking) 'plus one'. His youthfulness suggested that he might well be one of her students, although in fairness he was not carrying a skateboard.

The significant events continued to come thick and fast, as Evelyn gave birth to a honeymoon baby, a boy weighing seven pounds and eight ounces. They called him Peter. Seventeen months later they had another baby, this time a girl called Mia. In the meantime John's parents gave them a site at the far end of the farm and they built a fine dormer bungalow. (Sarah Creed had lots of ideas for its design. Too many, in fact. They incorporated many of them but Evelyn was wary of turning the house into a replica of her mother's.) When it was ready they moved out of Dublin and shortly afterwards Evelyn had her third baby, another girl whom they named Lily. At that point John and Evelyn had three children under the age of three. Later that year, John went to the Family Planning Centre in Galway where he underwent a little 'procedure'.

But did Evelyn and John, as in fairytales, live happily ever after? That can't be answered definitively because 'ever after' is happening right now. As they both approach the age of forty, they are in excellent spirits, within themselves and with each other.

Evelyn now works for an engineering consultancy in Galway but only part-time. The rest of her week is spent at home, some of it in a tiny room she likes to call her office. There she writes music reviews on a freelance basis for the *Connaught Tribune* and various women's magazines. She still hasn't heard a single new record that can match those made in the early 1980s and has yet to award anything five stars. Nevertheless she trawls MySpace and hypem.com and continues to listen out in hope.

Sometimes in a quiet moment she Googles her ex-boyfriend Shane and is relieved to discover that there is still no sign of his book being published. Sometimes she is moved to think about the baby she lost, sometimes also about her father. She lets those sensations wash over her, then flicks on the kettle for tea. While she's waiting she unloads the clothes dryer and pairs a few dozen little socks.

John, too, has taken a job-sharing arrangement. Jaded by the humdrum of pharmacy, counting tablets and managing grumpy customers, he now does just three ten-hour days one week, two the next. That reduces the amount of time Lily must spend in the crèche and means he can collect the other two kids (now in junior and senior infants) from school. Once home, they go out and play soccer and John has high hopes for both as he takes them to U6 training in the town once a week.

The reduced working week also allows John to help his father on the farm. Brendan Fallon is now seventy but age doesn't seem to wither him. Though he is several inches shorter than his son, he is at least as strong, if not stronger, when they are pushing a broken-down car, for instance, or hefting a piece of furniture – and most especially if they are catching sheep: then, in one fleeting movement, he still has the muscle and technique to grab and immobilize it, up on hind legs, in seconds.

John also likes to muck around in their garden, which is quite extensive. Only a few months ago he persuaded Evelyn that they needed a tractor mower for the lawn. He likes to drive it wearing an iPod, listening, as he winds among the apple trees, to the Ricky Gervais podcast.

But, of course, there are problems and worries too. Since the world's financial markets fell to pieces, the value of Evelyn and John's house is now 30 per cent below what they paid to build it. They've both had to take pay cuts, and on the earnings that remain, the taxes are higher. On the home front, although all three kids are generally blessed with good health, there is always one with a slight cough, an earache or a suspected infestation of head lice. Also slightly frustrating is the fact that Lily still won't sleep through the night, often waking them two or three times.

'It can't go on much longer,' Evelyn says.

'It can!' replies John. 'At least, according to that noted childcare expert Brian.'

Their marriage, just like the times that led up to it, is not quite a fairytale. Now and then there are disagreements, now and then strong words or a period of silence. But, overall, they have retained a lot of the magic, the chemistry, the spark, that brought them together. They are still very much in love. Partly this is because they still spend so much time talking to one another. Teasing and joking in an ongoing banter. It's also because they still have quite a bit of sex: at night before going to sleep (approximately) three times a week; in each and every room of the house at least once over the past four years; outside on the lawn, late on a summer's evening when the world wasn't looking; and, best of all, on a very occasional afternoon having asked someone nice to mind their children for a few hours. Then they can take their time and relax into it. Act as if there is nothing else in the whole wide world but themselves and each other.

*

So yes. For now, at least, they live happily ever after.

And for that they generally drink a toast each year on 5 May. To mark the early morning when they sat in a car together, stationary, somewhere near the M50, and tilted their heads and parted their lips and pulled one another close and . . .

51

. . . finally kissed. At first tentatively, gently, their lower lips slowly caressing, while Evelyn ran her hand through his hair and John brushed hers from her face.

Then, with faces pressed more tightly as deep breaths were taken and all hint of shyness fell away, her hand swept down across his neck and pressed his chest. John's reached across for her hip. Then dissolving into open passion as tongues entwined and hands began to explore everywhere, anywhere, places that only minutes previously had been utterly prohibited to touch.

There was only so long they could manage without breathing. After a few minutes, John switched from kissing Evelyn's mouth to nibbling her neck. While he was down there, she opened her eyes.

It wasn't as if she saw this kiss as being some kind of test. She was old enough and wise enough not to be crossing her fingers and hoping for a puff of smoke. When she opened her eyes, there was just the briefest moment when she registered that there was no transformation. John was still John. There was no special sign by which she might know with 100 per cent certainty that he was the prince.

It doesn't matter, she thought. This is real life, not a fairytale.

But just as she was about to close her eyes again, Evelyn caught sight of herself in the rear-view mirror. She saw her own face. She saw her own smile. And she was struck by a moment of revelation. About two things.

The first was the simple fact that she was not a princess. And that perhaps this went some way to explaining why none of the frogs she'd kissed had ever turned into a prince.

The second was even more important. It was made apparent by the sight of her own smile. A particularly intense I-can't-stop-smiling smile that she knew was not a regular visitor to her face. It was this that made her realize she'd been getting everything backwards. The kiss might not have changed John into a prince but it had worked a transformation. Of Evelyn herself.

And for that matter it wasn't even the kiss that was responsible. It was simply John. Just his presence. Being with him, talking with him, had a tendency to bring out the best in her. Something in the interaction between them meant that whenever they were together she automatically became funnier, more imaginative, cleverer, sexier, more full of bounce and more beautiful. More. More truly herself as she wanted to be.

Herself as she wanted to be . . .

The point was that there was more than one version of Evelyn. There was the one her mother knew (in essence still a teenager, rebellious and untidy) and then an entirely different one, which Shane had complained of (too serious, too responsible, too no-bloody-fun any more). Being with Michelle brought out a more girly part of her personality, while her efficient can-do side was emphasized when she was at work. Of all these possible Evelyns, however, the one she most liked to be was the one John inspired.

He had lots of great qualities but what set him apart

was that he was the catalyst she needed. She could be all those good things without him, of course, but only sporadically, like a flickering light bulb. John kept the electricity flowing, constant and strong. There had been other men in the past she had really liked, men for whom she'd had very positive feelings, but none had made her feel as positive about herself as John did. None had the magic ingredient that transformed her and made her feel like a . . .

John had no such moment of revelation. He just knew that he wanted her as he'd always wanted her, since the night they first met. Everything and everyone else that had got in the way was now totally irrelevant. There had always been a strong connection between them but it had been purely verbal. He wondered what the reaction would be if he were to open the buttons of her blouse, slip his hand inside and . . .

'Yes,' she whispered.

'Yeeeeeeeees.'

'Hey, driver.' Evelyn pulled back. 'Change of plan. I don't think you're going to the airport after all.'

'Indeed I am not,' said John, reaching for his mobile phone to switch it off. 'Or Cappataggle. I'll take us back to my apartment, okay, Ev?'

'No, Johnny.' Evelyn shook her head. 'I'm afraid I can't agree to that.'

'You can't?' He raised his eyebrows.

'No.' She smiled. 'It will take too long.'

She placed a hand on his thigh. Gliding slowly upwards.

'Oh . . . okay. Howzabout a hotel? There's a few up ahead.'

'No,' said Evelyn. 'No hotel needed. Just drive up a little way and I'll direct you.'

So they drove up past the M50 and John did not give any thought to Michelle, standing at the airport with her hands on her hips, her classically beautiful face increasingly cross. Neither did Evelyn consider her mother, waking up in hospital at that exact moment, saying, 'Good morning,' to Angela Vaughan and wondering what time would Evelyn come in for a visit.

They drove on to the next roundabout, where Evelyn directed John to take a right. That set them on a back road to Finglas across a large area of undeveloped countryside. Before very long, they found a quiet laneway. They drove down it for a few hundred yards until they were as near as made no difference to the middle of nowhere.

Then they got out of the car, sat in again to the back seat, locked the doors and pushed the seat downward into a horizontal position.

Acknowledgements

Thank you to my true main characters.
Jonah, Reuben, Seadhna,
Eliza, Daniel and Niamh.